THORN'S DOVE

ORC MATCHED BOOK 0.5

CARLOTTA HUGHES

WWW.AUTHORCARLOTTAHUGHES.COM

Cover art credited to Carlotta Hughes.

First Edition
ISBN: 978-0-9893799-8-4 [EBOOK]
ISBN: 978-0-9893799-9-1 [PRINT]

www.authorcarlottahughes.com

For my inner teenager.
Whose dreams got trampled by nearly everyone.
Fuck them all, we did the thing!

TABLE OF CONTENTS

Content Information

Map of Orc Rock Farm

Chapter 01   11

Chapter 02   17

Chapter 03*   27

Chapter 04   35

Chapter 05   47

Chapter 06*   65

Chapter 07*   77

Chapter 08   89

Chapter 09   99

Chapter 10*   109

Chapter 11   121

Chapter 12*   131

Chapter 13   141

Chapter 14   155

Chapter 15*   161

Chapter 16*   173

Chapter 17*   185

Chapter 18*   193

Chapter 19*   203

Chapter 20*   213

Chapter 21*   221

Chapter 22   235

Epilogue   241

Rhuger's Pearl Excerpt   245

Index & Pronunciation Guide   259

Content Awareness*   269

Acknowledgments   273

About the Author   275

CONTENT INFORMATION

Version Note:

Please note that this version of Thorn's Dove is an expanded version of the short story by the same name included in *Big Feels: A Monster Romance Anthology*.

Content Awareness:

Please note that there are aspects of the story that may be upsetting to some. It is my responsibility as an author to be transparent with my readers so that they have a comfortable experience.

Chapters in the Table of Contents with an asterisk are chapters that contain *explicit* sensitive content. For a full list of what chapters include what kind of sensitive content, please jump to the Content Awareness section at the back of the book. Please also note that I'm including *mentions* of sensitive content besides *explicit* scenes and they will be marked in the Content Awareness section, accordingly. A full list also exists on my website: *www.authorcarlottahughes.com*.

A Note On Orckin Culture:

Because of the decline in the orckin species, their once broad and varied culture was significantly affected. Oral traditions and education were altered or eradicated to keep the wanted narrative. This occurred rather easily, as the orckin industry revolves around trades, and not all orckin are taught to read and write. Thus, some of their traditions passed from common knowledge entirely or were only mentioned in old tales.

This includes alternate forms of life paths for both males and females and gender identity outside of the binary. As the series progresses and humans and orckin find their cridhe mates with one another, the pressures of species propagation significantly ease, allowing for traditions, genders, and philosophies that were stifled to resurface. Especially with humans reintroducing similar concepts with their mates.

It is important to note that while it is not *required* for females in the orckin culture to produce orclings; it is an expectation by their society and often seen as an honor. Not all the five clans approach this in the same way, and often manipulation is used. Which, of course, is not completely informed consent. Consent is a big factor in this series, and occasionally a point of conflict, as they reestablish rules of conduct within their culture.

Overall, as the orckin revive their lost culture, there will be outdated modes of thinking, harsh punishments, misunderstandings, heavy conflict, and compromises.

Teanga Dhubh or Black Tongue, the primary orckin language, is loosely based on Scots Gaelic. A pronunciation guide and index exist at the back of the book. You can find voice clips on my website courtesy of *https://learngaelic.scot/*

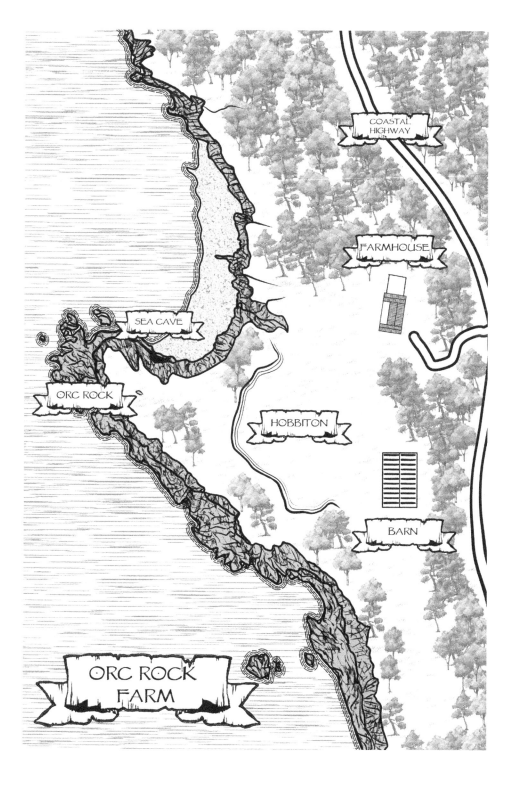

CHAPTER 01

RUTH - Northern California, USA. Summer 1974

When life kicks you in the gut as you're lying beaten on the floor, people cope in different ways. Some people go to therapy. Some go through a midlife crisis and buy a fancy car. Or get a divorce. Me? I bought a run-down coastal farm.

Something I could pour my time, energy, and love into and see tangible results. Unlike with people. People sucked rotten eggs.

I'd just left a hippie commune and was bereft of family. My parents had died in a car accident while I'd been listening to gurus and getting passed around like a joint while high as a kite. My experiences at the commune were mostly terrible, other than the skills I'd gained to help keep the commune functional. I'd taken my chance to get out the moment the opportunity presented itself.

Not long after, as I was coming down from the drugs I'd grown dependent on, I discovered that I'd become pregnant by one of the men in the commune. I wasn't sure which one. I couldn't stop throwing up and it had nothing to do with the detox or the morning sickness, as memories I'd blacked out resurfaced. The drugs that I had been on had harmed my baby, so I had made the agonizing decision to get an abortion. After I'd gone through with it, I'd discovered my parents' untimely death after their attorney found me. Unable to stomach it all, I sold their house. The dark haze of memory became one I forced back behind a door in my mind, desperate to move forward.

My comfort books, the works of Tolkien, sparked an idea as I struggled to cope with my lot without nose-diving back into drugs. I was going to use my inheritance to purchase some land I could turn into my very own slice of heaven. A place where I could escape from my past and build a future.

I couldn't imagine my luck when I'd found the listing. Twenty acres of land, a dilapidated farm, a private beach, and an old farmhouse all sold on the cheap. I'd sunk every penny into this land and my dream of having a Tolkien-inspired bed-and-breakfast. But, I had only six months to turn this ramshackle farm into a functional, income-generating attraction, or else I wouldn't be able to carry the mortgage. A race against time in a game of chance that would decide the course of the rest of my life. No pressure.

Today was the day my life would change for the better. The day my gamble with Lady Luck began. Today I got to move in.

With a grunt, I brought in the last box from the moving truck. I set it down just inside the door of my brand new farmhouse. Well, brand new to me. Peering around the dingy old place, I could see its potential. The Craftsman style farmhouse had good bones, but it needed some cosmetic changes and some structural reinforcing, but nothing too terrible. Nothing I couldn't manage on my own. The rest of the farm, though? It was going to take every iota of willpower I had to fix it up within my tight schedule.

When I was done, I wouldn't need to depend on anyone. I'd be able to smell the ocean and raise goats and chickens. Host guests and magical events. Celebrate weddings. Grow old watching others find their happily ever afters on my farm. All on my lonesome.

I wished I could find the love I'd only read about in books. The love Tolkien would write about. Enduring, poignant, and true. A little piece of me still hoped. But the world-weary cynic in me knew it was just a pipe dream. Just the prettiest of trips before the comedown.

Most people I'd dated in the past had been selfish, hurtful even. Always rushing me into things I wasn't ready for. Always making me wait for what they'd promised. The day I'd left the commune, I'd sworn that I was done waiting on men. Either I was worth it to them, or I wasn't.

With the last box safely inside, I moved towards the rear of the house through the kitchen and mudroom. Reaching the back door, I had to put my shoulder into it to get it unstuck. It swung wide with squealing hinges onto a breathtaking view. Clouds and fog obscured the summer sun, but I could see for miles out to sea. Taking a deep breath, I could smell eucalyptus, summer flowers, and brine as the ocean breeze lifted my wavy brown hair from my shoulders.

The back steps were wobbly and in desperate need of replacing. Gingerly, I eased down them and made my way down the gravel path that led to the cliff. Everything around me was an overgrown jungle, a wild tangle just like my heart. Turning on my heel, I looked back to survey my new domain.

The house looked a little saggy in some areas, like some supports needed to be reinforced. The roof was supposedly still sound, but it probably only had a year or two left in it. Salty Pacific air had done a number on the peeling paint, so that was another item to add to my ever-growing to-do list. Stripping the peeling paint alone would be a nightmare. But at least I'd be able to do it somewhere pretty.

Ivy, jasmine, and tea roses overflowed the stone-walled garden attached to the farmhouse and had even reached the tree line. It had grown over much of the house too, having run rampant for years. It was summer, so the salt-tinged air was heavy with the scent of roses and jasmine. Bees and butterflies frolicked amongst the blooms in the sunshine.

Beyond the house to my right lay a small barn that was falling to pieces, leaning more precariously than the Leaning Tower of Pisa. That would have to come down if it didn't fall with the next stiff breeze. A new barn could come later in my plans and would be a great space for wedding ceremonies. Fence posts turned green with mosses and lichen poked up through the overgrowth like broken teeth around the barn. Another thing to add to my list of things that needed replacing. There was an old chicken coop nearby I could renovate, and I could reuse the post holes from the old fence to create a new corral for goats.

Manzanita bushes, wild herbs, wildflowers, and dun-colored grasses covered the old fallow fields. But underneath all the overgrowth and work? There was so much potential. The vision was there. It was the honey-do list that was daunting. Turning my attention from the work I'd need to do to make my spaces livable, I shifted instead to the major project. The one that would bring in people, and with them, money. Hobbiton.

The hills just past the barn created a small bowl in the earth. Windswept cedars helped protect the lowlands from the high winds of the Pacific. I couldn't imagine a better place to put the hobbit hole cottages I would use for the bed-and-breakfast. Ideas flooded my mind. Everything from having a little outdoor bar I could call the Green Dragon to themes for each hobbit hole. I would definitely dedicate one to Rivendell.

Beyond the potential the place had and the dreams I had for it, the real gem of the entire property was the lovely strip of private beach you could reach by a winding path on the cliff face. There was even a sea cave I'd yet to explore nestled into a massive outcropping of stone that jutted out into the turbulent waters of the ocean. The beach would be the place that lured in visitors, especially for weddings. I knew I was tempting Lady Luck by thinking of all the ways I could make money without even starting. But I had to indulge in this fantastic future I was striving towards for encouragement before I buckled down and got to work.

I was facing a daunting task, fixing this place up in six months as I recovered. The overgrowth alone would take forever to cut back, and I didn't know what surprises I'd find with the farmhouse. I'd need to prioritize the creation of the hobbit holes to make the deadline. And if I couldn't find a contractor to help me, I'd be doing it all by myself. Not impossible, but I'd have a hell of a time.

Purchasing this property was a dream challenge. A way for me to test myself, my skills, and my determination to build the home of my dreams with my own two hands. To create something beautiful and enduring out of the ashes my life had become. Something I could pass down to my children if I ever had any.

The risks were high with this endeavor. Yet it was one I was going to take. So, with a half-mad grin and a deep breath, I rolled up my sleeves and headed back toward my new home.

CHAPTER 02

THORN - *Baile Coille, Oc'Dellor. Spring.*

I sat atop the highest branch of the Craobh Bean Glic, the massive tree that housed our temple and orphans. I stared off over the sharp stone spires that ringed the sunken forest city of Baile Coille to the wild forest beyond. On clear days, I could look out over the vast expanse of trees to the sea. Normally, seeing that vast strip of blue water was enough to bring me calm, even on the most upsetting days.

But not today.

My little sister, pregnant with her first orcling, had passed in the darkest hour of the night, succumbing to the plague. Her husband and my friend, Uther, was inconsolable. He had packed up and left Baile Coille without a word the moment Thisa's pyre had burned to ashes. I wasn't sure if I'd ever see my friend again.

Father had done what he did best, hidden his grief behind his duty as Rìgh, as king of our clan, the Oc'Dellor. Mother, Oc'Dellor's queen, and its Fear a Chì—its spiritual leader—had withdrawn deep into the Craobh Bean Glic longhouse to seek the wisdom of the gods on the disease that had swept through our people. The an'sgudal was a wasting illness that struck us orckin every few decades. It'd been a part of our history for centuries, with no known cause and no known cure. All we knew was that it seemed to strike whenever the dorcha'aon resurfaced from the dark, twisted places they spawned from.

Whether it was a disease brought by them or one they chased, we did not know. We didn't even know which came first. What we knew was this. With a population already weakened by plague, monstrous six-legged beasts with multiple glowing eyes who preyed on us at night was not something we needed. Where the an'sgudal struck our heart, our females and orclings, the dorcha'aon struck the unwary. Hungry for our hunters and our nocrys; giant felines that were our steeds.

I'd killed my first dorcha'aon months ago when the an'sgudal first crept through Baile Coille. The monster had sneaked past our sentries, through the stone spires of the Fàinne Sleagh, and sought to devour our nocrys. I'd been visiting Vagrin, my steed when it attacked.

Thoughts turning dark and twisted, I looked down at the thick ropes of newly healed scars that ran down my right arm. Vagrin and I nearly died that night. The dorcha'aon had devoured many nocrys and even a few orcs before I'd gotten close enough to fell it with my axe.

I was lucky I'd kept my arm.

It hadn't been the last dorcha'aon to think it could devour me, either. It was my duty to protect my people against this threat as its Leanabh Rìgh, its prince. My body was a patchwork of scars, proof of my dedication to my clan. Parting gifts from the monstrosities that now haunted my dreams.

With a heavy sigh, I looked up at the sky, where Talam's twin suns neared the horizon. I didn't want to move from my perch where I could let the wind blow my dark thoughts away. But I needed to check on what remained of my family before I sought my bed.

Climbing down the highest branches of Craobh Bean Glic was

as easy as breathing for me, having grown up playing amongst its leaves. I took the various platforms and connecting bridges at a run. I needed to feel the burn of my muscles and joints. To feel *something* after so much grief.

It wasn't like the grieving was even over. My future path, my frith-rathad, was bleak, and not just because my sister would no longer be a part of it. Bitterness was a sickening knife in my belly, resentment a hand at my throat as I lept from platform to platform as I sought to outrun my fate.

When the an'sgudal had struck this cycle, my father had reached out to our neighboring clan, the Oc'Turin, to seek an alliance. Binding our clans through marriage was the only option for peace in times like these. But the Oc'Turin were our near-enemies.

Whenever we were weakened, they would try to attack Baile Coille to steal what females we had. It was a barbaric practice only made worse by how poorly the Oc'Turin males treated their females. It wasn't a sustainable way to exist. But my father and the other three Rìgh of Talam wouldn't hear of altering our traditions. To give power over mating rights to the females, of whom there were so few left. Amongst the Oc'Dellor, there was barely one female per six males. The odds in some other clans were worse.

Oc'Veltas had only one female per ten males when they'd closed off their island spire city off the coast centuries ago. The Oc'Veltas had a Banrigh as ruler now and had sought to solve the problems of the demise of our species through technologies we couldn't possibly fathom. Their isolation and fortifications allowed them the time and space to put their greatest minds to the test.

They had flying machines that could visit the stars. I'd seen them myself. They didn't let anyone in. And they didn't share their technologies with the rest of us. Leaving us to our own devices. Just like our ancestors left the Oc'Veltas to their fate when the an'sgudal first struck.

I was the only option left for peace between our warring clans in the decline of our species. If that weren't bad enough, the Rìgh of the Oc'Turin wished his daughter to be married quickly. To merge our powers against inevitable attacks from the remaining two clans, The Oc'Blyre and the Oc'Sentan. In two days, I'd be traveling to the Oc'Turin capital of Cumail Cloiche to meet my future bride. And promptly marry her. I'd never met her. Yet I knew in my very marrow that she wasn't my cridhe. My one true mate.

And I yearned for a love I'd now never know.

With a snarl, I flung myself from the lowest platform, completely foregoing the stairs. Instead, I sailed out into the open air just below the canopy and began free-falling towards the hollow center of the Craobh Bean Glic where the heartwood used to be.

Passing a pulley, I snagged the rope and clutched it in one mighty fist. I wrapped the rope around my feet and continued my descent into the great hollow of the massive tree. I slid down it until I reached a platform built into the interior of the Hollow. Landing with a reverberating thud against the wooden boards, I slowly rose to my full height, cracking joints and rolling my neck. With a heavy sigh, my shoulders slumped, and I began weaving my way up the platforms of the tiny city lining the interior walls of the mighty tree.

Little heads poked out of some buildings dotting the interior and I ruffled an orcling's hair as I passed. The little huts were the homes of Baile Coille's orphans. The caretakers of the little ones lived in the tree homes built into the very tree itself along its outer trunk. My mother, the Fear a Chì, worked in the longhouse at the apex where the arms of the tree met. Where it overlooked Baile Coille and the Hollow where the orphans lived and played.

I mounted the stairs that would take me to the longhouse, footfalls heavy. Thisa's death had hit our mother the hardest. They'd been close. Thisa had been training to become Banrigh Ruksala's replacement, after all. Memories, at once sweet and warm, crowded close in my mind and I had to fight the tears that threatened to spill. My little sister had been such a bright light on Talam. Snuffed out far too soon.

The longhouse was quiet. The guards who stood to either side of the open doorway were solemn. Each wore an undyed cloth armband, signifying that they'd lost someone. Yet here they were. Still at their posts. Honorable orcs, both of them. I nodded to them before I entered the longhouse. It was quiet inside. The hearth was nothing but cold ashes. The windows shuttered, denying the filtered sunlight and open air of the canopy outside.

"Màthair?" I called into the gloom of the longhouse. Flickering light danced over the floorboards at the back of the building. It was the room where the Fear a Chì would cloister to converse with the Source of the universe. For wisdom. For guidance. Both were things my grieving, spiritual mother would look for.

I entered the small sanctum and found her kneeling in front of a giant crystal. Normally thrumming with vitality and power, my small mother was a veritable force of nature. But now? Now she sat there like an empty shell. A husk of the female who had birthed and raised my sister and me.

"Màthair," I called softly from the doorway.

She started and turned towards me slowly. As if she'd been sitting in that one position for hours and her joints were stiff and aching. I watched as the copper rings of her irises within the black expanses of her eyes hazed over and brightened. Then hazed over again. As if she was trying to focus between our world and the other.

"My son." My màthair croaked, and I handed her some water from a pitcher near the door. She looked at the cup vacantly for a moment before taking it from me. Downing the entire thing in a few gulps. "What brings you here?"

"I came to check on you."

"I'll be fine," she muttered automatically.

"You taught us not to lie," I admonished, and ushered her slight frame out into the open portion of the longhouse. Hoping to guide her to some food or sleep.

"I did."

"Then don't lie to me."

"I didn't." She gazed at me and her vision went hazy as if a cloud had scuttled across the sun of her irises. "I will be fine one day."

My heart broke anew.

"Sleep here. I'd like to have you close to me tonight." My mother patted my shoulder.

"As you will, Màthair," I murmured.

She turned from me then, returning to her post to stand with her hands on the crystal. A silent dismissal. My mother looked so small as if she'd shrunk inward with Thisa's death. With quiet footfalls, I crept from her inner sanctum and closed the door behind me. I walked across the narrow hallway to one of the guest rooms and retreated inside. Lighting a candle, I trudged over to the bed and sat down heavily. The day had been long. And I was a mess.

Kicking off my boots, I flopped back onto the bed and stared up at the ceiling's wooden beams. I'd lost my only sister and my best friend in one day. One to the an'sgudal, one to the whispering quiet of Noc'tal Forest. Plus the dozens of orckin who had passed from the plague, many of whom I'd known personally. It seemed as if I'd lost my parents to their grief, too.

And I'd lost myself. My hope that I'd find joy, my cridhe like my parents had, was snuffed out. An aching wisp of smoke was all that remained of it.

I blinked slowly, sorrow dragging me down behind my eyelids, and I succumbed to the waiting darkness of sleep.

I woke up gasping for air.

Sitting bolt upright, I realized I wasn't drowning underwater, staring at the face of a female I struggled to remember. Instead, I was alive, in a bed at the longhouse. Memories of the previous days rushed forward like waves with my waking. I was here because Màthair had asked me to stay close to her.

"You dreamed."

I jumped and swung my gaze to where my mother sat stock still in a chair next to my bed. Her gaze was soft, slightly hazy as if she had one foot here on Talam and one with the Source. My breathing evened, and I relaxed.

"Yes," I murmured.

"What did you dream about?" she asked, cocking her head as if listening to a distant song.

So I told her. I dreamed of a place so very different from Talam. Of a female who didn't look orckin. Her presence was just a whisper of feeling in my heart. Of the holy winged tree deep in Noc'tal Forest, the Craobh na Beatha. And of the Gaeta, the grand carved wall within the cave housed amongst the roots of the gargantuan tree. Of touching it.

And having the Gaeta come alive.

When I finished telling her about my dream, my petite mother placed a small hand against my cheek. The lines on her gray-skinned face had deepened, and I could have sworn some of the silvery hair amongst her black locks had not been there when I'd fallen asleep.

"This is a dream from the Source. You must follow it, meet that human woman. You must. Leave at dawn." Her hand slipped from my cheek, and I instantly felt its loss as she stood.

"What about the trip to meet the Oc'Turin Leanabh Banrigh? I'm supposed to leave the morning after tomorrow to meet her." I asked. Wait, had she just called the woman I described a human? A daonna? But those people were a myth. They only lived in the stories told to our orclings of those smaller, cunning beings from another world with their strange eyes and blunted teeth.

My màthair froze and looked at me. Her gaze bored into mine and the lovely rings of her irises became so thin her eyes looked like fathomless black pits.

"*Forget the Oc'Turin female. She is not for you.*" Her voice sounded simultaneously young and old, male and female. Terrifying in its timbre. "*Do not deny this call.*"

"What of Father?" I dared to ask.

"I'll deal with your father." My mother's eyes and her voice returned to normal, and I felt a shiver run up my spine. I'd never seen or heard of my mother doing this. It wasn't my mother who told me to forget the princess-the Leanabh Banrigh-of the Oc'Turin and to follow my dream instead.

It had been something other. Something connected to her through the universe, the Source. A power far beyond my mortal ken. Instances such as these were rare amongst my kind. Those who didn't follow the call brought a great calamity upon all orckin. Denying the call was how the an'sgudal first appeared on our planet. If our lore was to be believed.

I only knew it would have to be worth it, to follow this dream. Because I'd have one hell of a time explaining myself. If I were to fail at whatever task the Source was sending me on, it would undoubtedly spell the doom of clan Oc'Dellor.

For the Oc'Turin weren't to be slighted.

CHAPTER 03[*]

RUTH

"Look here, I just bought this place. I'm not about to sell it." I spat into the receiver.

"If you would just listen to our offer, you'd find it more than fair, Miss O'Daniels." Came the dry, onerous voice that had been calling me nearly every day.

"No," I said bluntly. "Do you not understand the meaning of the word? Are you, perchance, illiterate?"

"I have a degree from MIT, miss." Oh, the guy was not happy now. Seemed like uppity-pants didn't like being called stupid.

"Well, good for you. Though you couldn't pour water out of a boot if I wrote the instructions on the heel. Now, neither can I, nor will I, sell this place. Am I clear?" I was pacing, practically wearing a groove into the old hardwood floor that desperately needed a sanding.

"You've made that crystal clear." Their voice had gone completely cold.

"Good! Then do me a solid and *stop calling me* you uptight

square!" I slammed the phone down onto the receiver and screamed my anger out into the kitchen.

It hadn't been my day. But then, it hadn't been my week or year either. The same day I'd moved in, I'd gotten a call from the asshole I'd hung up on. He was calling on behalf of the government, 'The Man', to purchase the property from me. Unless, of course, they were just blowing smoke up my ass before they pulled Eminent Domain.

This guy was making my life hell in other ways than just annoying the hell out of me via a phone call. No, now rumors were cropping up about me in town. Claiming that I'm not only a hippie but a cult leader. Hippie? Yes. That I'd own up to. Cult leader? I'd rather lick a cheese grater. The last thing I needed was to be associated with cult activity.

I'd been on the phone all week. Trying to drum up a contractor to come out here to survey my property. To look over the farm's plans. But they all had refused to even hear me out once I gave them my name. If I couldn't make any headway, I was looking at losing the farm. And the future I desperately clung to.

This farm was mine. It would become an operational bed-and-breakfast in just under six months. Then I'd never need to depend on anyone again. Let alone a man.

Not that I inherently hated them or anything. I just couldn't trust them as far as I could throw them. At least that was my experience. Then here was this government man, making my life more of a nightmare than necessary.

"What am I gonna do?" I sighed and looked out the window to the ocean beyond. I wanted to keep this place, and I also really wanted the square to stop harassing me. But I would not figure out a plan with a head full of fire.

With a defeated snarl, I grabbed a cardigan. I headed out the back door, careful on the rickety steps. I tramped down the path from the house to the cliffs. If anything could soothe my tumultuous mind, it would be the crashing surf. The wind blew back my wavy brown hair and tugged at my bell-bottom jeans. Seagulls wheeled overhead and a few deer lifted their heads from the overgrown brush to stare blankly at me as I passed them in a stomping rage.

THORN

The sky overhead was a crystalline blue as my nocrys, Vagrin, leaped over a stream that bisected Noc'tal Forest. He was a sturdy beast, thick and powerful with muscle. Often used to sire new litters of nocrys cubs. He was a lovely deep charcoal grey, with bright gold feline eyes, sharp fangs, and claws. His plated scales were thick and his fur glossy with good health.

Vagrin was a noble companion. The closest thing I had to a friend since Uther had slipped off into the Noc'tal Forest. I wished I could speak to Uther about my dream. About the haunting half-image of a female, I'd never seen before. Who looked nothing like any female I'd ever known amongst the orckin. But Uther was so deep in his sorrows, he wouldn't have heard me had he stayed. Not that I could blame him. Thisa had been his heart and soul for as long as I could remember. They hadn't been cridhe, but they might as well have been.

It was a risk, bringing Vagrin, as the dorcha'aon's favorite food was nocrys. But he'd proven himself capable of fighting off the dorcha'aon. And I knew he wasn't stupid enough to be caught by one, either. If my mother Ruksala's words held any weight, I'd need to get to the Craobh na Beatha as quickly as possible to meet my frith-rathad, my destiny. That strange female I could neither fully remember nor completely forget. As if I'd glimpsed her through a hazy fog.

With her haunting my every heartbeat, we made good time. Reaching the Craobh na Beatha just before dusk. Normally, the trip took over two days on foot. I slid from the saddle, booted feet digging into the loam.

"Good boy, Vagrin. Geàrd." I gave him a good scratch on the cheek, his massive head tilting in bliss before I stepped up to the holy tree.

To say that the Craobh na Beatha was gargantuan would be an understatement. It was far taller and broader than even the Craobh Bean Glic. Clouds skimmed the topmost branches, catching amongst the boughs. The differences didn't end there either. The tree itself possessed six snow-white wings that fluttered and moved of their own accord. Large crystal acorns tinkled together amongst the boughs of the canopy, creating chiming music that cleared the mind. And down amongst the twisting roots was the entrance to a cave.

The reason I'd come.

I felt smaller than an insect as I stalked to the cave's entrance on quiet feet. I pulled a knife free from my bandolier. The Craobh na Beatha was on the border between Oc'Dellor and Oc'Turin lands. It wouldn't do to stumble upon one of the Oc'Turin unawares, as even impending marriage to their Leanabh Banrigh wouldn't spare me.

It became apparent rather quickly that the cave was empty. Abandoned for a long time. The decline of our kind and the lack of new cridhe mates forced many to give up hope. Most orckin didn't bother with the long journey to the Craobh na Beatha. Why would they, when they could honor the gods and the Source at their home altars and with their Fear a Chì?

I sheathed my knife and looked around. The walls of the cave were the ancient roots of the tree. Gaps in the winding roots allowed shafts of sunlight to filter down onto the walls and the hard-packed earthen floor that my ancestors had trodden all the way back in time to the birth of our people. I tread lightly, not wishing to anger my fore kin through clumsiness.

The massive carving on the back wall drew my gaze. It was awe-inspiring and, like everything else about the Craobh na Beatha, made me feel minuscule. It was a re-creation of the massive tree carved into the oddly flat wall. The canopy of the tree carving extended up into the ceiling. The roots were worked into the floor of the cave. A broad set of steps led up to the tree's trunk, into which someone had chiseled an arched doorway. Great rings with an ancient, long-lost language scrawled within them were engraved on the wall behind the tree carving.

And like the real Craobh na Beatha, this carving had six artfully posed wings carved down to the smallest feather. A shaft of light fell upon the arched doorway. Fourteen points of light shone amongst more of that scrawled language. And at the center of the seam that bisected the carved doorway lay three additional vertically placed points of light. One of them was dull and lackluster.

The points of light were the acorns from the Craobh na Beatha. Each one was large, easily the size of an egg, and crystalline. Reflecting light and rainbows onto any nearby surface.

Curious, I took to the stairs. I'd been in the cave many times with my mother. But I had never ascended the stairs to the gate. Spent candles and trinkets littered the curling roots and steps leading to the Geata and, more than once, I needed to pick my way through the offerings.

The offerings were like tiny prayers to the Source, to the holy tree, for a loved one's return, for healing, for honor. For love and finding one's cridhe. I'd left multiple offerings to find mine. And perhaps, if my dream was true, my offerings weren't in vain.

As I reached the top step, I looked up at the carving. I was one of the tallest Oc'Dellor, yet the lintel was far above my reach. Apprehension curled in my belly. What creature could be that tall to require so much clearance? How dangerous could the humans on the other side of the Geata be?

I only knew the oral histories passed down by the Fear a Chì. Tales of the Ancients and their interactions with humans. How there was once peace between our peoples, then war. Ending with the breaking of the Geata. Myths, I was told they were, stories to get the orclings to behave themselves and nothing more. But with that otherworldly human haunting me and the path set before my feet by the Source, I wasn't so sure they were just stories anymore.

My parents hadn't raised me as a coward. So I shoved down my apprehension and straightened my spine. Steeling my nerves, I looked at the seam in front of me. One question burned in my mind amongst the sea of queries regarding this Source-decreed quest.

How was I supposed to travel through the Geata? Especially if they were all broken?

The three crystal acorns glinted at me, one dim and dark, hardly reflecting any light at all. I let my eyes wander over the carvings, hoping to find any sort of sign from the universe. There was only echoing silence and that one dull acorn.

With a deep breath, I reached out and touched it.

For a moment, nothing happened. Then, the acorn blazed to life beneath my fingertips. Glowing with a pulsing light, each of the acorns awakened. I stood, frozen, as an explosion of rainbows scattered across the cave. The rings with their dead language carved into them shifted. Dust rained down on me and the uppermost stair, knocking over offerings as the rings shook off the dust of ages, grinding into motion. The carved tree shivered to life. Leaves and feathers fluttered and hummed from the vibrations of the moving rings. Then the seam in the center of the doorway cracked open onto the most glorious vision I'd ever laid my eyes on.

It was a tunnel of light and rainbow, filled with the high chiming sound of crystalline acorns and wind through leaves. As if it were the essence of life expressed in sound, sight, and touch. It was like time no longer mattered. Just this endless thrumming of the universe's life force.

I noticed it then. A red strand of light was tied to my pinky finger on my left hand. It ran up my arm to where my heart beat steadily in my chest. I touched the strand where it flowed into my breast and it shivered, a vibration running down my arm, out into the tunnel of light before me. Ripples of excitement left goosebumps on my skin as I realized that this was the sacred thread that tied me to my cridhe. The restlessness in my soul that I had felt my entire life suddenly stilled.

I stepped forth into that tunnel of light towards the other half of my being. A rushing wind pulled me forwards, propelling me through the tunnel of rainbow and life. The force of it was so strong I couldn't draw breath. Within moments, I saw a dark shifting wall rushing towards me. The Geata slammed shut behind me, and I plunged into a wall of saltwater and darkness. The impact expelled what little breath I had in my lungs. Frantic, I attempted to swim up to the surface but couldn't find it.

My lungs burned as a tide ripped me away from the Geata. I thrashed as I fought the current, but my limbs weren't cooperating. The tide sucked me deep through some tunnel, and I hit my arm against a sharp outcropping of rock. Sparks of light and pain exploded in my mind. My chest constricted as my body began to spasm with the need to breathe.

A sudden surge of tide shoved me back the way I'd come. It

slammed me against the Geata, my skull cracking on one of the three main acorns.

Everything went black.

CHAPTER 04

RUTH

To calm my nerves and untangle my thoughts, I made my way toward the cliff and the farm's private beach. I wanted to see it, feel the sand between my toes. To see the enormous cliff that resembled an orc up close and personal. A giant sentinel of stone that was carved by the elements.

Perhaps that's what I'd call it, my farm.

Orc Rock Farm.

A smile tugged at my lips at the thought. I stood atop the cliffs, staring down at Orc Rock. Its craggy profile was as rugged and ferocious-looking as the ocean that had been pounding against it all day. The tide had just gone out. Rushing water still churning in and out of a sea cave entrance.

The beach was hardly more than a strip of sand. Widening slowly with the retreat of the tide. Wrapping my cardigan closer to me, I ducked my head and began making my way down the path carved along the cliff face that would take me to the beach. The path was old, worn, and sketchy in a few spots. I'd need to add wooden walkways and railings in the future to make it safer for guests.

Several small switchbacks made things slow going. But it was worthwhile once I made it to the beach. Squinting against the blowing sand, sun, and sea spray, I couldn't help but grin at the stretch of sand that was mine. All mine.

My mind raced with thoughts about the draw the beach would have for the bed-and-breakfast and potential weddings. The beautiful ceremonies that could be held along this liminal space. How families would come down here to play. The opportunities felt endless.

My gaze landed on a large, odd form on the sand. It was half-submerged in the surf, the waves lazily lapping against it. Maybe a sea lion or some dead sea creature. Whatever it was, it was big.

Curious, I stepped forward, squinting against the blustery wind, my brain doing all sorts of mental gymnastics to explain what I was seeing. What on Earth was it? Horror slowed my steps while the realization dawned that I was looking at a pair of arms and a mop of black hair.

My heart nearly stopped as I recognized the unmoving form was a person. Adrenaline surged through my veins. I broke out into a sprint, sand flying behind me. Something I couldn't name gripped my heart in a vise, tightening with every heartbeat. Feeling as if I were about to lose something precious, tears pricked my eyes.

I reached the body, my feet splashing through the waves. He was clearly male, tall and broad-shouldered with heavily calloused hands. Red and pink spots bloomed on his waterlogged shirt. The ebb and flow of the surf moved his body, making it difficult to see if he was breathing. His skin was an alarming shade of gray, and my breath hitched, panic making my body shake. His coloring could mean one of many things. None of which were good. Was I too late? Did he catch hypothermia?

I lunged forward and got my hands under his massive shoulder. Heaving, I rolled him over onto his back. He flopped like a dead fish. Definitely not a good sign.

That's when I finally got a good look at his face. His features were strong, with a square jaw and a proud nose. The briny waters plastered his black hair against his skull and it lay like ribbons against his face. A full mouth, slightly open, tinged a darker gray instead of the blue I expected from hypothermia. That's when I saw his teeth. They were sharp like a predator's.

I scrambled back over the wet sand as the waves crashed over us both. A scream had lodged itself in my throat, and my chest heaved as I tried to breathe around it. He wasn't gray because of exposure, blood loss, or death.

He was gray because he wasn't human. No human had dark gray skin or a mouth full of wolf-sharp teeth. No human had pointed ears, either.

He coughed, and seawater poured from his mouth. I had to stifle another scream that bubbled up in my chest. A groan followed the water, but his eyes remained firmly shut. My body shook with unadulterated terror. Maybe finding a near-dead body on my beach broke my brain. Because either I'd lost my mind or Area 51 must've lost a resident.

I saw him twitch, one hand flung out towards me spasming as if grasping for something, and I couldn't take it anymore. I screamed. The sound echoed, startling nearby gulls into taking flight. Sitting in the crashing surf, eyes wide and unblinking, I stared openly at the unconscious body.

That he wasn't dead was a gods' damned miracle given the temperature of the water. My teeth were already chattering from the cold, and I was losing feeling in my toes. I got to my feet and retreated from the crashing waves. The brisk breeze was suddenly cutting, and my soaked clothes made it even worse.

Yet I couldn't take my eyes off of him.

Something tugged at my wreck of a heart, and I had to shake my head at my stupidity. But like the tides, I couldn't deny the pull I had towards this guy. I saw too much of my broken, discarded past in his situation. Knew he'd die without my help.

Without further hesitation, I stomped forward into the surf. I slipped my freezing hands under his armpits. I heaved his hulking form backward, using the surf's momentum to drag him out of the water.

I'd gotten my stubbornness from my Irish genes. It had always gotten me into trouble and gotten me out of it. So when I finally dragged him out of the surf and up onto the dry sand, I didn't let his immense size daunt me.

He was easily over seven feet tall and was pure muscle. Hell, the guy could probably snap me in half with his massive, clawed hands without breaking a sweat. He wore a kilt, a torn shirt, boots, and some sort of bandolier that must have carried weapons. I didn't spy any, and that gave me a small modicum of relief.

I pulled my gaze away from the giant at my feet and looked around at the debris that had washed ashore with the tide. A few long pieces of driftwood sparked an idea. I could make a travois to drag him up to the house. I slogged over to them in my wet clothes. Digging the driftwood out of the sand, I dragged them over to where he lay. A few more minutes of scavenging rewarded me with some salt-crusted rope, a small fishing net, and a sharp piece of glass.

When I'd lived in the commune, it had turned me into a handywoman, so it was quick work lashing the driftwood together with the scavenged rope. I turned the excess into a body harness to help distribute his weight and attached it to the travois's peak. Using the netting, I created a cradle between the two pieces of driftwood for him to lie on.

With my waning strength, I hoisted him face down onto the travois. The position wasn't ideal, but I was already tired. I still had to drag his gargantuan ass up the cliff. It would have to do, even if his knuckles dragged. I secured him to the frame with the rest of the net so he wouldn't roll off and go tumbling down the cliff as I maneuvered.

"Gods damn you, what did they feed you to get you this big?!" I grunted through clenched teeth. Bracing the peak of the travois on a knee, I pulled the shoulder straps over my body crosswise, then pulled my knee free and stood. His weight was far more bearable to carry this way.

Then I saw the storm brewing out at sea, dark smears of clouds bruising the horizon. I was certain the storm would hit before the sun fully set. Stubborn to the bone, I grasped the peak of the travois for leverage and leaned backward, using my lower center of gravity and thick thighs to help me drag the travois towards the cliff face. Once I'd pulled the travois out of the sand and onto the hard-packed clay and stone of the cliff path, my task got easier.

The wind picked up, and it cut through my wet clothes, making my teeth chatter. I started dragging his deadweight up the cliff. As I made my precarious way through a switchback, the mountain of muscle moved and groaned. The shift in his weight put too much pressure on part of the eroding path, and it gave way. Screaming, I held on for dear life as the travois slid, my fate tied to his. One of his dangling arms snagged on a rock, stopping the slide.

I sobbed in relief. Taking a deep breath, I channeled all my strength, planted my feet firmly in the clay soil, and hauled with every fiber of my being. Inch by inch, I pulled the unconscious guy from the edge of the buckled cliff. I screamed curses at the sky, fueling my body with pent-up, festering rage.

Rage at how I'd been passed around at the commune like a joint, high on too many drugs to notice. At my parents' death, and how I hadn't been there for them. How the FBI agent wouldn't stop harassing me as I tried to fulfill my dream. At the loss of the child who I'd failed. Everything I'd ever been angry about and tamped down into the dark recesses of my soul. Hell, even that time someone had pushed me into a duck pond in third grade. I dragged it forward and used that fury to fuel my body to get him up the cliff.

Suddenly, I fell backward, startled out of my red-hazed trance as I landed on my ass. Looking around, I realized I'd actually made it. Laughter bubbled up out of me and the adrenaline waned. I'd done it.

Once I caught my breath, I struggled to stand in my wet clothes. They were quickly stiffening from the salt, chafing my skin, and it made moving more difficult. I still needed to drag his ass all the way to the farmhouse. Raindrops pattered fitfully against my face and the clay earth at my feet. Shit.

With a half-mad chuckle, I grasped the peak of the travois in my now-bleeding hands. I groaned and pushed on, legs shuddering from the exertion. The rain became a drizzle and the wind bit through my soaked cardigan, plastering my hair to my head.

The rain was coming down in sheets by the time I dragged him up the rickety back steps into the mudroom. Panting, my breath puffing out in the quickly cooling air, I hauled on the travois one last time. It slid the rest of the way into the mudroom. I landed on my ass, my limbs shaking from all the strain. I crawled over the travois, grasped the doorknob, and closed the door before rain splattered against the hardwood floor.

I slumped against it and looked down at my shaking hands. Riddled with splinters, busted blisters, and smeared with blood. I'd done it. I still needed to get him warm, treat his wounds, and figure out what the hell I was going to do with him, but I'd done it.

Luckily, one of the previous owners of the farmhouse had seen fit to install a shower stall in the mudroom. I stumbled to my feet as the rain lashed against the windows. I snagged some scissors and cut the netting free. Grasping one side of the travois, I heaved, gently rolling him off of it and onto the tiled floor. I let the travois fall and weakly kicked it out of the way. Sliding his body across the cold tile of the mudroom, I got him into the stall, propping him against the tiled wall. So little of him fit in it. I huffed a laugh.

I removed his sodden leather boots. His feet were human-like except for his pointed black nails. Shaking my head at yet another oddity, I moved on to removing his clothes. I crouched down next to him, knees protesting, and with the hope that he wouldn't mind, I snagged the scissors and cut away his ragged shirt.

I braced myself to see injuries and some muscle. It did not prepare me for the rippling abs, scar-flecked torso, and tattooed shoulders that met my gaze. His arms were massive, like small tree trunks. Ropes of newly healed scars ran down his right arm, and his left sported a wicked-looking gash that probably warranted stitches. Wincing, I saw he was covered in lots of scrapes and bruises. I wasn't sure what caused them, but the tide and rocky shore were likely culprits.

Some blood trickled down his temple. Frowning, reaching up into his hair. My fingers brushed the cold tips of his pointed ears, and I tried not to flinch away from their strangeness. He groaned as my fingers found a sizable knot at the back of his skull. I froze. A few moments passed, and when I realized he would not wake, I removed my fingers.

"No wonder you're out cold. That thing's the size of a tennis ball. You're lucky to be alive, mister."

Glancing down, I realized I'd need to remove his leather kilt. Grimacing, I unbuckled the leather thongs that kept it in place around his narrow hips. I paused before removing it, unable to stop the flush that rushed to my cheeks.

"Fucking pathetic, Ruth. You've seen naked men chasing women around a gods' damned commune. What makes this any different?"

I shoved my uncomfortable feelings aside and his kilt along with it. I tugged and got the kilt out from under him, tossing it into the corner next to his boots. That's when I made the fatal mistake of looking back at him lying naked in my mudroom shower.

Eyes nearly bugging out of my head, I couldn't help how they zeroed in on his... package. He was hung like a fucking horse. Even flaccid, his dick hung nearly halfway down his muscled thigh. It was very similar to a human man's, but it was also very different. He had a sac, shaft, and tip. But that's where the similarities ended.

The shaft was oddly shaped. Instead of appearing as one cylindrical unit, four deep vertical grooves ran the length of it. A slight bulge at the center of his shaft boggled my mind. And there was ribbing along the top and bottom from base to crown.

Flustered and pissed at myself for ogling an unconscious man's junk, I shook my head and turned on the warm water. It took a few minutes for the water heater to kick in. But soon lukewarm water was spraying down on both of us. As our body temperatures rose with the water, I turned up the heat until we both felt normal to the touch.

Finally warm, I turned off the water and snagged some towels I'd left on the dryer. I brusquely dried him off and dropped a towel over his groin. I hesitated, glancing to make sure he was still unconscious before I stripped and wrapped a towel around myself.

"Sorry, dude. I gotta leave you here for a second and go get some clothes on. Don't want you waking up to us both naked." I blushed and ducked out of the mudroom. I left wet footprints on the worn hardwood floor as I made my way to my bedroom.

Within a few minutes, I'd dressed in some warm pajamas and had my wet hair tied up in a knot on top of my head. I stood looking down at the massive, half-dry, gray-skinned guy who lay sprawled in my mudroom shower with a towel over his... *monstrosity.*

My whole body ached and spasmed from the strain of getting him this far. But I didn't stop when I was tired. I stopped when I was done. So, with a heavy sigh, I reached down with protesting muscles and dragged him out of the shower. I got a good handle on him from under his armpits, his head lolling forward towards the floor as I pulled.

I had him halfway to the living room couch when I slipped on one of my wet footprints and went down. The wind huffed out of me in a rush as he landed on top of me. Naked.

It took a few moments for me to breathe again. He groaned above me, his mouth close to my ear, his voice gravelly and deep. My body came very much awake in a way I rarely experienced, and a low throbbing started in my core.

He breathed into my neck, his nose rubbing against the sensitive skin beneath my ear. I shuddered. I felt it then. The growing, hardening length of his cock as it pressed against my thigh. My breathing hitched, and his lips brushed my throat, inhaling before he groaned again. His cock twitched madly against me.

My heartbeat thundered in my chest, and I felt wetness flood between my thighs. I was getting majorly turned on by an inhuman guy breathing and groaning against my neck. What the ever-loving fuck was wrong with me?!

This guy, whoever he was, was fucking dangerous to my girly parts. And that was something I wasn't ready for. Not yet. Maybe never.

With a mewling sound, I shoved him off of me enough to drag

myself out from under him. A massive hand followed me and grasped firmly onto my own. His rough, calloused hand completely engulfed mine as I sat there on my ass on the hardwood floor next to him. His expression changed to one of sadness, a pained grunt slipped out from between his lips. Fingers tightened around mine briefly, as if he couldn't bear to let me go.

Confused, I gently extricated my hand from his. As soon as my fingers slipped from his grasp, his face grimaced in pain, and his hand clenched on nothing. Like my touch, my presence seemed soothing to him. I frowned down at the otherworldly man and pressed the hand he'd held over my racing heart.

I didn't like how easily my heartstrings were being tugged by someone who wasn't even awake. He wasn't faking me out, he'd fallen atop me and hadn't said boo. Standing up quickly, despite my protesting body, I decided I'd ignore my conflicting emotions. Instead, I staggered off to find a blanket. Snagging one from my armchair, I pulled him on top of it and used the blanket to drag him to the couch.

He dwarfed the six-foot couch, his limbs hanging off the arm and cushions. I arranged him as comfortably as I could before giving up on making him fit.

Utterly exhausted, I covered him up with a quilt and stumbled off to get the first aid kit from the closet. It took a bit of doing, but I bandaged up the scrapes he'd suffered. I also shakily removed the worst of the splinters from my aching hands and wrapped them up with some gauze and ointment.

It used up more of my supplies than I thought possible to treat us both. So I'd need to run to the pharmacy sometime soon. Just not today. Probably not tomorrow either, if I were honest. I was beat.

Wearily, I shuffled into the bedroom I'd made into a library. Something had been nagging me since I'd found him. As I'd brought him up from the beach and while I'd bandaged him up, I contemplated this wall of muscle. My gut was telling me to check something in my books before he woke up. And my gut instinct was rarely wrong.

Things were a little too coincidental for my liking. From how badly the FBI wanted to buy my farm, to the strange geological formation I'd started calling Orc Rock. To the non-human man, I'd found washed up on my beach and his distinctive features. A niggling at the back of my mind whispered that maybe, just maybe, he was an orc.

CHAPTER 05

RUTH

    I woke up to sunlight in my eyes and my whole body aching.

Sitting up, my joints and tendons cracked in protest from sleeping half-sprawled on my desk amongst piles of books. I rolled my shoulders and popped my neck, wincing at the feeling of my body realigning. Blinking blurry eyes, I stared out of the window with its crocheted drapes at clear skies. The storm had passed.

    Memories of the previous night, of the storm, the strange man on my couch, and my search for answers, made me freeze. My research pointed to a species I'd only thought existed in Tolkien's books. An Uruk-hai. An orc. It was almost insane to believe, but the proof was on my couch.

    I could hear some sort of rumbling out in the living room. I sighed in relief, realizing he wasn't dead. It sounded like he was still passed out, snoring like a bear. That was good. It would give me time to figure out what to do, and how I'd handle it when he woke up.

    I got to my feet and stretched. Glancing around my library, I couldn't find anything for a defensive weapon except a massive dictionary. My baseball bat was out in the living room. By the couch. I grimaced. Not my brightest moment.

What had driven me to save him from drowning and nearly thrown my back out by bringing him up to the house? Then get all horny over him being naked when he wasn't even human? I'd been grappling with that concept all night. I still wasn't sure I had an adequate answer. It boiled down to him being in trouble, and that I could help. Kind of naïve sounding, but true. The horny brain I couldn't explain away, though.

The orc represented an entire labyrinth of questions that I had no way of asking until he woke up. Maybe not even then, given the high chance of a language barrier. Something I both dreaded and found intriguing.

Would he be dangerous to me? His scars, teeth, claws, and sheer body mass showed that he definitely was dangerous. His scars proved he was a survivor. Whether he'd see me as a threat and attack me was something I'd only find out when he woke.

I wasn't a fan of The Man, big government, so I'd fought myself all night over whether to call the cops or reach out to that FBI agent who kept calling and harassing me. That's when I realized.

If I called the FBI or the cops, I'd probably lose the farm and they would likely take the orc to some top-secret facility. Where they'd experiment on him until he died. I couldn't have that on my conscience.

Instead, I was making the perilous choice to see what he was like awake. See if I could reason with him. Find out where he came from. See if I could help him get home with no one knowing. Calling the cops for help was Plan B.

Tiptoeing across the creaky hardwood floor, I made my way to the living room. He sprawled half on and half off the couch. His head hung back over the armrest, exposing the thick column of his throat and the winding black tattoos that crawled up it. I paused and studied him in the early morning light.

His face was an odd mix of craggy and finely sculpted. Rugged with a firm jaw, high cheekbones, and a straight, proud nose. His brows were thick but expressive, even in his sleep. A sculpted mouth that would have put Michelangelo's *David* to shame hung open to reveal his sharp teeth. Thick lashes fanned out across his cheekbones, and I couldn't help but wonder what his eyes looked like open.

His bared throat was powerful with corded muscle, juxtaposed with the light fluttering of his pulse, and inked with odd tribal-style-looking tattoos. Almost like Norse or Celtic knotwork mixed with Polynesian bold strokes. The tattoos curved down over his shoulders and his upper arms in a tide of inked waves. They were lovely and otherworldly, yet familiar, just like him.

Shaking my head to clear it of all the dirty thoughts that were creeping in, I padded my way over to where my wooden baseball bat leaned against the side table. Slowly, quietly, I picked up the bat. The good-looking orc kept snoring away. I crept to the kitchen, set the bat within reach on the counter, and began making coffee.

A loud rumbling ripped through the open space. Startled, I turned around, nearly dropping the canister of coffee grounds. The dude grunted in his sleep, scratching his belly. It had been his stomach rumbling.

Hand over my mouth to stifle my laughter, I set the coffee grounds down and went to open the fridge. I wasn't sure what an orc could eat. But offering him food once he woke up would be a good starting point to forging a truce. So I figured I'd do a bit of everything.

Eggs, bacon, sausage, pancakes, fruit... I got all the ingredients out and began cooking while the coffee brewed. I was so preoccupied that I hadn't noticed when he'd stopped snoring. All I knew was that it was suddenly silent.

A chill crept up my spine as I slowly turned around. The orc still lay sprawled out on the couch, but I could hear him sniffing as if the scents of my cooking were waking him up. Suddenly, I wasn't so sure about my plan of making him breakfast.

Snatching up the baseball bat from the counter where I'd left it. I crept forward and raised the bat high, ready to swing if he jumped at me. Standing over him, I could see his brow crease as he groaned. His eyelids slid open and the strangest eyes I'd ever seen, all black with copper rings for irises, blinked up at me.

I gasped, stumbling backward. Fast as lightning, his arm shot out and grasped my wrist before I could fall back onto my ass. With a sudden jerk, I fell forwards as he yanked me to him. The baseball bat slipped from my hands and crashed to the floor as I landed atop him, my breath rushing from me.

I opened my eyes, mere inches from his, and froze. I watched, utterly fascinated, as the copper irises in his black sclera contracted. His gaze focused on me as he finally registered our situation.

A flush exploded onto my cheeks as I did too.

His startling eyes darted down to where his hand grasped me and how I lay mostly sprawled on top of him. I watched in fascination as he seemed to drink in every tiny detail of my face and body like he was dying of thirst and I was a fountain brimming with clear, cool water.

Heat lit his gaze and something like recognition. Like he knew me. But that was impossible.

As was the swiftly stiffening, massive cock that was urgently pressing against me. How big was this thing erect?! A slow, sly, warm grin exposed his sharp teeth and a black tongue made for sin. He was shockingly handsome, with his expressive features.

Slowly, he reached up with his free hand and his black-clawed fingers gently brushed the hair back from my face. The move was so tender, the look in his eyes piercing and soft all at once, that it made my heart pound and my core ache.

"Och, fallen for me already, have you lass?" He asked, voice rumbling and gravelly.

My mind blanked for a moment. He... this orc... he just... spoke *English* with a *Scottish accent*. I could understand him!

What. The. Absolute. FUCK?!

THORN

A strange, earthy aroma penetrated the darkness of my mind. My mouth watered as I groaned, surfacing to wakefulness. Opening my eyes against the light, my head pounding, a shapely form coalesced from my blurred vision.

I heard a strangled gasp, and the blurry figure seemed to stumble. Without thought, I snapped an arm out and grasped their wrist, tugging them towards me to counteract their fall.

Something flew from their hands and landed with a rattling crash of wood on wood, just as the figure landed atop me with a rough exhalation of breath. Delectable softness pressed against me and my heartbeat quickened. I shook free the last vestiges of sleep, my eyes finally focusing on who lay atop me. I sucked in a sharp breath.

It was *her*.

The female from my dream. The one I'd traveled through the Gaeta to find and nearly drowned for my trouble. Her eyes met mine as we lay there frozen in this one timeless moment.

My heart began pounding against my ribs like a beast attempting to escape a cage. Her scent hit me, redolent of roses, sweetness, and something thicker, sharper, that I couldn't place. Her soft curves, so warm and inviting, different from the leaner orckin females, made my cock stir to life. The swiftly hardening length pressed against her as desire lit my veins like a wildfire.

And gods, her lovely face was mere inches from mine. Tangled tresses the color of dark honey obscured her strange eyes. Eyes surrounded by white instead of black. My body acted of its own volition, and I gently brushed her hair back with my free hand to see those eyes better. Warm sunlight caught in them, looking like luibh gaoil—the herb-spiked whiskey that caused us to go into a mating frenzy.

I wanted to drown in them. In her.

Her breath hitched and her strangely colored skin flushed a bright pink like rose petals. It was charming. Then I smelled a shift in her body, her arousal, and my mind almost blanked at the heady, intoxicating scent. I was suddenly completely aware of every inch of her that pressed against me. And I cursed the fabric between our skin.

"Och, fallen for me already, have you, lass?" I nearly growled into the space between us, voice rough from the saltwater I'd swallowed and the lust that pounded in my veins. I couldn't keep the grin from my face.

I did not know if humans could understand Common. But my smile and my body's reaction to hers? That she understood plenty.

Horror suffused her lovely features. In a flash, she sprung off of me, pushing against my chest and causing me to huff out my breath. I groaned, aching all over from nearly drowning. Aching with the loss of her curves against the hard planes of my body.

"You can speak English!" She nearly screeched as she backed

up and tripped over the long piece of wood she'd dropped before. Her voice struck a chord deep within as if I'd been searching for the sound of it all my life and had finally heard its sweet music.

"English?" I asked, taking a deep breath past the burning in my lungs. "Lass, I'm speaking Common."

"What the hell is Common supposed to be?" she asked, bewildered.

"It's a language our people have had since ages past. Per our histories, it was used to speak with beings from other worlds," I explained, cracking my aching neck.

"Yeah, but there's no way you could know one language out of the hundreds on Earth. Especially with the evolution of linguistics." The lass looked incredulous at the very concept.

"Well, perhaps it's something to do with the Geata? Look, I know a language that we orckin call Common. When I passed through the Gaeta, I arrived here and could speak to you." I shrugged, wishing suddenly for my mother's wisdom. But she was beyond the stars. A whispering husk filled with loss. I hoped she could see me here. "And what is Earth?"

"This planet. It's called Earth. Third planet from our sun in the Milky Way Galaxy." She relaxed a little more. As if being able to converse with me eased her fears. I liked that.

"Sun and not suns?" I asked, confused. It didn't sound right that a planet only had one sun.

"We only have one sun in this solar system. Earth has one moon," she said with a shrug.

"Only one moon?" I was utterly flabbergasted as I rubbed my neck. I couldn't imagine gazing up at the night sky to see only one moon nestled amongst the stars. Just one moon to light my way, instead of three.

It was then I realized my chleoc ring wasn't on my finger. It was an heirloom. And, if our histories were correct, it would allow me to look like the humans that our ancestors spent so much time with. Some long-lost magic that was fused into rings we only kept as keepsakes of a dying race.

Did she take it? I... didn't like how that thought settled harsh in my gut.

"Why do you sound so surprised?" she asked me.

"Well, Talam has two suns and three moons. There are other planets in our system, but none we've reached since ancient times," I explained. "I'm honestly not sure what a 'galakshi' is."

"A *galaxy*." She exaggerated her mouth movement as she said the word, so I could see how it formed in her mouth. It was then I saw her blunted teeth and pink tongue.

Riveted, I only nodded. So strange, her little mouth. I couldn't help but wonder what it would feel and taste like as I explored it. A thrill ran through me at the thought and my cock jumped.

Her eyes darted down to my waist and the pink in her cheeks suddenly spread to cover her entire face and neck, deepening to scarlet. I wondered if this was a human equivalent of a blush. Ours was just a brightening of our coloring. When I blushed, my skin turned a bright silver. Cocking an eyebrow, I looked down to see what had caught her attention.

Ah.

Well, it had been her doing. My dick had stirred to full attention and created a tent amongst the blankets she'd laid over me. It was then I realized I was fully naked beneath the covers. That the saltwater that had filled my lungs wasn't coating my skin, as if she'd washed me clean. That I was warm and safe in what appeared to be her home.

"It can't be that big," she whispered, gaze riveted.

I laughed. I couldn't help it. Her gaze flicked up to mine, and her face scrunched up.

"Och, want to see my cock for yourself then? See if it really is as big as it appears? I promise it's not so big as that stick you tripped on, but it's close." I couldn't help the slow grin that almost split my face in half, nor could I resist teasing her. Grasping the corner of the blanket that was tossed over me, I pretended to raise it.

"NO!" she cried and crouched down to grab the long pole. She held it defensively, hands in a tight grip, one foot forward. I paused as I caught a bitter scent wafting from her. She was afraid of me. I... didn't like that.

Slowly, I dropped the edge of the blanket and held up my hands. Studying her, I didn't move. She was a head's height shorter than me, at least. Her generous curves were on display in the soft loose pants and tunic she wore. With the way the large mounds of her breasts heaved as she breathed, I could tell she wore no support beneath. It was... enticing.

"Would you stop ogling me, you perv?!" she cried out and my gaze flicked up to hers, eyebrows high.

"Well, what do you expect a male to do when awoken by such a vision of a female?" I asked.

"Ugh!" she snarled and glared at me. "Typical."

"I promise you, nothing about me is 'typical,' lass." She only rolled her strange eyes at me.

"Do you have a name?" She grasped at the wooden stick in her hands.

"Yes," I replied. I reached up into my hair and found a sizable knot against my skull. It was tender but didn't sting nearly as badly as I'd expected. There was some sort of ointment on it, and my fingers felt greasy with it when I removed them.

"What is it?" she asked, obviously irritated. It was adorable. She was still frowning at me, but her body language had relaxed. I took that as a good sign. Being able to speak with her was a true blessing from the Source.

"Thorn Oc'Dellor," I said, sitting up and turning. I clutched the blankets to my midsection and placed my feet on the wooden floor. "Yours?"

"Watch it!" she snapped, raising the wooden pole high again and taking a step back. I shot her a droll look.

"Look, lass. If I wanted to hurt you, that measly stick wouldn't help you. You might as well put that down." I sighed and held her gaze.

"How am I supposed to trust you?" Her eyes narrowed to slits.

"Well, I guess you can't until I prove myself worthy, och? Can't exactly do that if I'm not given a chance to." I held up my hands in a helpless gesture and waited. Slowly, she set down her stick and stood tall.

"You get one chance," she murmured, looking uncertain despite her straight spine.

"Thank you. That's all I ask."

"My name is Ruth O'Daniels. You can call me Ruth." The words fell from her sweet-looking lips like the rarest of gems. That restlessness that had always pervaded my being, that had quieted when I'd seen my red thread of fate in the Gaeta, went absolutely silent.

"*Ruth.*" I breathed her name. The name of the female who'd brought me across worlds. The female I could only hope was my cridhe.

For what other purpose would the Source demand I travel through a broken Gaeta than for the cridhe bond—the strongest love bond an orckin could fathom?

Her scent changed again. This time, so ripe with arousal, I had to grit my teeth as I restrained myself from going to her. Worshiping her soft body as my instincts roared at me to do. But I was so much bigger than she was and I wouldn't risk harming her just to slake my lust.

"S-so what is a Gaeta?" she stammered and looked away from me. The pink was riding high on her cheeks again, and my mouth twitched in a small victorious smile. She liked how I'd said her name.

"Och, there's a Gaeta—a gate in Common—in the sea cave," I explained, running my claws through my tangled hair, attempting to comb it back. "They are gates between worlds. There are many on Talam, though they were all believed to be broken. Source called me to the Gaeta nearest my clan and when I touched it, it brought me here. I nearly drowned when I came through it."

"Why on earth would you come through a gate during high tide?" She cocked her head to the side as she stared at me with those deep uisge-beatha eyes of hers. I nearly drowned in them.

"I didn't know it was high tide, now did I? Thank you for saving me. May I have my clothes, please? I'd like to dress," I muttered and looked around. Unsure if I could continue talking to her while naked without falling to my knees at her clawless little bare feet. To offer her my heart and beg her to be my cridhe.

"Over there." She waved at a chair nearby. I stood, wrapping the blanket around my midsection, and stalked over to it. I reached for my clothes, then paused. Looking over my shoulder, I saw her still standing and staring at me. I tried not to smile.

"Do you mind turning around? I'd like a little privacy."

"Sorry," she muttered and swiftly spun on her heel. "Your shirt was so shredded, it wasn't worth saving. I'll have to find you another one, as mine are too small."

I chuckled and turned my back to her as well. I didn't actually mind if she saw me naked. It didn't take a genius to realize that she'd been the one to undress me and clean me, as I couldn't smell anyone else in her home.

It was that bitter scent of fear that I wanted to avoid. Perhaps I was too different. Wrong to her eyes. The idea was a painful one, and I had to push it aside as I buckled my leather kilt on.

"You didn't find a ring, did you? I seem to have lost one." My voice was tight. I hoped she wouldn't lie to me. I'd be able to smell it. Lies always smelled like hot metal. And I didn't want to get off on the wrong foot with the female I'd been drawn to meet.

"A ring?" Her tone was surprised. "No. I don't remember seeing one when I found you or when I got you cleaned up. What did it look like?"

I sniffed the air subtly and could only smell her sweet, natural aroma. I sighed in relief. She wasn't lying.

"It's old. Golden, with a symbol carved into a flat portion. It's an heirloom." It was best not to tell her about the ring's capabilities on the off chance they no longer worked.

"Like a signet ring?" she asked.

"I'm not sure what that is."

"It's a ring that's got a family crest on it. Usually passed down. Often used in old times by royalty and aristocracy."

"Ah." I couldn't help but smile as I buckled on my bandolier. I'd lost my knives, and I'd need to see about replacing them. I was glad I'd listened to my intuition and hadn't brought my sword and axe.

Weapons would have terrified her. "Yes, something like that."

"Shit!" she cried. I spun in alarm as she ran towards what appeared to be a kitchen and a smoking pan. The scent of charred meat had steadily built as we'd talked, but I'd been too distracted by her and her lovely fragrance to notice.

"What's wrong?" I asked as I prowled over to where she'd pulled a pan off of a metal box with four metal spirals on top. Three of them were black, and the fourth was red hot as she pulled the pan with slices of charred meat off of it.

"Ah!" she cried, and jumped, nearly dropping the pan. "Don't sneak up on me like that!"

"I apologize?" I hadn't meant to startle her, only aid her. Protect her.

I watched as she moved the smoking pan to a dark coil and turned off the bright red one. Slowly, the red faded towards black, and I reached out to touch it. Her tiny hand grasped my wrist, her fingers small enough that she couldn't wrap them completely around it, halting my movement.

"Be careful, it's hot!" she admonished, before releasing my wrist. I couldn't help but stare at her. The flesh of my wrist felt as if her fingers had branded me instead of the odd metal coil.

"What is this strange thing?" I asked, clearing my throat. I attempted to think of anything but her and how close she was standing. Of how badly I wanted to tangle my dark claws into her soft brown tresses and tilt her head back so I could taste that mouth of hers.

"It's a stove. It uses electricity to heat and cook food." She leaned over the nearby sink and opened a window so the smoke could blow out.

"Electricity?" I felt at a loss. Her world held mysteries and magics I couldn't fathom.

"Yeah, like lightning? We use electricity to run a lot of things. Including the lights at night." She shrugged as she looked at me. "I'll be honest, I'm not an engineer or a scientist, so I won't be able to explain it very well. I just know it works because it's science and people a lot smarter than me developed it."

"Science. Not magic?" I was skeptical. It seemed very much like magic.

"Not magic. Magic is just science we don't understand yet." She chuckled, and the loveliness of her smile struck me dumb. "Now get out of my kitchen so I can finish cooking. I take it you're hungry?"

"Very," I admitted, stomach rumbling at the mention of food. Ruth shooed me out of her kitchen with its science, and I let her. I went over and sat at a table next to the kitchen and watched as she cooked.

The scents were mesmerizing. Sweet, salty, fatty... she was cooking some sort of meat again, too. While the pan sizzled, she brought me an earthenware cup filled with some dark brown liquid that had the same earthy aroma I'd first smelled.

"This is coffee." She set down a small bowl with white cubes, a spoon, and a small container. "Humans drink it in the mornings. It'll give you energy. It is kind of bitter on its own, so you can add cream and sugar. If you don't like it, that's okay. I can get you some juice or milk."

"Thank you," I murmured, but she'd already moved back to her station in front of the stove. I sniffed at everything she'd set out for me. Picking up the earthenware cup, I took a hesitant sip and promptly spat it out.

"What is this?" I choked, face scrunching up in disgust. Setting the cup down, I wiped the back of my hand across my mouth, wishing I could rid myself of the bitter taste.

Ruth laughed. It was like the high chiming of festival bells and the tinkling of the acorns in the Craobh na Beatha. Mesmerized, I watched as she bent double, grasping at her stomach as she laughed at me. I couldn't find it in me to care. She could mock me for the rest of my days if she sounded like that. It was the most beautiful thing I'd ever heard.

"I'm so sorry!" She laughed, wiping at her eyes, grin wide, bright, and alive. "I warned you it was bitter!"

A bemused smile twitched at my mouth as she got her laughter under control. She came over, still chuckling, and added some white cubes and white liquid to my cup. The near-black potion turned into a lighter color as she mixed everything.

"Try it now." She smiled and pushed the cup to me.

Dubious, I cocked an eyebrow at her before sitting straight and lifting the cup to my mouth. I sniffed it and it didn't smell as bitter. Taking a careful sip, the sweetness and creaminess of whatever she added burst upon my tongue, mellowing out the acrid taste. I looked up at her, surprised.

"It's good!" I took another sip, and she patted my shoulder as she turned back to her cooking.

I couldn't help the way my body reacted to that small touch. Such a casual thing, but it set my heartbeat racing. I distracted myself by drinking some more of the coffee.

A few minutes later, she was bringing over plates of food. Meat and eggs stacked on one. Small cakes piled high on another. And a big bowl of cubed something in various colors. She set out plates and utensils for us to use. Then she sat down next to me at the table and pointed out items.

"So these long, crispy meat slices are bacon. It's salted pork. These tubes are sausages and are also pork. These are eggs. I wasn't sure how you'd like them cooked, so I made a few kinds. Then these are pancakes and I've got butter and maple syrup that goes on top. And this is a bowl of fruit. I cut up some strawberries, melon, and grapes."

"This is a feast, thank you," I told her, eyes wide on the variety of foods before me.

"Oh. You're welcome." A blush tinged her cheeks, and she looked away from me.

Taking my cue from her, I loaded my plate with a bit of everything. I picked up my fork and dug in. Explosions of flavor, some new and some familiar, burst upon my tongue. Groaning at the taste, I devoured what was on my plate.

The eggs and meat tasted familiar. Sausage and bacon warred for favorite meat. The cakes were like our caraiceag, except what she called 'maypel seerup' was a delicious addition. The fruit was the biggest surprise. Flavors bright and complex.

It was a delightful feast, and I refilled my plate to overflowing twice more. Ruth had finished and was watching me eat with a bemused smile on her face. She eventually stood and cleared away the dirty dishes.

Fatigue suddenly weighed on me. It dragged my limbs and eyes down as I sat at her table in nothing but my kilt, stomach bulging from the feast she'd prepared for me. My wounds ached under her careful bandaging and my head wouldn't stop throbbing. It was so indescribably sweet how she'd cared for me. The thought warmed my very soul.

"You look like you're about to pass out," Ruth murmured as she retrieved the last of the empty dishes. "I should probably check your bandages before you get some more rest."

"Och, they'll be fine in a few days. I heal quickly," I mumbled. "Just need some more sleep."

"Are you sure? They looked pretty bad." She sounded worried, and I found it endearing. Was she honestly worried about me? That warmed my heart even more.

I stood and staggered my way over to the couch. I felt like a terrible guest. Eating her food and sleeping on her couch, offering nothing in return. But I knew I was worthless until I'd recovered. I'd figure out how to repay her then.

"I'm sure." I groaned as I sat down and turned, bringing my legs up onto the couch and snagging the quilt. "Thank you, sweet Ruth."

Exhaustion pulled at my eyelids, and it was moments before I succumbed to oblivion.

CHAPTER 06[*]

RUTH

The next few days crawled past in a halting sort of way. Trepidation became my constant companion as I took on new tasks. Thorn had spent most of it sleeping. I only had the one mattress, but he didn't seem to mind sleeping on the tiny couch.

I passed the time either cooking for his massive appetite or out in the garden, trimming back the roses and jasmine as he slept. I'd wanted to stay close, in case he needed me. It'd been a near disaster the first time he'd gone to the bathroom.

I'd found him pissing by the back door and had to show him where the bathroom was. His kind had toilets and sinks back on his home planet. The mechanisms to get the water running were different. Which was why he'd just given up and had taken a leak outside. At least I could rest easy that he was house trained.

Regardless, I was worried that if I strayed too far, he'd somehow damage the house or himself. He'd been so ready to touch the stove coil that first morning... So, I went against my original plan and worked on the house first. The walled garden off the side of the house slowly revealed itself through my hard work and desperation to get the orc out of my mind.

I unearthed stone benches and fountains, pots, and stone pathways from the overgrowth. Whoever had owned the farm before had taken a lot of pride in the garden. Back before it had become a veritable jungle. I felt like I was peeling back layers of time and a contented sense of accomplishment and peace suffused my body. A feeling I hadn't had for longer than I cared to remember.

Checking Thorn's wounds had become one of my daily tasks. One we both seemed to enjoy and dread. I enjoyed caring for someone again, and he enjoyed flustering me. I dreaded how far my brain would dive into dirty thoughts, and he dreaded being seen as weak. Laughing at him, I told him he couldn't be weak if he tried. He'd liked that.

When I'd tried to do more than just clean his wounds, he'd waved me off, saying that he'd be right as rain with a few days' rest. I had little anyway in terms of supplies. Most of it I'd used up the first time I dressed his wounds. I was running low on food too, so a trip to the store in town was inevitable.

I was still apprehensive over whether to leave an orc sprawled asleep on my couch. What would happen if he ran off? Or if someone discovered Thorn, and the FBI showed up? These unhelpful thoughts tumbled around in my head like rocks in a dryer. But I couldn't live my life in fear anymore.

So with an anxious heart, I locked up the house as Thorn slept, got into my truck, and headed into town. Parking was easy, as was finding the medical supplies I needed at the pharmacy. People were staring at me, though, and I didn't like it. The pharmacist didn't seem concerned and just offered me a warm and understanding wink before sending me on my way.

Confused, but with a slow-burn understanding that something was very wrong with how the town perceived me, I headed to the grocery store. Men and women alike gawked at me as I walked down the aisles with my cart. They whispered words in derisive tones from behind their hands. Their mutterings followed me through the store like some insidious music.

I hadn't been close to my parents. But one thing my mother had taught me was that people would talk. If I just kept being true to myself, they'd eventually realize who I really was. I wasn't sure if her nugget of wisdom would help me in this little town. Not with the rude things they were saying loud enough for me to hear.

"I heard she was a whore."

"Dirty hippie...."

"She's the person who bought the old farm on the edge of town?"

"Going to start a cult right in our backyard, that's what I heard."

".... told me she was a part of ritual sacrifices to Satan...."

The last one had me laughing out loud. The whispers died out. I turned around near the cash registers and saw that everyone was staring at me in horror. I grinned at them and a few stepped back.

"You all are really that bored, huh?" I asked, turning so everyone could get a look at my smiling face. "Don't you have anything better to do than make up shit about the new girl? What are you, still in high school?"

Some folk had the decency to look properly chastised. I mean, it wasn't my first time in town. They'd been pleasant before and knew from my attire that I was a hippie. I was wearing bell-bottoms, a floral blouse, and my favorite fringed leather vest. It was hard to miss.

What got me was I wasn't entirely sure what had changed. Why were they suddenly acting like bullies? Someone had been talking smack, that's for sure. I wasn't sure who or what or why, but I knew I'd find out, eventually.

"I'm not going to hurt any of you, do you copy?" I sighed. "Don't know who told you all this, but I can assure you I won't start a cult. I don't worship Satan, and I just want to live my life and be left alone."

A few people nodded, others just glared at me. As if I were lying to them. Idiots. Shaking my head, I turned with my full cart and headed toward the cashier.

"Don't mind them. They're bored and will talk about someone else in a few days." The reserved cashier offered me a half-smile. "They did that to me when I showed up, too."

"Small town bullshit, eh?" I asked her with a self-deprecating half-smile.

"Tell me about it. You'd think they'd have better things to do than gossip." The cashier was around my age, pretty. "I'm Julia Franco, by the way."

"I'm Ruth O'Daniels. Nice to meet you." I grinned, unable to help it. It was nice to meet someone open to being friendly with me.

"Nice to meet you, too." She began ringing up my items and I helped bag them. "You haven't... noticed anything weird happening around here, have you?"

"Weird? Why do you ask?" I paused, a cold sweat breaking out on my skin. Did she know about Thorn?

"Well..." she trailed off, looking lost. "Never mind, it isn't important."

I couldn't help but watch Julia as she continued to ring up my groceries. She was quiet, introspective. Her brows were drawn together in worry and frustration. It became clear pretty quickly that she was asking because she had her own problems she was dealing with.

"You know..." I began, hefting the grocery bags into my cart. "I'm a spiritual person. I realize strange things happen all the time, things I can't explain. But just because I can't explain them doesn't mean I can't accept them or that there isn't a reason for them to happen how they do."

"You think?" she asked, gaze locking with mine in hope as I handed her the money.

"I do," I said, reaching into my purse and grabbing a pen. "Give me a bit of paper, will you?"

"Sure." She ripped off some excess receipt paper and handed it to me. I took it from her and began writing on it.

"This is my house number," I told her, jotting down my name and the row of digits of my number. I finished and stood straight again, handing her the bit of paper with a smile and a wink. "If you need to talk, call me. Us outcasts have to stick together in small towns like this one."

"Thanks. I just might." She gave me a small smile as she took the paper and traded me for my change. I gave her a small wave goodbye and made my way out to my truck.

Driving home, I kept thinking about Julia. Maybe she'd been experiencing weird things like I had. Perhaps she had her own orc holed up on her couch. Maybe this town was just a hub of weird activity. Like Sedona, Arizona.

Thorn had spoken repeatedly about some sort of gate down in the sea cave. Maybe he wasn't the only thing that had come through it. I'd need to ask Thorn to show me the gate now. I needed to learn more about the gate, in case someone else came knocking.

I turned off the two-lane highway onto the rutted gravel

driveway that led home. It wasn't even noon yet, and I was already tired. Pulling up to the house, I threw the truck in park and got out. It took me a few trips to get all the groceries into the house and put away. I could have woken Thorn and asked for his help, but I didn't mind. He was still recovering, anyway.

Later, I was out back trimming a stubborn patch of climbing roses. Just then, I heard the distinctive sound of tires on gravel. My body went instantly cold. Dread crept into my very bones as I rushed from the side garden to the mudroom. I ran inside to the front windows and peered through them. Who in the hell would come here?

A shiny new 1974 Chevy Impala rumbled over the potholes and ruts in my driveway, heading straight for the house. Straight for me and the orc on my couch. I knew that kind of car anywhere, knew the look. It was an FBI undercover car.

"Shit!" I bit out, snapping the front drapes closed. "Thorn! Thorn, wake up!"

I heard grumbling as I rushed around the house, closing the drapes in the kitchen and living room windows. Memories of the raid on the commune flashed behind my eyes. Agents had arrived at the commune in the same type of car. The agent driving it had nearly shot me.

Worry knotted itself up in my guts. What could they possibly want? I mean, I'd chewed out a G-Man on the phone just the other morning, but I doubt that warranted a house call. Unless... Unless they somehow knew about the orc snoring away on my couch.

"What's the matter?" Thorn went from groggy to alert in a flash. He sat up and watched me racing around the house like a chicken with my head chopped off.

"Sshhhh," I hissed as the sound of tires coming to a halt in the gravel reached us. A moment later, a car door opened and closed.

Panicking, I ran up to Thorn and pushed him towards the stairwell to the basement. "You need to hide!"

"Why?" he asked a little too loudly. I muffled his mouth with my hand. I shook my head and looked over my shoulder at the door, where I could hear someone approaching.

"No one can see you!" I whispered. Thorn pulled my fingers from his lips. "It's dangerous and won't end well for us if you don't hide right now! I'll explain more later!"

"You must promise me you'll call for me if you need protection." Thorn's gaze was like a brand. Unsettling in its intensity, making my stomach flutter.

"I promise!" I hissed. "Now go!"

With a final push, he reluctantly moved. Walking on catlike feet, he reached the door to the basement. He didn't even hesitate at the cramped space and entered it, closing the door behind him. It was creepy how such a large guy could be so quiet.

A knock rapped against the front door. I nearly jumped out of my skin. Pressing a hand to my chest where my heart thundered against my rib cage, I took a steadying breath. The knock came again, and irritation flared.

"I'm coming! Chill out, would ya?" I shouted and took a quick glance around. Nothing out of the ordinary, nothing that screamed a seven-foot-tall orc with gray skin was sleeping on my couch.

I could do this. Thorn was here, and he'd offered backup if things got hairy. I'd faced the invading police before. It sounded like only one car and one person. I could manage. I could survive.

Taking a deep breath, I steeled my nerves and stomped towards the door. I ripped it open and came face to face with a dark blue suit. The guy looked like every generic Joe on the block. Muddy brown hair, bland brown eyes, glasses, and indistinct features that could almost be handsome yet somehow seemed blurry. Then again, any features after Thorn's sharp, chiseled ones looked a little indistinct.

"And you are?" I asked the suit who stood so casually on my front porch.

"Agent Simms. We've spoken on the phone." His expression was a pleasant blank mask. But his eyes seemed to drink in every single detail. Of me, my house, and what he could see of the interior from his limited view. As if memorizing every iota of information he could.

I hated it.

"So you're the guy who doesn't understand the meaning of the word 'no'." I drawled.

He stiffened.

"Kinda rapey-sounding, isn't it?"

"I just wanted to meet the brave soul who'd purchased the property. Do you mind if I come in?" Agent Simms asked with a smile, an attempt to switch tactics and keep the conversation where he wanted it, no doubt.

"Yes, in fact, I do," I said. One hand on my hip, the other gripping the door, I itched to slam it in his face.

"I'm sure it would be more comfortable to have this conversation inside." His smile turned brittle. He clearly wasn't liking the fact that I was denying him. Entitled square.

"I'm sure it would be for you. But unless you have a warrant, you will not be entering my home. I don't know you and I don't trust you. Catch my drift?" My tone was flat, icy. "I've already told you, that I will not sell the farm to the government. So why you're pressing the matter is beyond me."

Agent Simms removed his spectacles and started cleaning them with a cloth, a self-satisfied smirk on his mouth. "We could just confiscate the property with Eminent Domain."

I called his bluff. "You'd have to prove that it would be for public use, provide just compensation, and I'd just file an inverse condemnation action. Plus, I highly doubt the town and county would appreciate the FBI executing Eminent Domain. There's a lot of pride in the local people. They'd rather see a hippie quietly living her life instead of the government strong-arming their way in," I replied. Agent Simms glared at me. "Honestly, what on Earth are you planning to do with this land? It's out of the way and isn't encroaching on any wildlife preserves. What's the value of a simple small farm to the government?"

Agent Simms regarded me anew as if finally seeing the intelligence behind my eyes and my lack of fear. "As part of Eminent Domain, I'm authorized to provide three times the market value for your farm."

"No, thanks," I replied.

"That's a lot of money to turn down, Miss O'Daniels."

"Money doesn't really do it for me, G-Man."

"If you can't carry your mortgage, you'll lose the farm to the bank and we'll purchase it, anyway. I know all about your little Tolkien project. Quaint. But it's not very practical." Agent Determined-Fucker straightened and pulled a card from the inside pocket of his suit coat. He held it out to me. "In case you change your mind."

"I won't."

He paused, clearly not used to being denied. Curling his lip, he flicked it at me and the card fluttered to the ground between us. Agent Simms pulled out a pair of shades and slipped them on. Over his glasses. What a fucking putz.

"Have a good day, Miss O'Daniels."

"Catch you on the flip side, G-Man," I called after him as he hastened back to his car.

I stood and watched as he got into his Impala, reversed, and drove out of sight down my rutted driveway. I closed the door and leaned against it, sighing and closing my eyes. What was I going to do? I didn't know what he wanted with the property and he was dead set on making my life hell.

Doubt crept in. I was having trouble getting contractors out here to look at my land. There were less than six months to transform this place, and I'd barely started on the house itself. I wasn't sure I could finish the bed-and-breakfast on time. I could work my fingers to the bone. But elbow grease would only get me so far.

"Is it safe?" a rumbling voice called, and I jumped.

"Y-yeah. He's gone," I replied, pushing off of the door. I headed into the kitchen to make some coffee to help settle my nerves.

Thorn exited the door to the basement. He had a hard time squeezing his colossal frame through the small doorway. Surprisingly, I was more comforted by his large presence than afraid of him.

"I could hear most of what you were talking about. But some of it I don't understand." Thorn crossed his tree-trunk-sized arms across his broad chest and my brain froze. That was a wwhooooole lot of man... Er... *male* presence right there. I'd never seen a man so ripped, and I was having a hard time processing it. I needed to buy the dude a gods damned shirt. If I could find one in his size. And that was a *huge* if.

"Okay, what don't you understand?" I asked, turning back to making coffee to hide the blush creeping up my neck.

"What is 'emmenetddomayn'?"

"Oh, Eminent Domain, it's where the government can seize someone's land if they want it. There are some rules to protect landowners. Few, though," I told him, while I put the kettle on the stove to heat. "Ever since I bought the farm, that FBI agent has been calling me every day. Bugging the hell out of me to sell it."

"What is 'FBI agent'?" His brow furrowed, and it was almost comically cute to see on someone so big.

"It's someone who works for the government." I sighed as the coffee pot thrummed with the force of the boiling water. "I'm afraid they might be after you. Or your kind. You said you came from another planet. Maybe they're after the gate, whatever that is."

"Och. When is low tide?" He asked, tilting his head in a thoughtful manner.

"Let me check." I took the whistling coffee pot off of the stove and set it aside before moving towards a chart I'd stuck to the fridge with all the local tide times. "In about an hour. Why?"

"I'll show you the Geata, and it will give me a chance to look for my chleoc ring." Thorn uncrossed his arms and seemed to relax. He frowned again. "Why are you so nervous, Ruth?"

"Because I don't want to lose this place before I've earned it." I shrugged as I poured myself a cup of coffee with shaking hands. I slowly set down the coffee pot before picking up my mug. Turning, I looked at Thorn in his weirdly black-sclera gaze. "Also... Agent Simms doesn't seem willing to take 'no' for an answer. I... don't have pleasant experiences with men who don't take 'no' for an answer."

A deafening silence cascaded around us, and my ears rang. Thorn had frozen, even stopped breathing. It was... alarming. Eerie. Suddenly, he drew in a deep breath. His chest swelled, and his face transformed into one of deadly surety. As if he'd become a warrior about to head into battle.

"Do you want me to kill him for you?" His voice ground out from between his wolf-like teeth. Quiet. Deadly.

"What?" I asked, nearly dropping my mug.

"Do you want me to kill him for you?" he repeated, enunciating clearly. I wasn't sure if he meant Agent Simms or whoever had hurt me in the past. I wasn't sure I cared. *No one* had ever respected my honor so much that they offered to murder someone for me. It was alarmingly flattering in a dark, twisted way.

How's a peace-loving girl supposed to take that?

"Um... no. I don't think killing Agent Simms would be a good idea. It would lead to more questions. More questions mean more people interested in the farm. And,"—I risked a glance up to his stoic gaze— "the others who hurt me are behind bars. They're in prison."

And they were. The commune leaders had been arrested thanks to some prime info I'd slipped the authorities. The government didn't like tax evasion.

Thorn took a deep breath and seemed to shake himself from his warrior mode.

"Amongst the Oc'Dellor, if a male has forced himself upon another, especially a female, they're culled and hung from the Traitor Tree." He sighed, expression turning almost defeated. "It's not the same for all five clans, though. Some clans uphold cruelty instead of justice."

"Well then, I'm glad you're from the Oc'Dellor." I offered him a weak smile, his clan name rolling off of my tongue in an easy cadence. His mouth twitched in return. Despite myself, I liked how a smile looked on his oddly handsome face. The desire to witness his smile again hit me swiftly, and I had to look away. What was wrong with me?

CHAPTER 07

THORN

I hated the stench of fear that permeated the kitchen and living room once the human male had left. It made my claws itch to rend flesh. I didn't like how he'd spoken to her, either. But it impressed me how she'd faced him and kicked him out.

His noisy metal beast rumbled as he rode away. Ruth had informed me that such contraptions were called 'cars'. Humans rode in them like orckin rode nocrys, only these beasts weren't *alive*. Yet they moved. Still, she claimed it was science and not magic that animated these metal monsters.

From what Ruth explained, it seemed her government wanted her land and the Geata. Perhaps even me, if they discovered my existence. She'd insisted I stay indoors all this time, but I knew she'd need to see the Geata for herself. To truly believe me when I told her of my home. So I offered. She'd accepted.

I'd also offered to end the life of any male who'd ever given her... *unpleasant* experiences. Who refused to accept her rejections. The pure, volcanically explosive rage that had flooded my system when she'd told me, I would have happily burned the world down for her.

She'd insisted that she was now safe, but I could smell that she didn't feel that way.

I'd do anything to help her feel safe. I would be patient with her. Offer her my protection and my heart. Earn her trust. Even if it meant pretending to be harmless when we both knew I wasn't.

Later, we left the house through the back door. Her stairs leading out of the house were rickety, and I nearly plunged my boot through a stair. I'd need to fix it when we returned. Ruth deserved to live in a safe home.

I followed her down a well-worn path towards the cliffs. The wind blew my tangled black hair out of my face and buffeted me with brine-tinged scents. I gawked at the sky where clouds were passing across a single sun and a lone moon hung on the horizon. The sky felt so empty without the many celestial bodies I was accustomed to. Glancing around at my surroundings, I noted the various plants and animals, some similar and others completely alien to what I knew from Talam.

"What are those?" I asked, pointing at some pale gray birds. They were plump, their plumage warm in tone, their call sad sounding as they cooed to one another amongst some trees.

"Those?" She looked at where I was pointing and smiled. "Those are mourning doves."

"Mourning doves."

"Yes, a type of dove, a bird. Pretty common around here." She shrugged and turned, about to keep moving, dismissing the wondrous sight.

"They remind me of you, Ruth." My words tumbled from my lips unbidden, and she froze. Her head turned, and she gave me a confused expression. I cleared my throat, feeling my cheeks burn a pale silver. "They're small and plump and lovely. You're like a little dove."

Ruth's cheeks turned a vibrant scarlet, her eyes round as the royal neamhnaid—pearls—my sister had worn. A bittersweet burst of love hit my heart like a knife. I missed my Thisa so much. She would have loved Ruth. It took little imagination to believe they would have been fast friends.

"I'm not small," my cridhe grumbled as she stomped away from me, ears bright red.

"To me, you are, little dove," I chuckled after her, and I could swear I saw her shiver.

We reached the cliffs, and sudden apprehension nipped at my heels as we followed the switchback trail to the sandy beach below. I'd have to tell her why I came to Earth. About the Source's call that had brought me here. I knew in my heart that she was my cridhe, that my red thread of fate had led me to her.

She'd found me on the beach that day. Had rescued me and tended to me when I was so different from her, when she hadn't any reason to. For that alone, I would wait for her approval until the day I died.

But I feared she wouldn't give me a chance.

When we reached the beach, I took the lead. I helped Ruth with her footing as we made our way into the cave. The tunnel was dark inside, but the ambient light was plenty to see by.

It quickly became obvious that, unlike me, Ruth couldn't see in the low light. Ruth's foot slipped on a rock, and she tumbled backward. Moving on instinct, I stepped towards her and caught her with one arm around her shoulders, one hand on her waist.

"I've got you," I murmured into the echoing cave. The sounds of clattering stones and shifting sand faded. Ruth looked up at me with surprise. I gazed at her for a long, enthralling moment. My breath quickened as I felt her softness in my arms once again. The urge to kiss her was overwhelming, and I couldn't resist looking down at her rose-colored lips.

"I-I'm alright." She leaped out of my arms, stumbling on the slime-coated stones. Her ears were a bright pink. Adorable.

She bravely strode into the cave, despite keeping her hands outstretched before her to help her find her way in the low light. I shook my head at her stubbornness and followed close behind. My hands itched to touch her once more, but I kept them at my sides. I'd let her lead and would catch her if she slipped again.

The tunnel opened up in the cave. Shafts of light cut through the stone overhead and lit up the lovely Geata, identical to the one on Talam. Carved into the very rock, it still glistened with the remnants of the tide. Ruth's gasp of surprise and awe was enough to warm the icy dread I felt.

I watched her approach the Geata. She'd endured so much at the hands of males. Her scent had spoken volumes more than her words. I didn't want to frighten her with the truth that I'd come here to find her. Yet I couldn't find it in me to lie to her, either.

Would she be able to see that I wasn't like them? That I would use my warrior's body to protect her, not harm her? I could only hope she'd see me for what I was. Who I was.

RUTH

It. Was. Stellar. Completely out of this world. Something out of some fantasy or science fiction tale. Almost like Tolkien's books come to life right before my eyes. As if I were staring at some lovely representation of the Tree of Gondor carved by elves who'd eaten far too many magic mushrooms.

I couldn't shake how strange it was. The massive carving was on a flat wall that extended along the floor and up onto the ceiling. There really should have been stalactites and stalagmites from millennia of erosion. There should have been signs of erosion from the elements on the carving. But nothing. Just this perfectly carved tree with such fine detail, it looked as if it'd been completed only yesterday.

"You came here through this?" I asked, awestruck.

"Yes."

"Did you want to see if you could open it to go home?" If I got him to go home, then the risk the FBI posed wouldn't be so dire. If he went home, I'd be alone again.

He looked at me with an unreadable expression. "I don't think I can."

"Why?"

"The Geata are broken. It's a miracle it worked and got me here in the first place." He crossed his arms over his broad chest. I had to look away or risk ogling him.

"Well, why not give it a try? It couldn't hurt."

"If it'll make you happy," he said. He didn't sound happy at all at the prospect, which confused the hell out of me. Why wouldn't someone in his position want to try to get home if they could?

Thorn walked up the stairs to the gate. Pressed one crystal, the dull-looking one in the middle, embedded into what looked like a doorway. His shoulders bunched as if he expected something to happen. When nothing but silence met us, he released a pent-up breath and turned to look at me.

"Looks like it doesn't work anymore." He told me with a half-shrug. "I don't think I can go home."

It bothered me how quickly he'd given up. Didn't he want to go home? Hadn't he said something about a call from the universe to do something? Accomplish something? Was he unable to go back because he hadn't completed his task yet?

"Why did you come here? What did the Source call you to do?" I asked. I was still skeptical about his story, but I worshiped gods and goddesses and had experienced strange things myself.

"When I touched the gate," he began, looking apprehensive but forcing himself to meet my gaze, "I saw my red thread of destiny. I believe the Source led me across the stars to you. My cridhe."

Silence weighed on us both. I could hear only the sough of the sea and our breathing. I stared at him, mouth falling open at the implication.

Fate. His fate. He thought *I* was his *fate*.

"Thorn," I rasped, clearing my throat before I continued. "What is a cridhe?"

His face tightened with what looked like worry, that full mouth of his flattening into a thin line, brows pulling together as he looked me in the eye.

"A cridhe is an orckin's soul-bound partner. The one person in all the universe who fits them perfectly. There are marks that appear when you've found your cridhe. Here." He held one massive, black, claw-tipped hand over his broad chest. Where there were no tattoos. No markings.

"But there are none. How do you know it's me?" Irritation at his surety was boiling up in my veins, and my limbs until I nearly shook with it.

"I know in my bones that you are my mate. My cridhe."

"You have got to be kidding," I barked a humorless laugh, smile wavering, then falling away. "You're *serious*. You think I'm your... your mate?"

"Not just a mate. Far more than just a mate."

"Your *soulmate*." I snapped, frustrated.

"Yes."

"So what, I'm supposed to just accept this and be your sex buddy for the rest of my life? Not have any say in the matter? Fuck off!" I bit out. Hurt flashed across Thorn's face.

"That's not what I'm telling you."

"Yes, it is! You're telling me that the damned *universe* chose *for me*! And it chose an alien from a different planct! We've only known each other for a few days, and you've been recovering for most of it! I don't even *know* you!" Tears trembled in my eyes as my breathing came faster, anger twisting into something akin to terror.

I felt trapped in the massive cave with this massive orc who had this massive, flirtatious personality, who had a massive *schlong*, and who evidently thought I was his universally aligned partner. I had to get out. Had to get away.

My breathing quickened, light and fast. Heart racing, I looked around for an exit. Spotting the tunnel, I made a mad dash for it, wet sand flying behind my tennis shoes. I had to slow down to make my way through the dark. The dark that hadn't seemed to bother Thorn one bit. It felt like the walls of the cave were closing in on me, going to crush me into a pulp.

A broken sob caught in my throat, and I finally saw light at the end of the tunnel. By the time I'd reached the mouth, I was practically dragging myself through it, hands scrabbling on the rock. I jogged out a few yards and stopped on the beach, gulping down air, trying desperately to slow my breathing and racing heart. I couldn't afford to blackout now.

"I will not force you!" I heard him call over the waves as they crashed against the sand and jagged rocks.

"You'd better not!" I screamed, turning to face him, fueled with a wave of sudden, bitter anger. "I don't belong to anyone! I am my own woman!"

"Ruth." He breathed my name, like a sinner beseeching a saint. Thorn's shoulders slumped, and he stood there, chest heaving with whatever emotion he was tangled up in, black and copper eyes imploring me to understand something far beyond me.

"How do you even *know*? How do you *know* I'm the one you're looking for?" I shouted, roughly shoving my hair out of my eyes.

"Because I saw your face!" he shouted. I almost flinched but kept my fear in check. He took a deep, fortifying breath before continuing. "The night before I arrived here, I had a dream of the Craobh na Beatha and the Geata within. Of this place. I saw your face. And when I came through the gate and woke up with your face mere inches from mine, I *knew* in my heart, Ruth."

"What am I supposed to say to this? We're not even the same species!"

"Say whatever you like!" He swept his scarred and tattooed arms wide. "I came here looking for my cridhe and I found you! I am stuck here. I cannot go back. My parents, my friends, my people, *all* of them are as good as dead to me now."

The raging storm within me stilled as I blinked at him. And then it truly registered. He was an alien orc from another planet. And he thought I was his mate. I couldn't fathom the mate aspect of everything, but I knew in my gut that I was his only friend. The only person who had his best interest at heart. I'd proved it from the minute I'd found him.

"I'm sorry," I whispered.

"Sorry for what?" he asked, brow furrowing and arms falling to his sides.

"That you can't go back. That you're stuck here. That you won't see your family or your people again." My voice was quiet, but he must have heard it with his pointed ears because he sighed and made his way over to me. "That I likely can't give you what you want."

And there it was. The truth.

It didn't take a genius to realize that what he'd said about mates and cridhe was only scratching the surface. He'd been wary of telling me at all. Probably because we both knew I was damaged goods. I couldn't give him what he'd traveled across the universe for.

"Ruth, I've lost a lot. My sister died of disease, my best friend lost to his grief. For Source's sake, I would have *married* a female, Leanabh Banrigh, from our neighboring clan. To combine forces and somehow withstand our species' demise. Because this disease is driving us to extinction." He stopped and stood an arm's length away from me. "My mother, the Banrigh and Fear a Chì, blessed my coming here after I dreamt of you. Meeting my fate and my cridhe means more to me than my own life. I trust in my mother and her visions. She would not lead me astray. If I must be here on Earth, then so be it. Whatever I endure, it will be worth it to be near you. Even if you never accept me as your cridhe."

The idea of him marrying someone else, even for political reasons, soured my stomach and made me furious. I pushed those feelings down deep. They wouldn't help me. I struggled to find words but found nothing. What could I possibly say to someone from another planet who was so willing to accept that he'd never go home just for the chance that I'd accept him?

"I don't expect you to accept me right away. Our ways are

different. Our people, worlds, and experiences are vastly different." He waved an arm out to encompass the world around us. "I don't know how these things work with humans. How you choose your mates. But I will get on my knees and *beg* you for the chance to prove my worth to you."

And gods be damned, he looked like he was ready to fall to his knees at my feet. His copper and onyx gaze was open, vulnerable, beseeching. Desperate, even.

"Please, Ruth. Let me prove to you I am serious. That I'm worthy to be your cridhe. I will help you build your bed-and-breakfast. I will help you do anything you want to do. I only ask for your friendship and the chance to prove myself to you. Please, little dove," he whispered the last, and I felt my cheeks heat with the sound of those two words.

Little dove. I'd never been called little in my life. Or given a pet name. I opened my mouth to speak. To give in and allow him his "chance" to woo me if he wanted. To be his friend. I found I couldn't say no to him if I tried. But he beat me to it.

"Let me start again. I am Thorn Oc'Dellor. I'm Leanabh Rìgh and heir to the Oc'Dellor clan of Talam." Thorn's voice was even, calm, his posture regal.

WAIT.

"You're the heir. Of your clan." I said flatly.

"Yes."

"So what, you're like a prince?" I asked, incredulous yet again.

"Technically, yes," Thorn smirked at my reaction, eyebrows cocked in amusement. Something in me snapped.

"You mean to tell me that a literal orc prince just *happened* to follow some sign from the universe to go through a supposedly broken gate on another planet in another galaxy to end up half-drowned on my beach? That I just *happened* to find you before you died of hypothermia? Then dragged your ass to my run-down farmhouse, have the literal *FBI* on my back because of this gate, you eat enough food in one sitting to feed a family of four, and then you have the utter *audacity* to claim that I'm your universe-appointed *mate*?" I stood panting, chest heaving, eyes wide with disbelief.

"Yes."

"*Would you please say anything else except yes*?!" I nearly shrieked.

"As you wish." Thorn's grin was absolutely vulpine.

I growled like a bobcat, startling myself. Thorn's gaze swiftly shifted to one of heat, and that pissed me off even more. I threw my hands in the air, spinning around to stomp into the crashing surf. The ice-cold water hit me up to my shins, and I huffed in a relieved breath at the shock of it. My anger and the cold Pacific water had me shivering in moments, shoes immediately waterlogged. Crossing my arms over my chest, I sought to rein in my temper, studiously ignoring the orc.

Having Thorn be just some orckin guy claiming I was his mate would be one thing. I had fallen so far in the last few years while at the commune. Outsiders hated counterculture and my ex-boyfriend, one of the commune leaders, had stolen every dollar I had. He'd kept me so high I never knew if it was him or someone else that had used my body. I could buy some alien dude being okay with that.

But his royal blood? No, I was no princess. I was hardly desired by my own kind. I wasn't worthy of being a prince's mate, so why the hell did he want me?

Tears rolled down my cheeks, and I refused to dash them away. I felt so adrift. What was I supposed to do?

"WHAT IN THE DEVIL IS THAT?!" We heard the cry from behind us and I whirled, heart beating a tattoo in my chest.

We turned to see a sheriff and a deputy at the base of the cliffs, not far from the path. We looked at them and they stared openly at Thorn. I panicked as I looked between the three guys, two of which had guns, one of which was a natural-born predator. We were so irreparably *fucked*.

CHAPTER 08

RUTH

"GET YOUR HANDS UP!" the deputy cried, fumbling to pull his gun from his holster. Thorn just cocked his head to the side, watching the pandemonium unfold. The Sheriff stood staring at Thorn like he'd seen him somewhere before. I threw my hands in the air, clearly the only one with some sense.

"Please don't shoot! We've done nothing wrong and he won't hurt anyone!" I cried, knowing it was a lie, hoping they'd believe it.

"That *thing* is not human!" the deputy hollered. Finally getting his pistol right way up in both hands. Though he was shaking hard enough to easily misfire if he wasn't careful. After nearly being shot once this past year, I could seriously do without a terrified deputy waving a gun around.

"Deputy." The sheriff's voice was strangely calm. Collected. Like he saw orcs on private beaches all the damn time. "Put away your sidearm."

"But Sheriff Brighton-!" The deputy began.

"I said, put it away Deputy Sanchez." The sheriff looked to his deputy who, after a few really tense seconds, swallowed, nodded, and holstered his gun. It impressed me, the respect Sheriff Brighton commanded of his deputy.

"Thank you," I whispered to whoever was looking out for me. To my deities and the universe. I kept my hands raised, though. Thorn, however? He just crossed his arms and stared curiously at the two men.

"Ruth? Who are these humans?" Thorn's voice rumbled over our little tableau like thunder. The deputy looked like he was about to shit himself. The sheriff's eyebrows shot up into his hairline. Guess he wasn't expecting Thorn to speak English. Er, Common. Whatever.

"These are officers of the law," I told him, hands raised and shaking.

"They uphold peace?" His black and copper gaze flicked between the two men. As if measuring them.

"Yes," I replied, tense. What would Thorn do if he found them lacking?

"Then why do you stink of fear, Ruth?" His words were frigid. Unyielding. Demanding an honest answer.

"Because I don't have wonderful memories of dealing with officers of the law," I admitted.

"Do you want me to kill them for you?" Again, that deadly tone from earlier.

"*No!*" I shouted and looked at him with my eyes wide, expression incredulous. "Why do you keep offering to kill people for me? We don't do that here!"

"Has this person killed anyone?" Sheriff Brighton asked sharply, his gaze narrowing on Thorn, hand drifting oh so casually towards his holstered gun.

"No!" I cried at the Sheriff, stress making my voice reach octaves I wasn't aware I could hit. "He's been mostly unconscious or eating me out of house and home!"

Thorn snorted and shook his head, but he couldn't hide the smile that curled his damnably tempting mouth. The sheriff relaxed a little. His deputy looked terrified.

"You can put your arms down now, miss." The sheriff called. I did, hesitantly. "I promise we won't hurt you or your... friend. If anything, we came here to clear a few things up."

"Things?" I called, wrapping my arms around myself. "What '*things*'?"

The sheriff walked over to us, body language loose and eyes glued warily on Thorn. The deputy followed like a good little duckling following his father duck. It would have been cute had I not been utterly petrified. There were so many ways this situation could go sideways, fast. Why on Earth was the sheriff not panicking like his deputy?

"Look, I'll make this quick and painless." The sheriff began, coming to a halt a few yards away. "I'm Sheriff Brighton and this is Deputy Sanchez and we're with the local sheriff's department. We got some anonymous tip about a dangerous person lurking on your land."

All eyes went to Thorn. He looked completely unbothered. As if getting accused of being a dangerous lurker was an everyday occurrence. The near-regal cant to his head was an open dare to the two much smaller human men. I wanted to hit him.

"We'd been hearing varying reports about you, Miss O'Daniels, and followed up with your attorney, Mr. Jensen. He informed us of what the FBI is attempting to do here. I wanted to come by to inform you we wouldn't be allowing bullying in our town. Now... as for your... friend. He's not human, is he?" Sheriff Brighton asked, hands resting on his gun belt in a very relaxed manner.

He was shorter than I was, stocky. His salt-and-pepper mustache and the weathered lines of his face put him somewhere in middle age. Deputy Sanchez was wiry and looked fresh out of the Academy. Baby-faced and clean-shaven, with thick black hair that most women would kill for. He attempted to mirror Sheriff Brighton's stance, to look at ease. He failed miserably. The poor little duckling was out of his depth, just like the rest of us.

"Um. No." I replied, absolutely baffled.

"What's your name, son?" The sheriff asked Thorn.

"My name is Thorn Oc'Dellor. I'm Leanabh Rìgh and heir to the Oc'Dellor clan of Talam. I'm orckin, not human." Thorn's voice was even, calm, his posture regal as he repeated his true identity. Regaining control over myself, I looked over at the sheriff and his cowering deputy. They both looked stunned, and I couldn't blame them. Being told you're in the presence of royalty isn't something we Americans were used to dealing with.

"So, I get why Deputy Sanchez looks like he's about to shit bricks, but why aren't you freaking out, Sheriff Brighton?"

"Well, miss, that's a funny tale." Sheriff Brighton scratched his balding head from under his cap. "My grandfather told me stories about this farm. About the cave. The strange things he'd seen in it when he was a boy. So, as much as I'm shocked by your friend Thorn's appearance, I'm not surprised."

He wasn't surprised. Well, he was the *only* one! I was beyond irritated at this point. Deciding I'd had enough for the moment, I snorted, turned, and stomped to the water's edge.

THORN

This whole day had slipped out of my grasp like water.

I couldn't tell if Ruth would accept me or my help. I had no way of knowing if she'd even allow me to stay. These peacekeeper humans had swiftly complicated matters. Now she was glowering at the crashing surf as if demanding it give her the answers to the universe.

"I'd like to see it." Sheriff Brighton called. I looked at him and saw the flinty determination in his gaze. He wasn't one to cower. He was brave, a warrior like I was. I could respect that.

"The Geata?" I asked him.

"Whatever is in the cave that my grandfather spoke about." He replied.

"I'm going to look for my ring and knives," I called out softly, figuring Ruth needed time to process what I'd told her. Perhaps my attempt at humor had done more harm than good. She lifted one arm and waved towards the sea cave in an irritated huff.

Taking that as permission, I caught the Sheriff's gaze and nodded towards the cave mouth. I walked towards it, spine straight, and heard the Sheriff and deputy following behind me, their footsteps noisy in the sand.

I wondered how peacekeepers could be warriors, yet make so much damned noise. Males of the orckin were raised from a young age to be swift and silent on their feet. Entire games orclings played revolved around stealth and quiet. Even amongst the females who would never grow to become warriors. The thought made me frown. Orckin once had fierce female warriors. But the an'sgudal, and the cursed dorcha'aon, removed that life path. As our kind dwindled, we reduced our females to the role of bringing about the next generation to keep us alive.

"Guy's quiet as the dead." I heard the deputy whisper to the sheriff, and I smirked.

The sheriff pulled something from his belt and made a clicking noise with it. Light, bright as the suns on Talam, lit up the dark tunnel. Hissing, I slammed my hands against my eyes. They'd already adjusted to the dark and the sudden light hurt.

"Oh! I'm sorry, son. My apologies." The light went out, and I lowered my hands, blinking until the light spots dissipated. "You can see in the dark?"

"Not total darkness. But my eyes can adjust to low light. What is that thing? What magic is this?"

"Magic? It's just a flashlight." Deputy Sanchez pipped up. Turning, I looked down at the small rod in Sheriff Brighton's hand.

"Flash... light?" I asked, bewildered.

"Yep. See, son, it uses batteries to light up." Brighton unscrewed one end and shorter, smaller rods slipped free.

"Batteries." The words were so foreign in my mouth. Words not made to be spoken with sharp teeth. "More of this 'science' that Ruth spoke of?"

"What did she say about science?" Deputy Sanchez stepped closer. His gaze was bright and curious.

"That it was magic that humans understood," I replied.

"She's not wrong." He grinned. "Most 'magic' from old times just turned out to be things we could explain with science."

"So, how does this work?"

"Well, the batteries contain chemical energy and convert it to electrical energy. This flashlight uses that electrical energy to power a light bulb." He pointed out areas of the flashlight as he explained.

Sheriff Brighton sighed and put the thing together again.

"You press this button here and it comes on." Brighton pointed the end with the light bulb towards the wall. "Might want to squint, son."

I did, and he clicked the button. The entire wall lit up again as if it held the power of the sun within that tiny rod and its science. Once my eyes adjusted, I looked at it. Wherever Brighton pointed the flashlight, it sent its beam of light. Shaking my head, I pressed on through the tunnel.

I had a lot to learn about humans and their creations. Just as advanced as the Oc'Veltas. The single clan amongst us all who had isolated themselves on their island fortress when the an'sgudal first hit. They rarely communicated with the other four clans. But what we'd seen them create was beyond any of us. Much resentment and hate had sprouted towards the Oc'Veltas, for they wouldn't share their advancements with the rest of us.

I wondered if it was the same with humans.

We came upon the cave's interior, and Sheriff Brighton turned off his flashlight. The pale shafts of light coming from the holes in the cave's roof bathed it in a soft glow.

"Well, I'll be," Brighton whispered as Sanchez exclaimed something in another language. I watched as they made their way carefully into the cave, booted feet leaving prints in the damp sand.

I left them to their explorations. Finding the chleoc ring and my knives were paramount. Hunting around amongst the rocks, I found my three knives. Each wickedly sharp and made of the strongest ore by the Oc'Dellor master smith. Even with days in the salty waters and at the mercy of the tides, my blades were undamaged, edges keen. Lacking even the slightest hint of rust. Sheathing them, I kept looking while the peacekeepers spoke to one another in hushed, awed tones.

"What are you looking for, Thorn?" I looked up to see Sanchez jog over to where I crouched by an outcropping of rock, shifting my fingers through the loose pebbles.

"A ring. It's an heirloom, and I lost it." I told him. "I found my knives, though."

"Oh, glad you found them." He said, and I nodded, turning back to my exhaustive search. Sanchez stood there for a moment. Watched me before he worked up the courage to speak again. "Do you need some help to look?"

"Och, I'd appreciate it, deputy." I smiled up at him, and Sanchez paled at my sharp teeth before nodding and calling over Brighton.

We spent a good amount of time scouring the cave for the ring. They were thorough. It wasn't long before we'd searched the entire cave with nothing to show for it. Unease gnawed at my belly. What if it washed out to sea? I couldn't very well walk amongst the humans without it. How would I live my life with Ruth if I couldn't find it or return to Talam?

"I'm sorry we couldn't find your ring." Brighton offered, and I thanked them both for their help.

We emerged from the cave sometime later empty-handed. Ruth now sat barefoot in the sand near the trail, her legs crossed beneath her, shoes perched on a rock. She faced us as we approached. Sheriff Brighton strode towards her and stopped at a respectful distance.

"Both Deputy Sanchez and I will keep this place a secret. We'll keep the FBI agent off your back," He proclaimed, and I watched in amusement as Ruth's eyebrows shot up into her hair in surprise. "You're a part of our town now, and we look after our own. I'll be letting folks know you're not sacrificing babies to Satan and that you like your privacy."

"Uh, thanks?" She said confusion etched on her lovely features.

"No problem. Keep this one out of sight, would you?" Sheriff Brighton jerked his thumb at Thorn with a smile, crinkling his eyes and twitching his mustache. "I don't think I need to warn you to keep this all a secret. If you need us, here's my card."

Ruth took the card and tucked it away into a pocket. "Thank you for not shooting us." She gave them both a lopsided smile.

"Our pleasure." Brighton chuckled. "We're excited about your Tolkien project, by the way. I'll keep an ear out for anyone willing to help you build your bed-and-breakfast. It'd be good for town tourism. We'll be in touch, Miss O'Daniels."

With a tip of his hat, he and Deputy Sanchez made their way up the cliff. When they'd gone, Ruth sighed and ran her fingers through her hair. Dread coiled in my gut. We were alone again, something that brought me joy, and made my heart soar. But that also meant that our unfinished conversation, and my heart, were in her small hands.

CHAPTER 09

RUTH

Deputy Sanchez and Sheriff Brighton had baffled me. They'd stopped by to speak to me regarding some strange claims made by the FBI agent who had been harassing me. They'd offered their protection and support for the bed-and-breakfast. I was having a hard time processing the fact that men in *authority* would help me.

Not to mention trying to process everything Thorn had dumped on my lap just before their arrival.

Thorn thought I was his mate. I was as alien to him as he was to me. Yet he still didn't balk at the thought of us being lifelong partners. I couldn't fathom that kind of acceptance and decisiveness. Especially so damn quick.

My thoughts inevitably drifted back to when I'd left my ex and the commune. To the betrayal. And how I'd whispered into the darkest night of my soul. How I'd beseeched my deities to send me my soulmate. My divine counterpart.

What if they'd been listening?

What if I'd called, and Thorn had answered?

I wasn't sure where this would lead, but I believed in synchronicities. I wasn't about to turn away just because he was different. I was tired of thinking I could comprehend what love was supposed to be, what it should look like. All I could handle right now was healing myself and creating my little Middle Earth. Everything else would work out somehow.

"Thorn," I said, turning my head to look at him. His expression as he faced me was wary. Something he was obviously not used to feeling. "I would very much appreciate your help to get the bed-and-breakfast finished. And your friendship."

The look of slack-jawed surprise warmed me, and I had to keep my face neutral.

"I can't promise you anything, okay?" I told him. "My experiences with men, males, aren't that great. But the gods, Source, the universe brought you here. Made it so I could buy the farm and find you. I'm not so much of a stubborn, blithering idiot as to deny that. But I don't know if I can give you what you want. You're more than welcome to stay here. To see if you can't get home to Talam. Okay?"

He nodded quickly. It must have been more than he'd expected. A small smile pulled at my mouth as I snagged my shoes and pulled them back on. They were still wet, but I didn't care.

"Did you find what you were looking for? Your ring?" I stood and dusted the sand off my ass.

"No. I worry it got swept out to sea." His hand raised to the leather strap he had on that crossed over his torso. I saw that there were now three wicked daggers sheathed along it. "Found my knives, of which I'm glad. These were specially made for me."

"Oh. I'm glad you found them then." I offered him a small smile, and he grinned openly back. "We'll try looking for your ring again. In the meantime, I'm hungry. You want some lunch?"

"Absolutely."

THORN

She hadn't turned me away. She hadn't accepted me as her cridhe either, but I would gladly take anything she'd give me. Ruth was offering me a chance to prove myself to her and to earn her love. It made my heart soar higher than I'd ever thought possible.

That day, at my prodding after lunch, she took me to her library and showed me her plans for the farm and the bed-and-breakfast. It was a wonderful concept. Small cottages built within the earth and themed after a series of tales she loved.

"This is interesting, building homes out of the earth instead of stone or wood. Do you have techniques to build them?" I asked, honestly curious. I'd helped Uther build a lovely house for my sister Thisa. It had been a work of incredible love and devotion. The result had earned our father's approval.

Normally, orckin could choose for themselves. But for Leanabh Banrigh and Leanabh Rìgh like me? We normally made our mating and marriages for the good of the clan. Unless we found our cridheachan.

It was the one thing that could trump a political engagement or marriage. The thought that finding my cridhe had the benefit of ending the political engagement was a relief. Though it was a moot point if I could never return to Talam.

"Wait, you have experience building houses?" she asked me, expression one of shock.

"Och. It's traditional for males to build their mates a home. Often we'll help one another with the basic construction and some of the detail work. Though our homes are built into trees." I gave her a half-shrug.

"You... orckin live in *treehouses*?" Ruth's slack-jawed expression made me chuckle.

"The Oc'Dellor do, och." I smiled, her awe making my heart flutter with joy. "Each of the clans builds their homes based on tradition and environment. The Oc'Turin live in homes built of stone and moss. Oc'Blyre carve their homes into the very mountains. The Oc'Veltas have an entire island city at sea made of glass and stone. And the traveling Oc'Sentan live in moving homes they take with them as they migrate. I've had some training in nearly all methods."

"That's amazing." Ruth gawped at me, stunned. A few moments passed and a foreign shyness crept into me.

"The techniques?" I asked, prodding her into action. She shook her head as if clearing her thoughts and turned to shuffle through a shelf filled full of books.

"Techniques. Right. I do have some books on earth-home building. Waterproofing is going to be the biggest concern. There is a workaround we can use, though." She carried over a stack of books, each bound with a colorful cover. She flipped one open and showed me fantastic illustrations of how such underground structures were built here on Earth.

"This is very doable if you have the materials. What is this here?" I asked, pointing to panels that had waves in them.

"That's corrugated steel sheeting. It's metal," she explained. "I can order some and have it delivered."

"Then we should get started, shouldn't we? The first part will be to choose your sites and start digging. We can start as soon as you'd like," I told her. "There may be things I don't know how to do to a human standard, but I'll learn."

For her. For her, I'd learn anything.

So, without hesitation, we went down the rickety back steps to survey the land and lay out where she wished her earth homes to be built. We outlined the area she wanted for each of the seven underground homes. She showed me where she kept her tools in a building off of the farmhouse she called the 'garage'. Some tools looked familiar, others were foreign. She had some that looked like weapons the Oc'Veltas would devise. One was called a 'chainsaw'. Ruth assured me it cut down trees and overgrowth.

I respectfully asked to use her axe instead. With an axe, I could fell trees, process them, carve wood, cook, shave, and kill enemies. A chainsaw looked like a death wish.

There was already a stack of beautifully dried straight boards and timbers, all perfectly the same length. Ruth explained they arrived that way, and I could only marvel at how effective their milling process was. There were also bags of cement, something similar to the concrait that we used.

After going over all the tools, resources, and materials, Ruth excused herself to make our dinner. Warmed by her thoughtfulness, I decided that today was as good as any to replace her back steps. I clapped my hands and got to work, quickly losing myself to the act of creation.

Ruth found me an hour later as I was recreating the steps that I'd easily ripped free from the house and the earth. I'd taken the entire thing to the garage instead of building it on-site, as I wanted to mimic the human-building techniques as closely as I could with the new tools. My favorite had to be the drill. Able to drill holes quickly and use metal nails with curves on them to hold the construct together. Screws, she'd called them.

"Well, you sure learn quick." She chuckled as she entered the garage. The sound was music to my ears.

"You're an excellent teacher. Most of the concepts are the same. Just fancier tools." I grinned, using the drill to screw the last of the railing in place. Learning to use the circular saw had been both a terrifying and thrilling experience. And a satisfying one. I'd swiftly measured and cut the wood I needed, quick as the wind.

"What are you making?" She asked, wiping her hands on an apron she'd donned.

"I'm making you new steps for the back of your house. You already fell for me once and nearly got injured. Don't need it happening again." I winked at her and she blushed.

"Cad." She muttered before looking closer at the original steps and the stumps of cement covered in dirt on the beams. "Thank you for making new ones. Did you just... *pull* it out of the ground?"

"Och, it was hardly in the ground at all. Barely attached to the house, even. Poor construction." Shrugging, I hefted the new steps onto my shoulder. Ruth startled and stepped out of my way as I walked out of the garage to install them. Her eyes round in her face as she stared after me.

"Dinner will be ready soon!" she called, and I waved an acknowledging hand. I'd impressed her. My chest swelled with pride and I felt like a preening iolaire-lasair, a proud predatory bird from Talam that flew on wings of fire.

Installing the stairs was trickier than I'd first expected, and I'd needed to make multiple trips to the garage to retrieve what I needed. The summer sun had set by the time I'd finished my work and entered the house on the now-solid steps. Leaving my boots in the mudroom, I entered the kitchen to a veritable feast at her table. Chicken, potatoes, and some kind of green she called kale. An orc could get used to being fed like this.

After I'd eaten, I pushed back from the dining table and the feast she'd prepared. Ruth had already left. She ate far less than I did and usually finished faster. Often taking the opportunity to shower while I finished eating. I padded to the bathroom just as she exited it, steam following in her wake. She was soft and pink and round in her fluffy bathrobe, wet waves knotted atop her head.

"Oh! The water's hot. I left some towels for you," she said looking up at me, her cheeks rosy from the heat. A bead of water slid from her hair down her jaw towards her neck.

The thought of hot, soapy water sluicing down her lush curves had me light-headed. My blood rushed from one head to another. My cock stiffened so quickly that it nearly hurt.

Something in my gaze registered, and she took a sharp breath. The heady fragrance of her arousal made me shiver. I desperately needed to bathe, and one question burned in my mind. Would she join me if I asked?

Fuck, I wanted to pull her towards me. To sink my claws into her hair and devour her mouth. Rip free her robe and drag her into the shower with me. To wrap her long legs around my waist as I pressed her against the wall. Moving with her under all that hot water as her blunt nails raked my back. As I gave into this building desire and plowed her until she screamed my name in release.

"Care to join me, little dove?" I nearly growled, lust riding high and obscuring my better judgment as I pulled off my bandolier. She noticed how my cock strained to tent my leather kilt.

My little dove's mouth softened, her tiny pink tongue darting out to lick her lips as her breathing quickened. I could see her pulse race at the base of her throat. A throat I wanted to sink my teeth into, to tease that line between pleasure and pain until she came undone.

"I'd better go get ready for story time." Before I could moan her name, she darted to her bedroom and shut the door.

Hissing, I ran my claws through my hair. I'd sworn to be patient, to wait for her acceptance, but every time we were close and her scent shifted, I felt like I was losing my mind. I nearly cursed the cridhe bond for causing me to think only of rutting her every time I laid eyes on her.

Snarling at my lack of control, I stripped off my kilt and entered the shower. Cleaning myself, I ignored the ache in my loins. I wasn't about to satisfy myself after potentially scaring off my mate.

Instead, I inspected my injuries. The wounds that I'd sustained from my arrival on Earth had scabbed over, healing nicely. The soap I scrubbed myself down with smelled nice, some sort of woodsy scent that helped clear my mind. When I got out of the shower and donned my kilt, I had a firm grasp on my control once again.

With a deep breath, I finger-combed my hair back from my face. I gripped the doorknob and twisted it, opening it with bated breath. Best I face my consequences quickly.

When I opened the door, Ruth was coming out of the library. She'd changed into soft pajamas and slippers, her hair still in a knot at the top of her head. We both froze in the hallway. Ruth gawked openly at my still-damp appearance. As if seeing me wet was doing to her what the mere thought of seeing her wet had done to me. The control I'd regained almost slipped entirely as I watched her body react to me.

Her throat bobbed, her breathing hitched and her skin flushed as she near devoured me with her eyes. I watched as her nipples pebbled beneath her top, her scent shifting again, ripening. I bit the inside of my cheek to stay sane. My sharp teeth sheared the flesh and flooded my mouth with the taste of blood as the pain grounded me.

After a tense moment, I made the first move. I closed the door to the bathroom behind me, standing in place. I nodded at the book in her hands. Not daring to take a step closer given the crackling tension between us. Neither of us needed my instincts to wrest control right now.

"What is that?"

"Would you like to hear the stories that inspired the bed-and-breakfast?" she asked quietly, shy as she gripped a leather-bound tome to her bosom, blocking my view. I wanted to hate the book on principle. It was separating me from my cridhe. "It's called *The Hobbit*."

"I'd like that very much." I swallowed thickly, relieved that my show of lust earlier hadn't ruined my chance with her.

She motioned to the couch and the small armchair that sat beside it. Two steaming cups of what smelled like herbal tea sat on the small side table between them. I hesitated but followed her as she went to sit down in her tiny armchair. My little dove looked adorable, curled up in the chair. I couldn't fit in it if I tried. I pulled a small blanket off of the arm of the sofa and unfolded it. She looked up at me in surprise as I draped it over her lap.

"Oh, thank you!"

"Can't have my storyteller getting cold." I smiled and sat back on the sofa and pulled my quilt up over me, settling in for what I hoped to be an epic tale.

She offered me a small smile in return before she dropped her gaze to the book in her lap and started reading aloud. As she read to me, her voice slipped into a melodic cadence. I found myself transported to the vibrant world of her tale. Full of colorful characters and incredible circumstances. My weary body, anxious heart, and lust-addled mind all fell away in the face of such a well-crafted story.

Eventually, with our mugs empty of tea, I drifted off. I half registered as she stood and encouraged me to lie down on the small couch. Complying without thought as she turned off the light, I fell asleep with the sound of her voice echoing in my mind.

CHAPTER 10*

THORN

Our days took on a rhythm over the course of the next few weeks.

We'd wake. Have our coffee and plan our day as we ate breakfast. Then we'd tackle that day's work. Often, we would split our tasks. Ruth was the only person able to deal with others, as my orckin appearance would have caused a panic. So she'd receive deliveries, take care of tasks at the farmhouse, and help me with projects.

When it came time to clear the land of brush and trees, she'd wielded the chainsaw like a warrior. I was secretly impressed. And afraid of what she could do with it if she got angry. I just stuck to my axe.

Clearing the land had been difficult, but not impossible. It was digging the holes that had proved challenging. She helped me, but I'd often ask her to do other smaller tasks on the farm so she wouldn't overexert herself. After all, her human stamina and strength weren't the same as mine. But I'd never tell her that.

We spent our evenings taking turns cooking and showering.

Then Ruth would open her book and read to me until I passed out. Sometimes she'd barely get a few pages into the story before I began to snore.

We had visits from Sheriff Brighton, Deputy Sanchez, and a female from town named Julia who Ruth had befriended. Julia hadn't learned of me yet and Ruth kept her to the farmhouse while I continued working on the foundations for the bed-and-breakfast. Ruth had bought me some shirts, some 'threads' as she'd called them, joking that it was to spare any womenfolk who might come across me as I worked. They did fit rather tightly, but they were the biggest she could find, and her thoughtfulness was touching.

When I'd first tried one on, her face had gotten that dazed look it did whenever she saw me fresh out of the shower. I wasn't sure if the T-shirts were better or worse for our strange courting dance. Because neither of us made a move after that night in the bathroom. A fact that both saddened me and kept hope alive.

The FBI agent who had shown up to terrify Ruth had disappeared. He'd even stopped calling to harass her about selling the farm. No one knew where he'd gone or if he'd come back. Ruth was hopeful he'd stay away. But I'd smelled his determination and how confident he'd been that day he'd shown up. I knew he was only biding his time.

One evening, we were sitting at the dinner table when the phone rang. Ruth got up and plucked the receiver out of the cradle.

"Hello?" her voice chirruped brightly as I continued to devour the delicious chicken and carrot dinner she'd prepared. "Hello…?" she asked again. I paused, fork halfway to my open mouth, and looked over to where she now stood with her back rigid. Hackles high like an angry nocrys ready to pounce. "Look, whoever you are, leave me alone, you damn creep! Don't call me again!"

Ruth slammed the phone back down onto the cradle and I found myself at her side, dinner forgotten.

"What happened?" I asked her, noting how she shivered, fists clenched at her sides as she stared down at the phone. The phone rang again, and she jumped. Before I could pick it up for her, she snatched it and yanked it to her ear.

"Hello?" she asked once more, her voice tight with fury. And fear. The bitter scent of it had me on edge. I couldn't make out what sound was coming from the receiver, so I gently took the phone from her trembling fingers and brought it to my pointed ear. I placed my other hand against Ruth's shoulders, a silent reminder that I was here. That she was safe with me.

Breathing. Heavy panting as if from someone scared… or aroused. A ragged groan exploded from the phone into my ear. A male voice. I could faintly hear a sound I knew far too well being a male. The sound of a hand working a cock, wet and messy. Rage ignited in my chest. Whoever this was, and I had a good idea who, was seeking release by terrifying my dove. That was a mistake.

A dark chuckle escaped me, and the sounds on the other end of the phone ceased abruptly. My chuckle deepened. A deadly edge to it as I let this sniveling smear of a male know I had caught him. Let him know he was pathetic and unworthy. Ruth jerked to look up at me, eyes wide with confusion. My gaze locked with hers and I winked to ease her fears. But then the smile dropped from my face.

"If you *ever* call here again," I began, voice rumbling like an oncoming storm. "If you *ever* bother Ruth again. I will hunt you down and flay the skin from that cock in your hand before force-feeding it to you. Ruth is under my protection. She is not alone. She is not for you. Do you understand?"

A long pause, then the line went dead. Static tone buzzing in my sensitive ear. I pulled the receiver away and looked down at it, scowling, before setting it back on the cradle. I heard a soft, hitching intake of breath and my gaze snapped up to Ruth. Tears wobbled in her eyes and I watched, transfixed, as they spilled over her lashes and cascaded down her cheeks. I watched one tear in particular as it slid down her soft skin to nestle next to the corner of that sinful mouth of hers. Unable to stop myself, I reached out slowly, curling my fingers until I gently scooped up the stray tear with the knuckle of my index finger.

Ruth stilled, her breath shuddering past her lips. She hadn't flinched when I'd touched her. Hadn't tensed or stepped away. I held the quivering droplet of her tear on my knuckle and looked up into those rich luibh gaoil eyes of hers. I froze. The relief I saw there, the raw emotion that I couldn't name, stole my breath. My body shuddered, instincts demanding I pull her to me, to crush her to my body, to kiss and lick her, to bury my face in her sweet cunt until she came undone and forgot all about her fear.

My heart and my dick throbbed in time as I lifted my knuckle to my mouth and slid my tongue out to lick away her tear. Her gaze dropped to watch, her scent shifting once again to that heady fragrance that made me weak in the face of my primal urges. The taste of her tear exploded on my tongue, salty and strangely sweet all at once. How I imagined she must taste elsewhere. A ragged growl ripped through my chest as my instincts screamed to claim her. To mate her. To truly make her *my* little dove.

Ruth's breathing hitched again, and I saw her nipples peak beneath the shirt she wore with no bra. She'd liked it, my growl. Some primal instinct roared at the triumph of the tiny victory. My mouth watered at the sight of her and I fought the urge to pick her up and carry her to the table, to rip her clothes from her body and lay her out on it like my own personal feast. My breathing grew ragged as I strained against my self-imposed leash, just as my cock strained against my kilt. I'd sworn to myself that I'd let her lead. That I'd wait until she was ready. I'd never been one to revel in pain, but waiting for her to decide was a delicious, knife-sharp agony that grazed against my soul. One that I delighted in.

Every moment like this was equal parts pain and ecstasy.

Ruth jerked and turned away from me suddenly, pressing a hand to her chest as she stepped away and fought her breathing. I waited, eyes now riveted on the beautiful sight of her generous, round ass in her sweatpants. I gritted my teeth and tore my gaze from her, grabbing a glass and filling it full of water to do something, anything, with my hands. Hands that were shaking in desperation to sink into her softness. Without thinking, I downed the water, then refilled it. Stepping away from the sink, I moved towards her, the pull she had on me drawing me to her like a moth to a flame. I stopped a few feet from her and held out the glass.

She looked up at me then, tears gone, yet that emotion still shining from her like a beacon. She looked down at my hand and gingerly took the glass from me. Raising it to her lips, Ruth slowly drank the water I gave her. A deep-seated need I didn't know I had was abruptly sated by her accepting what I provided.

She tipped the glass back, swallowing all of it in long droughts. I watched the elegant column of her throat bob and a stray droplet of water ran over her chin to plummet down her throat, over her collarbones, and down into the valley between her breasts under the collar of her shirt. I bit back a hungry groan.

Pulling the now empty glass from her lips, she wiped her chin with the back of her fist before handing it back to me. I grasped it, our fingers brushing, and a jolt of electricity sparked between us. She paused in surprise before pulling her hand back quickly. Coughing, I turned and placed the glass in the sink.

"Thank you." Her voice, rough with emotion, was like a hand caressing the back of my neck. I just jerked a nod before turning back to face her.

"Has this happened before?" I asked her as I ushered her into the living room to sit down in her chair. She was still shaking, from fear or anger... or arousal... I couldn't tell.

"Yes." Her whisper was almost a hiss.

"When?" I asked sharply, "How often?"

"It's normally during the day when you're out working on the hobbit holes." She said as she sat down in her chair, sinking back into it with a defeated sigh. "It's happened about a dozen times. This was the first time it happened at night."

"Why didn't you tell me sooner?" I near-growled and she looked at me sharply. I moved and grabbed the quilt off the couch and laid it over her, tucking the edges in. My treacherous heart delighted in how maddeningly soft she was where my hands pressed against her as I made sure she was snug under the comfort of the quilt.

"I didn't want to make a big deal out of it." She bit out. "Creeps are creeps."

"If you do nothing, say nothing, then males like that will take it as an invitation to continue." I bit out. Not angry with her, but with the situation. Frustrated that she hadn't come to me the first time it happened. "Regardless of what you say to them, they won't listen to you."

"Because they only respect what other men say?" She snapped, and I flicked my gaze up to hers. We were so close, her mouth mere inches from mine. This human female, this woman, was going to be the death of me. I moved in front of her and braced my hands on the armrests of her chair. She leaned back as I leaned forward until our noses nearly touched.

"Yes." I snarled. "Males like that? They are *vile* and only think of females as property. Will only respect the word and power of another male. Regardless of how strong the female is." Anger rippled under my skin like heat over a fire. He should have stopped when she told him to. She should have come to me when he didn't. How was I to protect her when she kept things like this from me? Did she not trust me to protect her? Did she not see me as a male? "Your choice, your boundaries, should be respected. But not all males are honorable, little dove. And *you...*"

I trailed off, gaze moving so slowly from hers, roaming her face, her neck, her chest where her sharp breaths heaved her bosom against the thin fabric of her shirt.

"And I?" she asked, voice both hard and breathy at once. I glared up at her from under my brows. Twin spots of color rode high on her cheeks even as she glowered at me. So lovely, even in her ire.

"And you... with that fiery spirit of yours and that damnable kindness..." I leaned forward, sinking my face into her brown waves until her ear was a hair's breadth from my mouth. She gasped, almost a moan, as my breath tickled the shell of her rounded ear. "... combined with this lush body of yours... your *scent...*" I breathed deep, groaning as I gripped the armrests in my massive hands, the wood creaking and threatening to splinter. "You'd drive any male *mad* with hunger," I growled, and a moan escaped her then. A high, gasping sound that burned a furious line of need from my ear near her mouth, down to my groin. My voice dropped lower, softer, longing staining it despite myself. "Wear his honor threadbare until just a glance from you would be all it took to shred it to nothing."

A shudder wracked her body and I could see how her pulse raced against the hollow of her throat. A throat I longed to lick, to kiss, to bite. I could feel her gasping hot breaths against my neck and shoulder and gods if I didn't wonder what those blunt teeth would feel like sinking into my flesh.

"You are a *bane*." I snarled, desire muddling my mind as I grew intoxicated by her smell. My frustrated need was so intense that my feelings for her rode that fine line between love and hate. "And a *blessing*."

It took every iota of self-control, discipline, and willpower to drag myself away from her. To release the protesting armrests and stand slowly to my full height, gaze never leaving hers. Her mouth hung open, eyes slightly unfocused, hands fisted into the quilt as she panted in her chair. I'd told her one look would shred my honor. And Source be damned if the last remnant of it didn't rip with the way she stared at me.

Grinding my teeth, I stalked from the room on silent feet, fleeing the woman who held my heart and my desire in her tiny hands. I had to get out. Had to seek release somewhere or truly risk madness. I felt my honor shear further as she gasped, a tiny moan behind me at the loss of my presence. I'd never run from anything. Yet here I was, running from the very female the Source had sent me across the universe to find.

I barely remembered throwing the back door wide and stomping down the stairs out into the night. Unable to think beyond the dual needs to flee and to fuck, I found myself in the woods near the barn. Shaking, I nearly ripped the leather of my kilt as I tore it from my body. I threw it aside in anger, not caring where it landed and looked down. Panting and snarling, I snatched my cock in my hand, retracting my claws. My dick was so swollen with the need to plow my cridhe that I couldn't wrap my fingers entirely around it. My knot ached abominably and my seed near-poured out of my tip, leaving a string of wetness to my belly where it had been straining against it. I moaned loud and long as I grasped it, that light pressure alone almost enough to send me spurting.

Growling, I set to work, stroking myself with both hands, occasionally dipping one down to fondle my bollocks. Every stroke over my straining knot had me shivering closer to release. I wrapped both hands around myself, creating a tunnel of sorts. Closing my eyes, I imagined it was Ruth touching me, that it was Ruth's pussy I'd sunk into, not my fists. My hips snapped forward of their own accord and I fucked my fists like an orc possessed. I squeezed down, imagining it was her cunt as she came for me and I roared, flying over the edge of orgasm. Ropes of cum shot from between my fingers and splattered against a nearby tree. The entire forest, the windswept hills, all went silent at the sound of my wild roar.

But it wasn't enough. It'd never be enough.

So I began again, finding release almost as quickly as before. But again, it wasn't enough. So I took myself in hand again. And again. And again. Until my seed dripped obscenely from the trunk of the tree and from between my fingers to pool at my feet. Imagining all the ways in which I wanted to possess my cridhe after she'd so thoroughly possessed me. Snarling and growling like a wild beast each time I climaxed.

Eventually, I stopped, donned my kilt once more, and looked back at the farmhouse. My orckin eyes could see well in the dim light of Earth's single moon. The house was still. I crept back into the house, being quiet so as not to wake Ruth. My malehood was still throbbing in need, but at least I was mostly sated now. A state in which I felt I was safe enough to be under the same roof as her once more.

But then I heard it as I made my way into the living room. A soft, breathy gasp, a quiet moan from the other side of her bedroom door. I stopped breathing as I stood and listened. The quiet moan came again and my mind blanked. She was pleasuring herself. She'd been as turned on by our steamy encounter as I'd been.

I longed to go to her room, throw open her door and her thighs, to plant myself between them, and *never* fucking leave.

Instead, I made my steps noisy as I stalked back into the living room so she could hear me. The sounds from behind her door ceased, and a wicked idea wormed its way up from my pleasure-addled mind. I sat down heavily on the couch and sighed loudly. Then made a fuss of noisily unbuckling my kilt. I flung it open and gazed down at my swiftly swelling shaft. I took it into my hand once more and let my thighs fall wide, leaning back and making myself comfortable. If I couldn't show her how badly I wanted her, I'd let her hear it.

I threw my head back over the back of the couch and let out a growl as I stroked myself. My knot was already full of cum once more, the thought of her listening to me sate myself, making me ready quicker than I thought possible. Closing my eyes, I imagined her lying in her bed, hand pressed desperately against the apex of those thick, juicy thighs of hers. I let my thoughts tumble and burn. And I let my mouth and throat speak and moan and growl as they saw fit, lost to my imaginings.

That's when I heard it. A shaky, soft moan from her room. I snarled in satisfaction, grateful beyond all sense that my hearing was so sharp. That she liked what she heard. Enough so to continue seeking her own release. A thrill sparked up my spine, and I redoubled my efforts. Matching her moan for moan as the tempo we shared, though separated by a door, picked up its throbbing pace. I was close, gasping as I stared at her door hard enough to bore a hole through it.

"*Ruth.*" I moaned her name into the air and wood that separated us. Longing and need and love, cutting a desperate edge to her name. Her breathing quickened, and I heard her move under her blankets. Heard her scream even as she sought to silence it in a pillow.

I came then. With a shuddering, relentless groan as waves of pleasure rippled through me. My body jerked and spasmed as my knot constricted, shooting cum into the air to splatter against my bare thighs. Against the floorboards at my feet. Her screaming stopped, changing to a heavy panting as ragged as mine. I flopped back against the sofa, utterly spent and finally sated.

Coming with her, despite the distance and barriers between us, had been the single most pleasurable moment in my life. And the most satisfying. Source save me if she ever surrendered to me.

CHAPTER 11

RUTH

The past few months had been grueling. The end of summer held heavy and hot. Even the roses drooped in the heat. But that couldn't compare to the heat that had been sizzling between Thorn and me. After that wicked night, we'd kept to our routine, not speaking of it, often unable to be close to one another for long.

It was driving me insane in the most delicious way imaginable.

To distract ourselves from it, we both poured our time and energy into building the bed-and-breakfast. Digging the depressions in the earth for the hobbit holes had been a nightmare. The soil was heavy clay with a lot of boulders. Had I been doing this by myself, I would have failed. But with Thorn's crazy strength, we made huge strides in a short amount of time. We were almost ready to lay the foundations and erect the posts. Both were crucial things to complete as soon as possible. That way, we could finish waterproofing the corrugated steel before the winter rains arrived.

Sheriff Brighton and Deputy Sanchez came by often in their spare time to help us with construction. They were good men, and I was happy to befriend them. Sanchez was a bachelor with boundless energy, and Brighton had worked in construction when he was younger. His knowledge helped us a great deal. Brighton and Thorn often debated construction options with Sanchez helping with troubleshooting. Sanchez also had a way about him that made gaining what we needed a lot smoother.

His family owned and operated the hardware supply store a few towns over, so he could order things for me that no one here in town would sell to me. Brighton knew someone down at the permitting office who was happy to help us get the permits that we needed. Evidently, they were a Tolkien fan. One offer for a free stay had them hastily approving every form we would need.

The nasty rumors about me kept circulating, as they do in small towns. Julia had been helpful on that front. She also occasionally came over to help fix up the house. And have some quality girl-time. It'd been really nice having a gal pal again. I hadn't had one since before the commune.

Eventually, I told her about Thorn. Told her about the night he'd taken the phone from me and spoke to the creep who'd been calling to terrify me for weeks. And threatened him. How those calls had ceased because of him. And how he'd made my heart nearly tumble out of my chest when he'd declared I was under his protection. How… hot and heavy things had gotten between us. I told Julia all of that. But left out the part about the gate and his alien looks. Gods only knew how she'd take that, and I didn't want to lose my friend.

What I couldn't possibly tell her was how that night, after Thorn had stalked from my house, I'd heard him roar outside. Heard it again. And again. How I'd quickly realized what he was doing. And how fucking turned on it made me. I'd rushed to my room as wetness soaked my panties and my sweats, slamming my door as I nearly dove into bed. I couldn't sink my hand under my waistband fast enough, and with his next roar, I was crying out, too.

But once wasn't enough. Just as it seemed, it wasn't enough for him either. I'd never been so damned horny in all my life and I ruthlessly sought my release repeatedly. Time passed, and I was still lost in my lust when I heard Thorn enter the house. I'd froze, not wanting him to hear me, but straining to hear him.

He sighed and sat on the sofa. I'd heard him unbuckle his kilt and *moan* softly. I had to bite my lip to keep from moaning, too. In the quiet, I could hear him moan and growl and pant low in the living room. I couldn't stop my fingers from their dance if I tried as they flickered in all the ways that felt good. Thorn was always so quiet in nearly everything that he did that his noisiness surprised me. And then it registered.

He knew. He *knew* what I was doing. I'd bet good money he could smell me at it, too. He wanted me to hear him as he masturbated. Wanted me to know that it was me he was thinking of.

My core clenched hard on nothing as my fingers began a blistering pace between my thighs. I knew, no matter what, that he'd be able to hear me in here with those pointed ears of his. Still, I was afraid that if I was too loud that he'd take it as an invitation and break down my door. That thought had me groaning softly into my pillow. How the hell was his brutish nature so damned sexy? How was it possible that I wanted this orc, this male of another species, so damned badly?

"*Ruth.*" I heard my name from the living room and I stilled, so damnably close to release. The *tone* of his voice as he moaned my name nearly undid me. Not just lusty, but full of a longing that leveled whatever defenses my heart had left.

My name on his lips as he picked up his pace had me skyrocketing towards climax. I rolled over beneath sheets I suddenly wished he was under with me and screamed my orgasm into my pillow as I bucked wildly against my hand. I knew he'd heard me. His long, low moan as he came in *my* living room, on *my* couch, at the sound of *my* orgasm, was the sexiest thing I'd ever heard in my life.

Yeah, not exactly something I could comfortably share with my new best friend.

"GIRL. You mean to tell me you *haven't* fucked his brains out yet?" Julia asked, tossing a cloth she was using to stain the hardwood floor in the living room into a bucket.

We'd spent all morning sanding it down until it was smooth as silk. I'd stacked the furniture in the mudroom and I prayed Thorn needed nothing from it. I always told him when Julia would be at the house. That way, he'd know to stay clear until I came to get him. It was an opportunity to talk to another girl, one I needed.

He was respectful of it and I appreciated his acceptance. It was strange having my needs honored. I wasn't used to it, but I could get used to it.

"Look, I told you what I endured. I'm trying to focus on healing and this bed-and-breakfast, okay?" I sighed. My broken record ass must have repeated that a hundred times over the last few months.

"You can do that and let him shag you until you walk bow-legged." She gave me a withering look. "You've got a man who mysteriously showed up and offered his help to build your dream life *for free*. He's gorgeous enough that you're *hiding him from me*. And he wants to make your fantasies come true, too?"

Seems like I couldn't get anything past her. She'd seen through my ruses. She was right, of course. I didn't want her to see Thorn, but not for the reason she was thinking. I let her think about it that way, anyway.

"Look, I like him, okay? I admit it!" I huffed, wiping my face with a clean rag. The heat was oppressive even with the doors and windows open. There was no sea breeze today to help cool us off, so we'd resorted to hooking up an old fan I'd found in the attic. All it did was blow the hot air around.

"When was the last time you got laid?" Julia asked bluntly, staring dead at me.

"When was the last time *you* got laid?" I snapped back. I'd gotten off plenty, but that wasn't the same as getting my brains fucked out, and I knew it.

"Last week, actually. Did wonders. Now answer my question."

I stared up at the ceiling. Beseeching the gods why I had the bright idea to tell her about Thorn. Oh yeah, she was the only person in this gods forsaken town who'd talk to me like a human being. And I knew she'd help me navigate this tricky situation. She was a good person who gave good advice.

"Not since before I left the commune... eight months ago," I murmured.

"It's been a long time. You told me what you went through. And also how badly you want Thorn in a carnal way. It sounds like he respects you enough to stop when you say no." Her voice had gone quiet, her expression knowing. "If he's that dead set on you, it might be worth a try with him. If you don't face being intimate soon, the idea of sex is going to haunt you, and terrify you. Trust me on that. You can try again with someone who obviously respects you."

I swallowed thickly. She was right. The longer I'd waited, the more my old memories blended with my current situation. The more my anxiety over intimacy grew and the more paralyzed I became whenever Thorn came onto me.

If I were honest with myself, I'd wanted Thorn in the biblical sense since I first dragged him into my mudroom. He'd been unconscious then, and I'd had no idea who or what he was. Yet my body reacted to him as it had never had to anyone else. Anytime he'd offered intimacy towards me and I'd shown even the slightest hint of stress or anxiety, he'd immediately backed off. Left me to my own devices. He was waiting for me to make the first move. And I respected him for it.

"I'm not trying to pressure you into it. You don't have to if you don't wanna. But it sounds like you genuinely want to. And you don't have to bang him immediately. Hell, it would be a gigantic step if you even kissed him." Julia shrugged and dipped her rag back into the can of stain before wiping it onto the floorboards. "Just think about it."

And boy did I ever.

When the floors were stained, Julia hugged me and promised to call on her next day off before heading home in her little orange Pontiac GT-37 Hardtop coupe. I knew I needed to face this problem head-on. Exactly like I did with everything else that stood in my way.

So, swallowing my fear and ignoring how badly my heart pounded in my chest, I went around back towards the hobbit holes. The footings had been poured and properly set. I could see in the distance that Thorn was now starting on constructing the framework that the corrugated steel sheets would cover. He had over-engineered the thing to make sure it would endure the test of time. Like everything orckin, he'd said.

The male was impressive. He'd taken to building my hobbit holes like a Took to adventuring, adapting his knowledge with what he learned from my books. He was learning to read and enjoyed listening to me read to him. It had endeared him to me more than I'd ever admit.

I found him in one of the seven hobbit holes. He was hefting beams into place that would support the roof. He'd stripped off his T-shirt and stood in his kilt and boots, adjusting the beam before screwing it into place. His back muscles bunched and moved. Sweat glistened on his skin and it was sweet torture to watch a bead of it run down the length of his spine.

How the hell could a non-human male be so damned sexy? Just standing around, *sweating* in the sun? It was almost as dangerous as whenever he came out of the shower, still dripping wet and smelling like my cedar soap. I made a small grunt of frustration, and Thorn glanced over his shoulder at me.

"You alright there, little dove? You've been awfully quiet since you arrived." He cocked an eyebrow at me in curiosity. Of course, he'd heard me walk up. He could hear a mouse fart three rooms over with those pointy ears of his. Had heard me every time I tried to orgasm quietly in my room. My cheeks heated.

Then it hit me as our eyes met. He really was genuinely concerned for me and anything that bothered me. Not just now, but since he'd arrived. He actually *cared*.

When I didn't respond, he turned to face me, chest heaving with his harsh breaths. He grabbed his T-shirt to wipe off his face and neck. It pulled the muscles at his abdomen and my breath caught at the sight of all that gray glistening skin that ended in a vicious V right above the waistband of his leather kilt. He tilted his head at me, gaze raking over me as he inhaled deeply. He froze the moment he smelled my soaked panties, already slick with my desire. I realized early on that he could smell it whenever I got turned on.

Which made living with him a hellish inconvenience.

"Ruth?" His voice dropped into a deep rumble. It felt like an invisible hand gliding against my skin. My desire for him, finally openly acknowledged, flashed into a wildfire in my veins. A pounding began at the apex of my thighs, my knees felt like limp noodles, and I nearly moaned.

"Thorn." His name slipped from my lips as I wrung my hands together. "I've been thinking about why you're here. I've been thinking about what you said about us being mates... a lot if I'm honest. And I...

I..."

I couldn't finish my thought. At a loss for words. Sweat poured off of him as he panted in the heat. His strange eyes, like twin copper stars in the dark expanse of his gaze, sparked with a sudden understanding.

"Little dove," he whispered, taking a slow, powerful step forward.

My heartbeat ratcheted up until no room existed in my ribcage for my lungs to breathe. Suddenly, he was all I could see, all I could sense as he enveloped my vision. His scent, like whiskey and leather and my cedar soap, overpowered the air I breathed until I was drunk on it.

Slowly, he reached one calloused and scar-flecked hand up to my face. My breathing hitched as he slipped his fingers into my hair to brush back my riotous waves. His claws scraped gently against my scalp before loosely fisting the strands between his fingers at the back of my head.

"Thorn," my moan was barely a whisper, but those pointed ears of his picked it up over the breeze and the crashing surf.

"Say it again," he growled, his voice gone raspy and deep and slurred. As if he was as drunk off of me as I was off of him. I opened my eyes and looked up at him from under my lashes, helpless at the power he had over me. "Say my name again."

He looked barely restrained, his expression near-feral and vulnerable all at once. Just like he had that night. His fingers tightening in my hair, I gasped and tilted my head back so I could look at him straight on. The effect my gasp had on him was staggering to witness. Frozen in place, a shudder wracked his entire body before he stilled again, mouth ajar.

A deep, hard throbbing pounded between my legs. Barely able

to breathe through the fog of lust that had overtaken me, I licked my lips. His gaze snapped down to my mouth. Thorn moaned deep in his throat.

I wondered how he'd respond to hearing his name on my lips again. The heady realization that I held the power here, I held the cards, suffused my heart. I'd never held such power over someone else before. It seemed only I could give him what he needed. And it was as easy as breathing to give it to him.

"Thorn," I breathed. His copper and black gaze snapped up to mine.

"What do you want, little dove?" The words a command. A caress in and of themselves.

"Kiss me," I demanded, without thinking. A tremor wracked him as he growled. Between one moment and the next, he'd bent down and claimed my mouth. The soft feel of those lips I'd been fantasizing about for months nearly undid me. I moaned against his mouth, and he opened for me. His long, black, ridged tongue met my soft pink one in a hungry dance. His sharp teeth were so very careful on my lips as we finally tasted one another.

The kiss was desperate, decadent. It made my body go loose and taut all at once. He held my head where he wanted it, as he practically feasted on my mouth like a starving man.

My hands met his chest, and they explored the slick expanse of his skin. Thorn pulled back enough to meet my eyes. When I nodded, he moaned my name and crushed me to him. His mouth found mine again, and I wrapped my arms up around his neck.

His hand skirted under my T-shirt, pointed claws gently scraping my flesh as his fingers brushed the sensitive skin at the small of my back. I arched into the touch, breasts grazing against his torso when he suddenly froze. Baffled, I pulled back to look into his eyes. I couldn't string together words, only make mewling noises of protest, quietly begging him with my eyes and my body to keep going. But he didn't.

"What's that sound?" Thorn cocked his head as if to hear something better. "I don't like it."

Shaking my head to shake loose my horny thoughts, I focused on listening. That's when I heard it. In the distance and getting closer, louder, with every passing moment.

"Sirens," I sighed.

There was only one person who would come charging onto my property like he owned it. I was going to knock that FBI agent's dick in the dirt for cutting this make-out session short. I was so horny, I was furious.

Couldn't he have waited until tomorrow? Maybe next week? *Never?*

"You'd better find someplace to hide where they can't find you," I said, shoving at Thorn's chest. "We don't have a lot of time. I'll keep them busy on the farm, okay?"

"Will you be safe?" he growled, hand still fisted delightfully in my hair.

"I'll do my best," I told him, pushing at him again. "Go."

Thorn hesitated, then darted in. His mouth met mine once more, and I practically melted against him. Then he was gone, fingers releasing my hair as he bounded over the hills to the cliffs.

CHAPTER 12*

RUTH

Worry and irritation warred for top emotion as I stormed my way back to the house. I was hoping Agent Simms hadn't been sneaking onto my property and gotten evidence of Thorn's existence. I wouldn't have put it past that damned G-Man. Whatever he thought he had, I'd make sure he didn't. You don't interrupt a kiss that damned good and get away with it.

Because holy hell, it had been... well. Easily the best kiss I'd ever had.

Police cars with their lights flashing, and that distinctive 1974 Chevy Impala, were parked haphazardly in front of my house. The posse had just exited their cars and were loitering by my front door. Sheriff Brighton caught sight of me and waved.

"Hello, Miss O'Daniels." He said with a nod. I didn't let his cool welcome deter me. The man had been over to my house to help so often he'd become addicted to my hazelnut cookies.

"Hello, Sheriff. What's going on?" I asked as I watched Agent Simms try to direct a group of grumpy officers from the Sheriff's department and police departments from the surrounding areas. It was like watching a very distraught cat sitter try to herd a bunch of independently-minded cats. There was even a forensics team there with photography equipment.

Apprehension knotted my gut. What if they discovered the gate? My gaze flicked around the scene, taking in as much detail as possible without looking conspicuous. There wasn't a vehicle substantial enough to transport Thorn in amongst the lineup, a minor relief.

"Drug bust, apparently." He rolled his eyes at me. "Claims you're growing marijuana on your property."

"Pfft. Really." I sighed and pretended to be more annoyed than I was.

Agent Simms caught sight of me then. He grinned widely and met me halfway to the house, practically prancing. He was so giddy. It was the weirdest shit to witness a blandly handsome government man in a suit do. That, more than anything else, creeped me right the fuck out. He came to a halt in front of me, well within my personal space. I refused to step back and relinquish ground.

"Hello, Ruth. We meet again." His smile was as plastic as his personality. But something smoldered in his gaze that I didn't like. It made my hackles rise and my face twist into a scowl. He was slimy in a way that I was all too familiar with.

"It's Miss O'Daniels to you, G-Man," I sneered.

"Oh, so formal? I thought we were beyond formalities." His smile broadened into a grin and I got the distinct impression he got his rocks off by making me angry.

"Why do you feel the need to make that sound so damned gross? I don't know you. And I wouldn't touch you with a ten-foot cattle prod. So don't make it sound like you *know* me like that." I made a disgusted sound in my throat and looked away.

"I'm here with a warrant to search your property for the illegal growing, distribution, and use of marijuana." With that, he held up an official-looking document, and I resisted the urge to roll my eyes.

"That's *all*?" I asked, crossing my arms. "All you had to do was ask."

"Oh, that's all that we'll be searching for with the warrant. But it won't be the only thing we'll see, I'm sure." He drawled as his gaze wandered lower than was polite. Absolute fucking ick. He was slimier than the ooze from a thousand snails.

It was then that I understood precisely where I knew his brand of sliminess from. His eyes sparkled in a way that I'd seen before at the commune. My intuition kicked me hard in the gut. It was the look of a man so desperate to catch someone that they'd do whatever it took to trap them. To win.

We'd see about that.

I turned to Sheriff Brighton. "Would you mind patting down Agent Simms before he enters my home? I don't want him to, uh, *misplace* anything that belongs to him."

The thing I liked most about Brighton? He wasn't slow on the uptake. I saw the understanding spark in his eyes as he turned to Agent Simms.

"Why, Miss O'Daniels, it would be a delightful honor." His peppered mustache stretched wide with his smile.

"Don't you dare or I'll make sure your badge is pulled and you're forced to resign without your pension." Agent Simms's expression turned dark so quickly it made my head spin and panic flare within my chest. Who thought hiring this unstable guy at the FBI would be a good idea?

"If I don't and we find illegal substances on the premises, I would be complicit in a false arrest. I would be in dereliction of duty as Sheriff. Not accommodating a simple request by the homeowner, who has offered a complaint regarding your behavior and slander, would mean I wasn't fit to be Sheriff." He settled his hands on his gun belt, framing his belt buckle. A twitch began in Agent Simms's eye.

"Been taking one too many tabs of LSD, Agent Simms? You're making it sound like a conspiracy theory," I quipped.

Agent Simms curled his lip at me before turning on his heel and stalking back to the milling police. I followed close behind. Had to love the hate-hate relationship the local police had with the feds. It was obvious to anyone with eyeballs that the local boys wished they could be anywhere else. I invited the officers inside.

"Do you guys like cookies?" I asked cheerily as I moved towards the kitchen. "I make some radical hazelnut cookies. Free of weed, I promise."

A few of them chuckled as the forensics team joined them.

"Now, I'll be straight with you. I keep a small amount of weed for when I get migraines. It's in the jar on the mantle," I admitted.

One officer had taken up a post nearby and was watching me like a hawk. I started getting out ingredients and utensils to make my cookies. It was as if he wanted first dibs on the cookies when they came out of the oven. But also wanted to ensure I wouldn't sneak in the devil's lettuce as a special ingredient, either. Cute.

Another officer had pulled down the jar I'd pointed to and opened it. Inside the jar, there was a tiny plastic baggie with maybe one whole bud in there. When I'd left the commune, *I'd left it* in nearly every sense of the word. The only holdovers from that life were memories I'd rather burn from my mind with a brand and the occasional joint to help with bodily ills.

I knew showing them the weed I had was risky. But I knew it would be riskier if I wasn't honest with them and they found it. Or if Simms managed to plant something.

Brighton walked in with the pain in the ass in question, glowering behind him. On his bland features, he looked like a petulant toddler instead of an angry man. The officer with my jar held it up to Brighton, who nodded. The officers and forensics unit spent the next several hours scouring my house, under my house, the garage, the nearly collapsed barn, and the grounds. Other than the small bit of weed I'd told them about, they'd found nothing.

They hadn't found Thorn either, thank the gods.

"I won't confiscate this. This is less than what we find on teenagers at the mall," said Brighton, sighing. "This has been a colossal waste of time, Agent Simms."

Agent Simms pretended not to hear him and gave me the hairy eyeball. As if I'd magicked away all the evidence he'd made up in his damned noggin. I pulled out the last batch of hazelnut cookies with a smile plastered on my face. I shucked them off of the baking sheet with a spatula, put the baking sheet to cool on top of the stove, and turned off the oven. A beatific vision of domesticity, blithely ignoring the cantankerous bastard who'd cut the best kiss of my life short. I hummed as I filled little baggies full of cookies.

Eat *shit*, Agent Simms!

"Don't forget to take some cookies with you!" I called with a smile at the officers and forensics. They all cheered and grabbed a baggie, making noises of appreciation as they ate them while walking out the door.

"Thank you for your time, Miss O'Daniels, and your cookies." Sheriff Brighton smiled kindly at me and took a baggie. He herded Agent Simms out my front door. Brighton's kindness hit me again, as he made sure Simms got into his car and even followed him off of my property and onto the coastal highway. An escort for a very grumpy federal agent. When the last of the police cars turned onto the coastal highway, I let out a sigh of relief. Hours of baking to hide your worry over your alien orc... *friend*... while police raided your house really took it out of a girl.

"What smells so good?" a familiar voice called. I screamed bloody murder, turning on my heel, arms flailing. Thorn stood there in the afternoon light, coming in through the open door of the mudroom.

"You scared me!" I cried, and he gave me a crooked grin.

"Sorry about that." He scratched at the back of his head and my brain blanked at how lovely his abdominal muscles moved. It wasn't fair that between his personality and his looks, I couldn't find it in me to stay mad at him for more than a few minutes.

"Want a cookie?" I sighed in defeat and held up a plate with cookies on it.

"What's a cookie?" he asked, cocking his head in interest. Brighton and Sanchez had always made off with the cookies, joking that they were too good for Thorn. As Thorn was getting other kinds of sweets from me.

"A sweet treat for good orc boys," I said with a smirk, and Thorn's gaze heated.

"Good orc boys, och?" he asked, voice deepening. "Does that mean I've been good?"

"You somehow avoided a group of cops, so yes. You've been good." My cheeks heated, and I refused to look him in the eye again. Thorn came in and accepted a cookie from the plate. The noise of pleasure he made once he'd bitten into it had my core pulsing between my thighs. How the hell could a guy just *sound* so damned sexy?

It wasn't fair!

I wasn't ready for commitment so soon after my misadventures at the commune and the wreck my life had become after. But I also knew that our situation would only get harder. I mean... more difficult, from here on. Not like it hadn't become difficult after that night we'd come together in separate rooms.

The lid to Pandora's box had blown off the second I'd demanded he kiss me, let him touch me. Did I still want to kiss him? Hells yes. Did I know it would lead me down a path I wasn't prepared for? Also yes.

So I'd need to keep this tempting orc the hell away from my lady bits until I knew I could face intimacy without balking. He deserved that much respect from me at least.

A few days later, I was busy in the kitchen, cooking up some hot dogs, corn on the cob, and potato salad for dinner. I'd just bought a radio, a small splurge to help relieve stress, and had turned it on to lighten my mood as I cooked. The visit from Agent Simms had gotten under my skin more than I'd like to admit, and getting to listen to music again was a balm.

A tremendous crash sounded and the back door nearly sailed off its hinges as Thorn came busting through the doorway like a Viking berserker. I froze, caught being a closet disco queen, and we stared at one another wide-eyed as *Ain't No Mountain High Enough* by Marvin Gaye and Tammi Terrell kept playing in the background. He was panting, wild-eyed, and sweating as if he'd run the entire way here. Looking damned fine silhouetted by the sun.

"You're safe?" Thorn growled, eyes flicking between me and the inside of the house, apparently looking for intruders.

"Yes?" I asked him, bewildered.

"What's that noise?" He asked, still on high alert.

"It's the radio?" I pointed to the contraption in question as his brow furrowed and he cocked his head at it.

"What is 'raydyo'?" His shoulders eased, and he strode over to look at it.

"It's..." I began, but quickly realized I wasn't equipped to explain the technology behind how radios worked. So I shrugged and kept it simple. "It plays music."

Thorn picked it up and was tilting it from side to side. I gently took it from him and set it back down on the counter. It wouldn't do to have him break it after I'd just bought it.

"Where are the players? The instruments?" He asked, looking at me in complete bafflement.

"Ah... more science." I gave him a sheepish smile. Thorn nodded sagely, probably convinced it was magic. Just then, the song changed, and *Hooked on a Feeling* by Blue Swede came on.

Thorn jumped, surprised at the intro. Then, as the vocals hit, his eyes dilated, and a grin grew on that sinful mouth of his. He bobbed his head and then boogied as the chorus hit. Watching him move like that blanked my brain.

"I like it!" He cried over the trumpets, grinning at me with those wolf's teeth of his. I couldn't keep my giggle back at his discovery of human music. He was like a little kid at Christmas. We stared at one another as the next section of the song came on, talking about a mouth candy sweet that could make the singer drunk.

"The words remind me of you, Ruth!" His smile was bright as the sun as he looked at me with love in his eyes. I froze, my face exploding into a blush. Fuck... He was reminiscing over our kiss from the other day! I was not ready for this kind of thing!

Knowing I was safe and loving the music, he sang along entirely off-key, missing half the words as he walked to the sink. He got himself some water and chugged it. I shook my head as I got back to work cooking dinner. More than once, while the song played, I caught him staring at me with something akin to wistful adoration on his face.

Before I knew it, dinner was ready, and all of my stress had melted away. As we ate, I told him a bit about our music and dances and it intrigued him. Evidently the orckin highly prized dancing and he was curious to see what kinds of dances I knew.

We forewent story time that night and instead, we spent the night teaching one another dances from our respective cultures. I taught him how to do the Hustle, the Mashed Potato, the Twist, and even a waltz. It was the most fun I'd had in ages as we fumbled over the dance moves and sang along with whatever came on the radio.

As songs on the radio often do, *Hooked on a Feeling* came back on, but we were so tired, that I taught him how to slow dance instead. Thorn kept his hand on my waist, instead of letting it wander like I'd expected, which surprised the hell out of me. My heart thundered in my chest as he curled his massive clawed hand around my much smaller one and held it to his heart. Where I could feel the solid, steady beat of it.

Thorn sang along with the song, his voice a deep hypnotic rumble, his lips brushing the top of my head. I'd never been so damned flustered in my entire life. I knew if I looked up at him, I'd kiss him. And I knew I wasn't ready for that again so soon because it would lead to more than just a kiss. So instead, I rested my head on his chest and sighed as the rest of the song filtered past us out into the starry night.

CHAPTER 13

THORN

Weeks passed, late summer gave way to early autumn, and the roses began losing their petals. Rose hips ripened on the trailing thorny masses. The dun-colored hills of the coast turned golden in the rich autumn light. The scents changed, deepening, redolent of loam, eucalyptus, and oak.

We spent the first part of autumn dancing around our first kiss. Literally danced around it the first time I'd ever seen a radio and had the blissful experience of dancing the night away with Ruth. I'd desperately wanted to kiss her as we danced slowly to *Hooked on a Feeling.* But I'd sworn to myself that I would not take the lead. Only flirt with Ruth. She would come to me when she was ready. If she was ever ready. Source be damned if I didn't crave her constantly, though.

Beyond that sweet torture, Agent Simms was a genuine threat that hung over us like a dark cloud as we pushed to complete the hobbit holes on schedule. Progress continued on them and one by one, they were slowly coming together. We'd just completed the framework on all seven of the little earth cottages. Now we could move forward with the waterproofing.

At night, Ruth would continue telling me the tales by Tolkien in her soft, melodious voice. I wasn't fond of Tolkien's take on orcs in his stories. Ruth and I often discussed the differences between actual orckin culture and the vestiges of human knowledge. It was clear that Tolkien had created the orcs in the spirit of how ancient humans saw us before the breaking of the Geata. Ruth's openness and acceptance of my criticism, point of view, and cultural corrections surprised me. She offered to read something else, but knowing she accepted me and my actual culture, I told her I wished to hear the rest of the story.

Samhain, or Halloween, came and went with children dressing up and begging Ruth for sweets. A strange ritual founded in darker times that now brought joy. Ruth got into the spirit of Samhain, dressing as a witch. She was delighted to pass out candy to the children, surprised considering the slanderous rumors still circulating about her.

Her strange conical hat was silly, but the dress that hung off of her soft, round shoulders and the belt that cinched her waist was a temptation beyond measure. More than once, I had to leave the room or risk succumbing to the need to discover what delights existed under the sway of her skirts. Strangely enough, I could be present in the house. Most of the children thought my appearance was a fantastic costume. Some even shrieked in delight when I answered the door to give them candy.

Samhain came and went. Ruth's cooking transitioned to stews and heartier meals as the weather cooled. Autumn deepened, and the colorful foliage fell, leaving bare branches like spears aimed at the sky. Another human holiday loomed closer, one that Ruth was conflicted about.

Thanksgiving. She told me the origins of the holiday and it was something that made us both uneasy. Because it stank of greed and oppression, instead of the thankful and innocent facade it used.

Regardless of the holiday's origins, Ruth explained it was a time for families to gather and celebrate.

One day, Deputy Sanchez called Ruth on the phone. I couldn't help but eavesdrop with my sharp hearing. I watched her from the kitchen table as I reviewed some plans for the hobbit holes.

"Would you like to join us for Thanksgiving, Ruth? My family will have a feast, and you're more than welcome," Sanchez asked.

"Oh, thank you, but no. I appreciate the thought, though!" she replied cheerily.

"The offer stands. You don't have any family here, right? My Abuela would adopt you immediately." Sanchez said.

"No, I don't. And I don't doubt it, from the way you talk about her. She sounds like a gem. But I'll be okay. I don't celebrate Thanksgiving, anyway." Ruth smiled and wrapped her cardigan around her before she hung up the phone. With her hair piled atop her head in its usual knot, loose tendrils brushed her neck as she returned to making dinner.

My heart nearly stopped. She was so lovely. My pretty little dove.

She cooked a soup made from a vegetable called a pumpkin. The same kind we carved faces into on Samhain. It smelled delicious. Fresh, crusty bread and iced tea complimented the savory soup. If it weren't for all the hard labor, I would have easily gained weight with how she fed me.

Ruth blew on a spoonful of soup. Her lips were so close to it as she breathed on it, I ached. The kiss we'd shared so many weeks ago was haunting me. Every day, it became harder to resist kissing her again.

"So why did you decline Sanchez's offer to join his family on

Thanksgiving?" I asked, to distract myself from her mouth. Ruth shrugged and ate her soup.

"My family was never big on holidays. I feel like I missed out. It would be nice to have Thanksgiving with a large family. But what about you? It wouldn't be right for me to leave you here all alone on your first Thanksgiving."

Her words hit straight into my heart. Stunned, I stared at her as she dunked her bread into her soup and continued eating as if she hadn't just shaken the foundations of my world. Did she care that much about me? Was I slowly winning her over?

I could only hope so.

RUTH

I was excited to spend Thanksgiving with Thorn. My folks hadn't been into holidays, and at the commune, we only celebrated certain pagan holidays from varying faiths. So I'd gotten a few cooking magazines, poured over my cookbooks, and planned out a meal fit for a king. Or, literally, a prince.

If it was going to be our first Thanksgiving, then I was going to make it amazing. Thanksgiving day came, and I forbade Thorn from going outside to work. We'd been working on the bed-and-breakfast every day. Both of us needed a day off. So instead of working on the hobbit holes, he helped me in the kitchen.

The meal itself was insane once we'd finished cooking. I'd set up the island counter as a buffet, and we helped ourselves. There was turkey, sausage cornbread stuffing, pies, spiced cranberry relish, oysters casino, and Jell-O.

I'd taken one look at the California Waldorf salad recipe in one of the cooking magazines and wanted to puke. I liked Jell-O in certain ways. But packing it full of both fruit *and* vegetables, then insisting on pouring Jell-O onion soup mix into it just... ew.

Who the hell lacked taste buds and thought this would be a tasty combination? Instead, we made it with fruit so it would be a nice, light, refreshing side dish. It wasn't half bad, but it wasn't really half good either.

When we'd both filled ourselves to bursting, I broke out the whiskey. We deserved to celebrate a little. We were ahead of schedule, after all, and it was primarily thanks to Thorn's tireless hard work.

Thorn had expanded the back steps and added a deck where we could sit outside on warm evenings and enjoy the sunset. Sometimes, I'd even read to him out there instead of inside next to the fireplace. The orc was a damned sweetheart, and I had a hard time holding back. I stopped counting the times I'd nearly grabbed him by the shirt to yank him down for a kiss. Because that single kiss we'd shared? It wasn't enough.

But I didn't want to lead Thorn on. If I wasn't certain I could be his mate for life, I refused to make a move. It wasn't fair to him. Or to me. I knew one thing, though; I was healing. Slow but sure, bits of my heart, broken by my ex and time at the commune, by the abortion, and those shards from losing my parents, were being pieced back together and healing over. All because of Thorn's patience and company. His friendship.

We sat there in Adirondack chairs on the porch, staring at the stars. Orion hung above us, and I smiled as the sky glittered like an expanse of diamond-encrusted velvet. Curling into my quilt, I popped the top on some Jameson and poured us both a few fingers' worth.

"What's this?" Thorn asked as I corked the bottle and handed him his glass.

"Irish whiskey. If I'm going to introduce you to human whiskey, it'll be with this." I chuckled. Holding my glass between my fingers, I watched Thorn as he sniffed at the amber liquid in his glass. He took a small sip, swished the contents around in his mouth, and swallowed it. I watched, entranced, as his throat bobbed. "So?"

"Not bad. Pretty light, if I'm honest," he shrugged and downed the rest like it was water. My eyebrows rose in surprise.

"Excuse me, light?" I blinked a few times. "I mean, it isn't the highest-proof whiskey in existence, but it's not like that's lemonade in your glass."

Thorn grinned at me. Sharp teeth, luscious lips, and that hypnotizing onyx and copper stare transfixed me. I was a sucker for his smile and his laugh. He shrugged and grabbed the bottle, pouring himself another glass.

"I'm used to stronger stuff," he told me haughtily, cocking an eyebrow my way as he nursed his drink. I had to look away to keep my wits about me.

"It was nice of Sanchez to invite me over for Thanksgiving with his family." A smile tugged at my mouth at the thought.

"Do you regret not going?" he asked, rolling the whiskey in his tumbler, watching how it clung to the glass.

"Well..." I paused, took a bracing sip of the whiskey, and stared Thorn dead in the eye. "My family is here, isn't it?"

I swear he wasn't breathing. Then he laughed, shaking his head and releasing a defeated sigh.

"You keep saying things like that, Ruth, and I'm going to think you're serious about me. Then you'll really be stuck with me."

I didn't respond, a little shaken.

"Thorn…" I began, and he turned to look at me, eyebrow cocked. I couldn't move, could barely breathe through the lump in my throat. He was so dead set on me being his mate, I didn't think it was right not to tell him about what I'd gone through. What I'd done. "I have something to say. You will not like it."

"Say it, lass." Thorn's gaze raked over me, assessing me and how tightly I gripped the arms of the Adirondack chair, so tight my knuckles were white. He was wary, but not upset. I knew that was about to change and it near-shattered my heart.

I swallowed, stared ahead at the moon, and began.

I told him about living in the commune. How I'd been lured in on promises and ideals of a utopian life. How it'd started off amazing. And how it'd quickly devolved. How I'd become hooked on various drugs. That the leaders of the commune, including my ex, had pimped the women who'd joined out to those in the community and beyond. Stating it was for the good of the commune when it was only good for their dicks and their pockets.

Silence met my words as I finally told my story. I refused to look at Thorn, but I could see him in my peripheral vision, see that he'd set down his glass and was watching me. With shaking hands and a wounded heart, I told him the rest. I told him about the memories that had resurfaced. Of how I'd discovered I'd been pregnant. And my choice.

"With the passing of Roe v Wade, with abortion being legalized, I sought care. I was told that because of the drugs I'd partaken of and the lifestyle I'd led, it was extremely likely my child would be born with significant health defects. That they might not survive, and even if they did, I knew I was in no position to care for a sick child." I murmured, staring off into the night, lost to the haze of memory. "Despite all of my ideologies of free love, I'd always wanted a family. A man who loved me and a few kids. Only the little ones would run in fields of wildflowers instead of behind picket fences. But with no one to help me through the pregnancy and raise a child, knowing that my child would be born and suffer their entire lives because of what I'd done..."

I took a deep, shaking breath and watched as my exhalation plumed into the night like smoke.

"I already loved that child more than my own life. I would have died happy had it meant my child would live a healthy life. But that wasn't the case. So I got the abortion, no matter what it would cost me. I chose mercy for my child." I swallowed thickly and took a sip of whiskey.

More than once, I'd tried explaining to others how I saw what I did as an act of mercy. Julia had been the only one to understand. Life was miserable at the best of times. My child didn't deserve to have extra helpings of anguish, pain, and suffering because of *my* poor choices. I would forever love and mourn my child. That was my burden. One I was grateful for.

Thorn was still quiet, waiting for me to continue. Granting me the time and space to talk. So I did.

"When I'd gone in for the procedure, there were people outside holding signs. Christians who saw what I was doing as a sin against their god, instead of the act of mercy, I saw it as. As if I were doing it on a whim and not on the soul shredding decision it was. They told me I was going to hell. I told them to have the end they deserved." I bit out. "Then I had the abortion, discovered my parents died in a car accident, got fully clean, and bought this farm with my inheritance. You know the rest."

There was a heavy silence, even the wind not daring to blow. My cheeks itched, and I realized I'd been crying. I set my empty glass down on the armrest of the chair and used my sleeves to scrub the tears away.

"You are..." Thorn began and stopped, swallowing hard. I turned my head to look at him, terrified of what I'd see. The judgment I feared, marring the expression of the space orc I thought of as my dear friend. As possibly something more. My gaze reluctantly met his and what I saw ripped the ground out from under me.

He was crying.

Tracts of tears were shining against his storm grey skin. His copper eyes were bright as stars in the darkness with his unshed tears. Coughing, he brushed them away as if they were nothing. When somehow, I knew they were everything.

"You are the strongest female I've ever had the grace to know." Thorn's voice was deep and grave as he spoke. "To be tricked and used and to make the choice that you did. To survive all you have faced and still be handed more sorrow. Only to take that sorrow and transform all of it into this dream you are making a reality. Truly, your mettle is greater than any warrior I've ever met."

That was *not* what I'd expected him to say. I sat staring at him, dumbfounded, reeling from his words.

"You don't... judge me for what I did?" I whispered the question.

"How could I?" He rasped. "You made a choice no female should ever be put in a position to make. Amongst the orckin, because of how our kind is dying out, orclings are highly prized. But not at the expense of the female's life. Not if the bairn is sick while in the womb. Not all clans approach how females should be treated the same. Some don't treat them well at all. But it is the female's choice to carry an orcling. Most find it an honor to do so. But it is *her* life that is important to keep if something goes wrong with the pregnancy. I don't understand how humans don't see the sacredness of a female's existence in the world."

Fresh tears spilled from my eyes as he spoke and I made a keening, choking sound deep in my throat. He saw me. He understood in the limited way he could and he did not judge me for my choice. The thought that somewhere in the universe, a woman's life, her body, and choice, were respected, even imperfectly... seared a line of hope in my veins that one day too, we could honor it here on Earth.

"I truly admire you, Ruth." He murmured, voice stark and honest, his piercing gaze open for me to see the veracity of his feelings. I swallowed hard.

"Thank you for listening, Thorn. And for not judging me." I gave him a broken smile. One that he returned. "I admire you too, you know."

Thorn chuckled and shook his head, a bright silver color exploding over his cheeks. It was charming and endearing. I'd made him blush and a part of me longed to make him blush again.

"Admiring you is like admiring the stars. You don't expect them to admire you back." He murmured. We sat there in comforting silence as we stared at one another for a long moment. My heart stuttered in my chest like an old tractor engine. Did he truly think of me like that? Morrigan take my soul...

To break the silence, he smirked and lifted his glass. "I'm going to have to distill some uisge-beatha for you. So you can have some *real* whiskey."

"You make your own whiskey?" I asked, honestly impressed. Relieved at the change in topic.

"Och. Came up with the recipe myself. I apprenticed to the clan's head distiller. I did it for fun and to have an outlet." Thorn shrugged. "Sometimes the pressures of being Leanabh Rìgh were too heavy."

"I'm so sorry," I murmured, brow furrowing. "Like marrying

the princess of your rival clan?"

"You're adorable when you're jealous, little dove," Thorn chuckled and gave me a sly smile.

"I never said I was jealous!" I protested, smacking his arm. He just laughed harder, his sharp-toothed smile striking my heart.

Okay, maybe I was just a teensy bit jealous.

"Och, marrying princesses I'd never met, although marriage is normally reserved for fertile couples. Fighting the dorcha'aon, helping the sick who'd contracted the an'sgudal." The smile faded bit by bit from his face. "Burning my sister's pyre. Babe yet unborn within her."

His face shut down, and he swallowed the last of the whiskey in his glass, reaching for the bottle and refilling it three knuckles deep.

"You've been through so much. I'm sorry." He gave me a noncommittal shrug. Needing him to understand, I reached out a hand and placed it over his. He froze, glass partially raised, gaze zeroing in on where my hand barely covered the back of his palm. "It must be difficult to be gone from them. Your people. You were brave to do all that you've done. I'm proud of you."

He sighed heavily and set his glass aside.

"It can be sometimes. You humans are strange and your world is so very different from mine. At times, it's almost too much to bear." He ran his free hand through his shoulder-length hair. I couldn't help but watch in fascination as the thick strands slid against one another like sheets of silk. "But being here with you. Learning from you. Helping you build your future while you piece yourself together bit by bit? It heals wounds I didn't realize I had."

Now I was the one who couldn't breathe. Him helping me heal was healing him? Gods, I could almost feel how easily we'd slipped our jagged edges together. The deep valleys and sharp peaks of our souls just... sliding into place without effort. I wasn't sure how to accept it. How to deal with it or how to move forward.

"You're making it sound like you're planning on sticking around for a long while," I said around the lump in my throat.

"Forever if you'd have me," he said, copper-and-onyx gaze sliding to me as he took a long swallow from his tumbler of whiskey. He lowered his glass and I could see a bead of it still on his full bottom lip.

A lip I suddenly wanted to kiss.

Forever.

No one had ever declared forever for me. Or stuck around. Or busted their ass on my behalf just to prove themselves to me. Treated me as if I was worthy of such attention.

All I knew was that if Thorn ever left, the bar would be impossible for anyone else to reach. And not just because of his size. That thought made me pause, glass halfway to my mouth. I didn't *want* him to leave.

Swallowing thickly, I lowered my glass and looked at him. I really, truly looked at him. As if genuinely seeing him for the first time. Not as some washed-up piece of flotsam that needed rescuing. But as the male who was so dead set on me being his forever.

The male could rip a log in half like a superhero and easily crush anyone who stood against him. Yet he called me his little dove like I was the most precious thing in the entire universe to him. He treated me like I'd always wanted to be treated. He *cherished* me.

The dude had kissed me in a way that still turned me on whenever I thought about it. Like right now. I knew he could smell the shift, but he tried to hide it like always. Tried to respect me and my boundaries in the only way he knew how.

I'd somehow, without meaning to, utterly and irrevocably fallen for an alien orc prince from across the universe. A charming, flirtatious, strong, intelligent, handsome, and honorable one at that. And it had taken me *months* to do so.

I was a fucking idiot. And it was going to be up to me to make the first move.

Shit.

CHAPTER 14

THORN

My heart was sore for my cridhe. All that she had gone through and endured. I'd scented her fear of males, her wariness even around ones she trusted since the day I'd met her. Having her trust me enough with her history, hearing it in its entirety, my heart broke for her. She was truly the most amazing female I'd ever met.

"There's something I'd like to do," I told Ruth softly as we sat beneath the stars. We'd sat in thoughtful silence for a time after I'd told her I'd stay forever if she'd have me. Ruth shook herself back to the present and looked my way. "Back home on Talam, we would go to the Craobh na Beatha every triple moon cycle. It was a time of peace between the clans. Where the Fear a Chì and the devout traveled to leave offerings. I lost my sister the day before I arrived here, and I would like to light a candle for her and the baby she lost."

"Oh, Thorn..." Her expression was filled with heartache, not pity. That she had room for my woes despite the enormity of her own spoke to her strength of heart. "I'm so sorry for your losses. We can go down to the sea cave. I have some spare candles and we can bring something as an offering."

"You're very kind," I told her, my mouth twitching into a small smile. I didn't know when the cycle had closed back on Talam. It was just a guess based on my time here on Earth. The Source would forgive me for missing the holy day. I wasn't sure if I could forgive myself, though.

She stood and made her way inside. I followed close behind, carrying the blankets and empty glasses. She immediately checked the tide timetable and gathered candles, flashlights, and a bag of cookies. My heart swelled watching her do this for me. Her kindness made my heart and my knees weak.

Ruth was a very loving woman. Smart, hardworking, and brave. Any male would be lucky to have her as his mate. I'd been hoping it was me, but without the cridhe marks to prove it, that hope was wearing thin. Even with the passionate kiss that sang between us like truth. In the end, cridhe marks or no, I was hers just as she was mine. I was completely and inescapably in love with her. I hoped she would feel the same way I did for her one day.

We made our way to the sea cave, and I helped her navigate the slick, rocky ground. Once we'd entered the cavern, she turned off her flashlight, and we made our way towards the Geata. When I turned to her, she wordlessly handed me the candle, a lighter, and the cookies. Her smile was sad. Nodding my thanks, I ascended the steps and lit the candle. I placed it against the seam of the door, cookies piled carefully around it, hoping that my dear sister and her orcling could feel it in the afterlife.

Standing tall, I pressed my hands together palm to palm, one with my fingers pointed to the ground, the other towards the ceiling. I began speaking an Oc'Dellor prayer to the Source and the variety of gods we worshiped. Beseeching them to see that my sister and her babe made it to our afterlife. It was a prayer our mother had taught us. And one Thisa was preparing to use as the Fear a Chì-in-training before she fell ill. Tears choked me as I finished the prayer and lowered my hands.

"What language is that?" my little dove asked softly when I'd finished the prayer and moved back to her side. "I've heard you say things in it or sing in it before."

"It's Teanga Dhubh, black-tongue in Common. It's our native language." I swallowed thickly, thankful for her distraction.

"It sounds so melodic and pretty. Why call it black-tongue?" Ruth's confusion was adorable.

"Simply put, because orckin have black tongues." I grinned wolfishly at her. Then I stuck my tongue out at its full length, lashing it back and forth. It easily fell past my chin.

"Oh gods, put that thing away!" she laughed, looking away from me with her face bright red.

"Och? You want to get a closer look, you say?" I leaned in close to her cheek and she made an adorable squeak. Ruth attempted to push me away, but I kept making noises and faked trying to lick her face. Probably not the most respectful thing to do after speaking a holy prayer and lighting a candle for Thisa and her bairn. But I knew Thisa's sweet heart would not have begrudged me making my cridhe laugh.

Especially after such a heavy evening of truths.

Suddenly, Ruth froze. "What's that?" she asked, the laughter gone from her voice. A lilt of curiosity limned her tone. Her arms had slackened, and my tongue licked the rounded shell of her ear. She made a whimpering sound and shivered, a reaction I liked. But her single-minded focus across the cave caught my attention.

"What's what?" I asked. I couldn't seem to pinpoint what she was looking at.

"Something is glinting over there," she pointed, and I leaned in close to look over her shoulder. Ruth shivered again, and I had to resist the urge to bend my head down and kiss along it. Gods, she was distracting.

"I don't see it," I admitted. Which was odd, considering my eyesight was better than hers.

Ruth hustled away from me, down the stairs, and over to the direction, she'd been pointing. She walked up to the rough wall there and reached into a small hollow in the rocks, worn smooth by small stones over the millennia to form a little cubby. Her hand completely disappeared. I waited as she dug around in the opening for a moment, tongue pressed between her lips in concentration. She cried out in victory and removed her hand.

"What is it?" I called. She was silent for a while.

"I think I found it," Ruth said softly, her words echoing in the cavern.

"Found what?" I asked, about ready to move towards her. She then turned away from the cavern wall and trotted over to me.

"Hold out your hand," she demanded, and I did so without a second thought. Lifting her hand, she dropped a familiar weight into my scarred palm. My breath caught in my chest. Looking up at me, she took her hand back. "Is that your ring?"

"It is," I whispered. Her grin was so bright it was like looking at the sun. Gazing back down at the ring, I huffed a laugh. Leave it to my cridhe to be the one to find it.

"Well?" Ruth asked, pushing at my arm. "Put it on!"

So I did.

At first, there was nothing as I slipped my ring onto my finger, where it settled against the indent in my finger on my left hand. It was an heirloom I'd worn with pride since I was old enough for it to fit.

The rings did nothing to us back on Talam. So we didn't know if they worked anymore. But per the histories passed down by the Fear a Chì, they would allow us to look human once we passed through the Geata. I hoped it was true.

Suddenly, a strange shiver washed over my skin, from my pointed ears to my clawed toes. It felt like an aftershock, an echo of what passing through the Geata had felt like. Like liquid life was being poured over my form.

I stared down at my hand and watched as my skin changed. The gray lightened and morphed to a warm tone like bronze. My fingertips itched slightly and the claws simply disappeared. I looked down at myself and placed my hands on my body, marveling at how I appeared as a human. I was still my normal size. But my defining characteristics as an orckin had vanished. With steady fingers, I touched my ears, now tipless and curved like Ruth's. My teeth were blunt and my tongue felt strange in my mouth. Too slick.

Ruth's gasp had my gaze snapping to hers. Her hand was partially over her mouth and she was blushing. She scanned me over and over in the moonlight as it filtered in from above, and I smirked.

"Like what you see, little dove?" I asked, and she shivered. Oh, she liked what she saw, alright. The thought that she liked me better this way was like a knife blade in my gut, though.

"Holy shit, it *worked*!" she whispered. "I mean, it was stellar to watch it happen! You really have magic!"

"Och, it worked." The smile I gave her was brittle. "Do you think I'll pass as a human now?"

"Pass? Hell, you'll probably get recruited to be a model or an actor!" She huffed a laugh and shook her head. We stood there on the top stair of the Geata, facing one another. Taking one another in. Her bemused smile was sharp and lovely at once.

"I can finally stand beside you," I whispered, voice cracking. Anywhere she went, I could now follow without risking it all.

"What are you talking about?" Ruth whispered, brows furrowing together. My pained expression must have registered, her frown deepening as she understood my meaning. She placed a small hand against my cheek, and I shuddered at the contact.

"Oh, Thorn..." she murmured and pulled me down for a kiss. I bent down, capturing her lovely mouth with mine. Groaning at her taste, one I'd craved since before I'd passed through the Geata, I stepped forward until her back pressed against the carved wall that had brought me to her.

I told myself it didn't matter if she'd only accept me like this. It would be worth it to be with my cridhe. I hoped it wasn't a lie.

CHAPTER 15*

RUTH

It was strange having him look so human after falling in love with him as an orc. I didn't mind it. Gods, he was staggeringly handsome as a human. His facial and body structure was the same, his skin tone a lovely creamy honey color. Same proud nose and full mouth. But his teeth were blunt, tongue pink, and so very human. His ears were rounded now, the points gone. And his eyes. There was no fathomless black surrounding the iris and pupil. Just normal, human, average white. Even the bright copper of his irises mellowed to a light amber color. Thorn was drop-dead gorgeous.

But I hadn't fallen in love with this vision of him. And I didn't want him to think I only wanted him because he appeared human. His words had burned. Thorn only thought he was worthy of me when he looked human. Thought I'd only want him when he looked like me. It was a load of bollocks I would not allow taking further root between us.

"Take it off," I whispered, pulling back from our blistering kiss. He began unbuttoning his shirt with trembling fingers, and I placed my hand on them to get him to stop. "Not that. Well, maybe in a minute. Take off your ring."

Thorn froze, his human gaze meeting mine in shock. "You wish to have me as I am? As an orc and not a human?"

"I'll take you either way." I couldn't keep my voice from shaking. "I want you to be who you are."

There was a heavy pause, rife with words unspoken, as we stared at one another. Then, in a flurry of motion, he ripped the ring from his finger and held it up to me. The magic in the chleoc ring faded from his features and the very human-looking guy before me shifted into the orc I'd fallen head over heels for.

"It's yours," he rasped, and I took it, slipping it onto my thumb for safekeeping. "Are you sure?"

"Sure, as the sun rises and sets." I lifted my hands to his face and pulled his head down to mine. Our lips brushed and within one heartbeat and the next, he was devouring my mouth.

The ridges on Thorn's tongue were such a delightful contrast to the slick smoothness of my own. One I'd fantasized about. I cried out into his mouth, and he growled in response. His hands reached up to rip free his button-down, sending the buttons flying and scattering amongst the stone roots carved into the cave floor.

Thorn was done being patient. He'd been patient for months. Hell, so had I. He moved forward, pressing me against the carving. I gasped as my back met the doorway where he'd entered my world from his own across the universe.

Mouth still ravenous on mine, he ran his clawed hands up under my sweater. His fingers chilled from the cold cave air, made my nipples harden and peak in anticipation. His claws gently scraped against the soft curves of my stomach before they cupped my waist and moved inexorably higher, inch by inch. As if he were memorizing the feel of my skin.

"Gods, you're so fucking soft," he growled against my lips,

knuckles moving against the undersides of my breasts in the barest whisper of a caress. "So impossibly soft."

Our gazes locked, and he slowly raised his hands to cup my breasts. I cried out as they filled his palms, his rough calluses scraping against my overly sensitive nipples. My hips bucked hard against him.

He snarled then, pressing his massive muscled thigh between my legs, his giant cock pressing into my stomach from beneath his kilt. I shamelessly ground my sopping wet mound against his thigh through my jeans. The throbbing of my core demanded more. I jerked against his leg while he fondled my breasts and breathed against my neck. My jeans were already completely soaked with my juices. I couldn't find it in me to care.

"I need to be buried inside of you, Ruth. Can't take it anymore. I'm going to go absolutely mad at how badly I need you." Thorn's voice was a harsh, grating rasp that skipped across my skin like another hand. Lighting up my body even more. He licked and sucked and nibbled at the sensitive skin along the column of my throat.

"*Thorn.*" I moaned his name, and he groaned in reply, body melting and pressing hard against mine. My shoulder blades dug into the cold carving. But I was too drunk with pleasure to even register the discomfort.

"Say my name again, Ruth. Let me worship you like the goddess you are." He ran his sharp teeth against my earlobe, sending a shiver down my spine and a rush of wetness from my pussy.

"Thorn!" I cried out as he flicked both of my nipples and gently bit down on my neck. Fuck, he felt so gods damned good I couldn't help but dig my nails into his shoulders. "Please!"

With a primal roar, he ripped my sweater apart in a matter of moments with his black claws; the remnants slipping down my arms to the stone. Chest bared to him, nipples taut and aching, goosebumps pricked my skin. Thorn's eyes were a scorching copper brand, roving over my body as his hands explored. Shivering with more than cold, I made a desperate, needy noise in my throat.

He bared his teeth as he inhaled deeply, gaze settling at the apex of my thighs where I was grinding it shamelessly against his thigh. Thorn drew his hands down my waist to grip my hips.

His breathing grew ragged as he fumbled at my waistband. I wasn't much better as I set about unbuckling his kilt with shaking hands. As soon as I was done, he flung it aside and pressed against me again. The long, thick, and heavy weight of his cock pressed hard against my bare belly. The copious amounts of pre-cum felt slick as it pressed into my softness.

He was still struggling with my pants, snarling in his frustration. So I quickly pushed him back, unbuttoned my jeans, and shimmied out of them. As soon as I'd kicked them aside, he was on me. Mouth on mine before he kissed his way down my neck. Teeth scraping against my collarbone, he growled as he got to his knees in front of me, head even with my chest. He moaned as he buried his face between my breasts. Everywhere he touched, he left a trail of fire and a need for more.

I sunk my fingers into his hair, breath hitching as Thorn took the tip of my nipple into his mouth with his long, black tongue. Shuddering at the heat of his mouth and the cold of the Geata behind me, I writhed and gasped as he cupped, licked, and suckled at first one breast, then the other. His lashes were dark fans against his cheeks. His hands grasped and released my curves as they roamed up and down my sides. Gods, I could feel wetness trailing down the insides of my thighs as I moaned for him.

Thorn trailed his hands down along the curves of my waist and hips, claws gently raking against my flesh, leaving shivers in their wake. He followed the curves of my thighs inward, thumbs slipping between my quivering legs. Pausing at the slickness he found, the dark rumble of his laugh against my belly was like a bolt of lightning to my clit and my pussy clenched on nothing, dripping more of my juices onto his thumbs.

"So wet for me. Are you ready, mo cridhe?" he growled at me from where he sat on his heels, lips and ridged black tongue brushing my navel. All I could do was moan and sink my fingers further into his hair.

I cried out in surprise as Thorn flung one of my legs, then the other, over his shoulders. He hefted me until he was comfortable, holding my waist until he'd settled, sitting bare-ass naked on his knees in the cave. I pressed my back into the carving behind me and, as I looked down the soft curves of my body, I could see his black and copper gaze riveted on how I trembled in his grasp. He bent his head to my core.

Transfixed, I watched as he inhaled deeply, eyes rolling back and closing as he moaned.

"I love the way you smell, Ruth. So damned sweet and musky and delicious." His gravelly whisper blew air against my wet curls, and I gasped. Thorn's eyes snapped open and focused on my face. "I'm going to *devour* you, my sweet little dove."

And with my thighs wrapped around his head over his shoulders, my back pressed against the wall of the gate, my orc gripped my hips in his clawed hands and stared into my soul as he pressed his mouth against my mound. It was so fucking erotic, I couldn't help it. I bucked against him. My hips jerked as he slid that magnificently long and ridged tongue from my dripping core up to my throbbing clit. I cried out as each ridge on his tongue ran over the sensitive little nub, thighs trembling around his head.

"Ruth," he moaned, eyes now hazy with lust and mouth slick

with my juices, "you taste like heaven, my dove."

With barely a shaky breath, he closed his eyes and feasted on my pussy. The orc used every ridge on that nubile tongue of his to tease every inch of aching flesh. He slid it up and down each side of my labia. Curled it around my clit over and over. Heartbeat hammering in my chest, I panted, feeling my orgasm on the horizon.

"Thorn..." I moaned his name like a prayer. Growling, he slipped that magnificent tongue of his into my core. Parting the tight, slick flesh and flickering it back and forth, he pushed his way inside of me. I cried out, so close, nails digging into his scalp.

Thorn undulated his tongue inside me, the ridges rubbing against my inner walls. My panting became cries as my climax loomed. He moaned gutturally against me then, his tongue vibrating as it plunged in and out of my core over and over. The orgasm hit like an explosion of stars. My back arched, and he had to clutch me to him as I pressed his face between my thighs. My screams of ecstasy echoed in the sea cave as the orgasm crashed over me in waves. Thorn didn't stop. He wrung it out of me, extending it as long as possible with his writhing tongue.

When I'd finally stopped bucking and released my death grip on his head, he slipped his tongue from my still-clenching pussy and took a deep breath. His face was slick with my juices and I watched completely dazed as he ran his tongue over his lips and chin, licking up every drop. Then he gently took each of my legs and set me back on my feet. I had to lean back against the Geata for support or risk falling over.

And *fuck me* if I wasn't still desperate for him.

"Thorn," I moaned as he stood before me, my thighs shaking, "I need you inside of me. *Now.*"

"As my little dove wishes," he snarled, standing and reaching down, grasping my ass and hoisting me until I could wrap my legs around his hips. His massive cock pressed against my slick folds. Obsidian-and-copper eyes nearly shimmered with heat as they devoured the sight before him. "Oh, little dove. You're so beautiful. Perfection."

I whimpered in response, thighs clenching around his waist, desperate to get any friction between us. He chuckled, a lopsided, predatory smirk near splitting his face. Pulling his hips back, he slid his dick up and down along my folds. The odd four grooves and the ridges rubbed against my swollen flesh and I choked back a desperate sob. *Fuck*, he felt so good. When he began speaking in his native language, words lilting and dripping from his mouth like honey, I nearly came undone.

"Thorn! Please!" I panted, hands scrabbling against his forearms. I needed him inside of me now, as deep as I could get him.

"I love it when you beg, little dove." Thorn's vicious growl rent the air.

"Please!" I nearly screamed.

"Good lass." With one massive hand grasping my ass for leverage, he slipped his other between us, guiding himself to my clenching core. Feeling him pressed there, I threw my head back against the Geata, moaning. "Look at me, Ruth."

His demand pulled at me until I looked at him from under my lashes. My body was hungry for him in a way I'd never felt for anyone else. With our eyes locked together, he pushed himself inside me. I gasped and held onto his forearms, nails digging into his gray flesh.

Fuck, he was so damned big. I was so wet and ready that I made room for him. But it skirted that edge of pain deliciously and nearly had me coming. Who knew feeling like you're being split in half could feel so euphoric? Thorn openly moaned as he sank himself deeper inside of me, inch by slow inch. He sunk enough inside of me that, at first, I thought he'd slid in to the hilt. But I was wrong.

Thorn snarled as he continued to push. It was then I realized he'd only reached the bulge in his cock that was halfway down its length. He was only *halfway* inside of me. My legs started shaking, and he grasped my hips in both hands again.

"You're so tight, Ruth. So fucking hot and tight," he hissed, body tense and breathing ragged, as he continued to push. "And so damned *wet*. You feel so *fucking good*, little dove."

With an involuntary jerk of his hips and a moan, he sunk himself entirely inside me, his knot filling me. I cried out, feeling him hit a spot deep inside I didn't know existed. It felt so good it left me quaking.

We stayed like that for a minute. Him sunk inside of me, panting and eyes raking over my body while I shivered and adjusted to the thick heft of him. Then, with a moan, he slid out, and I hissed. He slipped out just past the bulge and then thrust hard. The bulge pushed in, ridges rubbing along the sensitive spots inside of me. His hips met mine, and he ground in hard, expression feral. I cried out, already so close to orgasm.

"I'm going to fuck you against every inch of this cave," he breathed. I just moaned helplessly as he thrust into me again and again, his massive cock hitting that deep spot with each thrust. The way he ground his hips each time he sank to the hilt gave my clit a bit of friction. It wasn't long before I slipped over the edge of climax. He sunk himself deep inside as I screamed his name to the stone ceiling. He bent forward and claimed my mouth, swallowing his name on my lips.

"*Fuck*," he groaned as he pulled away from the kiss. My body slowed its jerking as I spiraled back into my body. "Nearly had me spending inside you already, Ruth."

"You didn't come?" I asked through my panting, looking up into his heated gaze that seared my very soul.

"Oh, we orckin are built to last, little dove," he growled. "What kind of male would I be if I couldn't wring every drop of pleasure from you before I seek my release?"

"A human one?" I gasped as he ground against my hips. He chuckled as he slid an arm behind me and clutched me to him. He then sank to his knees on the steps.

"Ah, but I'm not human, am I?" he growled.

He pressed one hand against the Geata behind me, his other hand cradling my head, arm bracing my back. I slipped my legs from around his waist, planting my feet on either side of him on the floor. I undulated my hips, rolling against him. Thorn hissed, face inches from mine as I slipped my arms around his neck, pulling his face to mine in a blistering kiss.

We rocked together as we kissed, tongues dancing, not yet willing to separate. Thorn slid his hand from the Geata and bore me to the ground. He released the kiss, hands sliding down my waist to spread my thighs wide. He rose to his knees, still planted inside of me, my thighs hooked over his forearms.

Gods, he was so slow and steady with his rhythm as he knelt before me, watching me writhe and clutch at the stone. His hands were holding onto my hips while my shoulder blades braced me against the floor. From this angle, I could see his cock each time he slid home. Seeing it pressed against the flesh of my tummy from the inside out sent me skyrocketing to the edge of another orgasm. I panted and moaned and ground against him as much as I could in this position.

Thorn *tsked* at me. He stopped moving, and I wanted to scream in frustration. That wolfish smile of his flickered on his sinful mouth. The damned tease.

"Not so fast, my dove. I want to dance you along that edge until you're mad with the need for my seed inside of you," he murmured, gaze hot.

"I already am!" I cried, attempting to buck against his hips to get any friction possible. He just chuckled and gripped my hips harder, pressing firmly into my pussy so I couldn't move.

"You want my seed? Want me to fill your womb? Stay firmly inside of you until you swell with our child?" I swear I could feel that knot in the center of his cock swell with every word. Filling me up, thick and heavy and delicious. Thorn's breathing became ragged and his tone more guttural with each word that fell from that mouth I loved so much. He was so close to losing his control, and I wanted nothing more than for him to fuck the soul out of me.

"*Yes!*" I screamed.

"My beautiful dove. My mate," he moaned and then pounded the fuck out of me. Within two strokes, I was screaming my orgasm to the ceiling. But he kept pumping, thrusts turning erratic and gaze wild as he watched me thrash in his grip. "Come for me again! Say my name!"

The slick sound of our flesh slapping together as his hips snapped him home inside of me was so heavenly. The orgasm he'd thrown me into built higher and higher until something broke within me.

"Thorn!" I shrieked, nails biting into his forearms as my back bowed. He wrapped an arm around me and pulled me up against him as he continued to pound into me, breathing ragged. The orgasm just kept going, and I screamed his name repeatedly. It was as if the world around me shattered into a million glittering pieces as I rode the waves.

With a roar, Thorn sank his teeth into my exposed shoulder, pain and pleasure mixing, and thrust one last time. I could feel the wash of hot, sticky cum as he came deep inside of me. As he filled my womb. A sharp comparison to the quickly cooling blood that trickled down my collarbone. It all felt so fantastic I cried, hot tears slipping from my eyes.

When we'd both stopped shuddering out our orgasms, Thorn sank to his heels, still inside of me. He pulled his mouth from my shoulder with such tenderness that a sob lodged itself in my throat. Pulling back with a satisfied smile on his face, he froze as soon as he noticed my tears.

"Dove?" he whispered, face paling to a light gray. Not the bright flush of a blush, but something ghostly. "Dove? Did I hurt you?"

I shook my head vigorously but winced as the movement pulled at the bite mark on my shoulder. Noticing the flicker of pain, his expression turned to one of utter desolation. His gaze dropped from mine, hands still gripping my back. With a hiss, he slid out of me, setting me gently down on the top step of the Geata.

"Thorn! No!" He froze, but wouldn't look at me. "The bite was a surprise, but I... well, I liked it."

"If you liked it, then why are you crying, Ruth?" He shook his dark head and backed away from me, bending to scoop up his kilt. His shoulders slumped in shame, and it pissed me right off.

"You colossal *idiot!*" I cried, dashing away my tears as he buckled on his kilt. He froze again and looked at me as I got to my feet on wobbly legs. "I'm not crying because you hurt me! I'm crying because *I love you!*"

Those three words rang against every surface of the cave, echoing out into infinity. A truth I'd been holding back now for months. Because it was true. I loved him.

Despite our differences and our origins, I loved Thorn with everything that I was. He'd worked his way into my heart in such a way that I didn't think I'd survive it if he ever left.

"You love me?" he whispered in disbelief, his hard, pained expression softening. Leaning against the Geata for support, I glared at him with every stubborn bit of me.

"Yes! I do! I didn't think I could ever love *anyone* ever again! And then you just showed up in my life, coughing up half the Pacific, and made me fall in love with you! Just now? You gave me the best sex I've ever had and I've got so many emotions happening all at once right now and..."

Before I could continue, he stalked over to me and hoisted me up into his arms. I flung my arms around his neck, scared that he might drop me. But without another word, Thorn began making for the tunnel leading out of the cave.

"Where are we going?" I asked, shivering from the cold.

"Home," was all he said.

"But we're not done talking!" I sniffed up at him, his features firm and determined.

"Oh, you can keep talking if you like. But I'm taking my mate home, where she'll be warm and comfortable." His gaze snapped down to mine as we exited the cave into the crisp, bright light of the early autumn morning. "And then I'm going to show her that the 'best sex of her life' was just a warmup."

My face burned, I blushed so hard.

CHAPTER 16*

THORN

I kicked open the rear door to Ruth's house. *Our* house. We were mates now. I'd be damned if I ever spent another night on that couch again. I'd spend every night worshiping Ruth in *our* bed until she screamed. And Source, did I love it when she screamed my name to the skies.

Kicking the door closed behind me, I carried Ruth into the dark living room. The early morning light had yet to penetrate the curtains. I set her reverently on that damned couch and wrapped her in the quilt. Her eyes were enormous in her perfect face, color riding high on cheeks I longed to kiss.

But my desire could wait. It'd been cold in the sea cave when she'd touched me, kissed me, opened herself to me, and then told me she *loved me*. She loved me.

Gods, the wait had been worth it. Worth every night for months that I ached to hold her, craved her touch. And had to slink off to slake my lust with my hand so she wouldn't hear me. I'd never burned so for a female before. If that wasn't proof she was my cridhe, then I was lost.

When a cridhe pair came together, when their marks appeared, the mating frenzy took over. A full triple moon cycle where the pair couldn't keep their hands off of one another. Some ancient feral instinct that demanded to mate, demanded the making of offspring. Even pregnant females succumbed to the frenzy when it took over.

A highly honored time in an orckin's life. When they were granted peace and were left to their pleasures, their instincts. Because to disturb a territorial orckin male while lost to the mating frenzy, the overwhelming need to rut his mate, was to court death. Cridhe, Clan, and Family were the three priceless treasures that a male orckin could protect. And the three things he was instinctively territorial over.

The moment Ruth had touched me so sweetly, I knew I was lost to the cridhe frenzy. Marks or no marks. It felt like my blood was boiling, my nerves thrummed, and every sense I possessed was vitally aware. And my cock, gods it ached something fierce. Even after just sating myself inside of Ruth minutes ago, it pressed eagerly against the heavy leather panels of my kilt, demanding to plow her sweet, tight little cunt. To fill her womb full of my seed until she conceived. Gods, knowing that she indeed wanted bairns, despite her past, made my very being crackle with the desire to fuck her ragged. The need was so blistering I'd have ripped anyone who stood in my way apart with my claws. Without hesitation.

Except for Ruth. If she had told me to stop. I would have. I might be a prince, but she was the Banrigh, the queen, of my heart, body, and soul. Whatever she decreed, I'd make it so.

And to honor her, I'd make sure she was warm, first. The fire we'd built earlier that evening had died down to embers. I snagged a few logs and some kindling from the cubby by the fireplace. In a matter of minutes, I had the fire curling warmth into the living room. The entire time, I could feel Ruth's eyes on me as if they were her hands. Her scent and the combined aroma of our mating made my blood heat and my cock throb.

When the fire built to a cherry crackling roar, I looked over my shoulder at her. She sat there wrapped up in the quilt, mouth open slightly and eyes heavy-lidded with lust. A shiver rippled over her curves and my mouth watered.

"Come here, little dove." I held out my hand as my voice rumbled from my chest in a gravelly growl. "Let me warm you up."

She slipped her hand into mine, a spark shimmering between us. I laid down on the sheepskin rug she had on the floor. It was soft and comfortable, like her. And some primal part of me longed to snuggle down into her plush body in front of the fire. To lavish her with my attentions, the fire mirroring my passion for her.

Ruth slipped from the couch onto her knees next to me, the quilt trailing behind her, revealing her thick thighs in such a way that had my groin straining against my kilt as if it could punch through it. Her gaze raked over me, fanning the flames of my desire.

"My chubby body doesn't bother you?" She whispered, firelight dancing in her whiskey sweet eyes as she finally looked at my face.

"Why would it bother me?" I frowned up at her. She couldn't seem to find the words to explain. Her cheeks stained pink as she struggled to express her reasoning, with my thumb rubbing against the back of her knuckles.

"I'm soft, fat?" She finally half laughed, trying to pull the quilt closer around her. To hide herself.

Whoever told her she should cover herself up, who told her she was anything less than gorgeous... I wanted to shove my booted foot right up their ass. Her fat, her curves and valleys, her dimples and stretch marks were all a work of art. A masterpiece that I could spend the rest of my life studying and never tire of.

"Ruth." I put an edge in my voice so she'd look at me. "I've had a lifetime of hard things. I can't tell you how badly I've needed all of your softness."

Her mouth opened and closed as she gaped at me, then turned so red. Ducking her head, she tried to hide behind her hair. So I reached up and tucked the silken strands of her brown locks behind her rounded human ear. The firelight set the strands to copper and gold between my fingers. I caressed her cheek with my thumb and then slipped my fingers under her chin. I tilted her head up so she would look at me, truly see me, and hear my words.

"I have an enormous appetite, little dove. And you are a plump, delectable meal I long to feast on for the rest of my life. You are stunning. The best possible kind of distraction. I love your body because it's yours. You're my *cridhe*, my mate, and if you think I'm going to allow what another person thinks of your body to dictate how I'm going to love you, you're sorely mistaken." I sat up then and pulled her to me, twisting so I bore her down into the fluffy rug, my arms braced above her head. "I'm going to show you how much I love you and your body and nothing is going to change my mind."

The lovely blush on her cheeks and the soft gasp she made had me slowly bending my head down to tease and nibble and kiss that addictive mouth of hers. As the kiss deepened, her body went loose and taut against the hard planes of my body. I couldn't hold back the smile that curled my mouth and the chuckle that escaped me. She pulled back and looked up at me in confusion.

"I love how you react to me, dove," I growled. "It makes me... *hungry* for more."

To prove my point, I braced my weight on one hand and began tracing the pillowy softness of her side with my claws. My lips barely brushed hers as she shuddered at my touch, nipples hardening before my eyes. Trailing my lips along her skin, I kissed my way down the elegant column of her throat, over her collarbones, and down between her breasts. Her nails sunk into my hair and her breathing hitched, thighs spreading wide for me as she released the quilt. I took first one pebbled nipple into my mouth, licking it round and round with my tongue, then the other.

While I lavished her breasts with my mouth, I slowly dragged my hand down her stomach. I lightly scraped my claws into the nest of short curls at the apex of her thighs. They were drenched with our juices, and I moaned against her chest.

"Y-Your claws..." Ruth stuttered. I looked up at her, cocking an eyebrow as I gave her a lopsided grin.

"What claws?" I retracted them, then slid my thick fingers between her folds. She gasped as I stroked the sensitive little nub above her core. She quivered and cried out in surprise. "They're retractable, dove."

It was as if all the tension in her body, the fear of pain, just evaporated as she melted into the fluffy rug. Then I remembered that she'd been mistreated in the past and I sobered. She was learning what it meant to be with someone who prized her pleasure and hated her pain. And I was going to show her exactly how much I prized her: every cry, every buck, every tremulous moan. So I plunged first one finger inside of her core, then a second. Slowly, I flickered my fingers against that sensitive spot inside of her as my thumb gently massaged her clit.

Bracing on my forearm, I kissed every inch of her I could reach, licked every scar and freckle and stretch mark as if she were a decadent feast I wanted to savor. Her thighs fell wide open, and she rolled her hips to meet my hand as her cries hit a fevered pitch. Within moments, she was screaming and bucking wildly beneath me. I claimed her mouth with mine, drinking her down like fine whiskey.

When she'd stopped clenching on my fingers and lay there

panting in a soft, mewling melody, I gently pulled them from her. Pulling back, I brought her fingers to my mouth and licked them with my black tongue. Her eyes locked onto my mouth as I stuck my fingers, slick with her pleasure, inside and sucked them clean. I could taste both her juices and my seed. The combination was heady, intoxicating. Made my knot swell so hard it made me lightheaded. Breathing harsh, I pulled my fingers from my mouth and sat back on my knees, claws extending once more.

I stared down at her panting, sex drunk form, as she lay there with firelight dancing along her quivering flesh. I couldn't take it anymore. If I didn't sink my cock inside of her soon, I'd likely go mad. So I unbuckled my kilt and ripped it from me, near tearing the leather. I sat there on my heels between her thighs, cock straining, knot throbbing, and tip leaking like a busted pipe.

"Ruth," I growled, guttural and feral.

"How do you want me?" She whispered, biting her kiss-swollen bottom lip. I couldn't answer her, eyes tracking every movement her lips made. As desperate not to fall onto her like a wild animal as I was to rut her.

She surprised me then because she pulled up her knees and rolled onto her stomach. Sliding her body against the sheepskin rug, she maneuvered herself so her thighs spread wide on either side of my knees, then pushed back. Her perfect ass lifted into the air as she kept her chest and face buried in the fleecy fluff.

"Like this?" She asked, voice gone deep and sultry. Ruth's lubh-gaoil eyes near-glowed in the firelight as she looked at me over her rounded shoulder.

"*Yes.*" I hissed through my teeth, clawed hands grasping and kneading her ass. My shaft rested in the valley between her cheeks, pre-cum dripping down the crease to glaze her curls. Ruth's expression heated as she watched me, her hair fanned out over the rug. The look in her eyes had me nearly coming all over her backside.

"Then what are you waiting for?" Giving her ass a little wiggle, she sent me into a furor.

I got to my knees, grasped her ass, and with a primal snarl, I sunk myself up to the knot in one swift stroke. She cried out and arched her back further, a silent plea for me to sink myself inside of her entirely. So I did. With one more thrust, I sunk myself to the hilt inside of her. Her slick heat and quivering walls had me moaning already. I began a punishing rhythm, hips slapping against her lush ass, fingers sunk into her yielding flesh. I couldn't keep my eyes off of her. How her curves rippled with every hard thrust, how her face contorted in pleasure as she cried and wailed for me, and how her lovely little hands grasped and scrabbled for purchase against the rug.

Already, I was close to spending inside of her. She had me feeling like a green youth. Because she didn't just hold still while I rutted her. No. This woman met me stroke for stroke, moan for moan. She gave as good as she got. I'd never been with a female who wanted me so badly. I felt more virile and powerful as I fucked her than I'd ever had before on Talam with anyone else.

I had Ruth's juicy thighs and ass pressed tight against me as I finally came. I roared, staring down at her ass as it twitched and she bucked against me. The knot in my cock still swelling with seed even as I emptied it inside of her. I couldn't pull myself free of her until the knot had subsided. And I sure as hell didn't want to. Not with how she kept clenching down on me as she shrieked her orgasm into the sheepskin rug. My eyes rolled back into my head as I rode out our climax, panting her name as we slowly came down from the heights of our pleasure.

I bent double over her and panted against her shoulder blades, offering kisses and murmuring to her in Teanga Dhubh. Eventually, the knot softened, I pulled free of her and held her as I righted us both onto our knees.

"That was... Mmh." I chuckled into her hair as I held her close, kissing her shoulder.

"Good?" She laughed breathlessly.

"Och, amazing."

"Thorn?" she murmured in question.

"Och, little dove?"

"I'm, um... still horny," Ruth muttered, blush riding high on her cheeks and ears.

"Oh are you, now? Still not sated after that proper fucking, I just gave you?" I laughed, delighted.

"N-no. Not yet." She was so sweet when she was embarrassed.

"As my mate wishes." So I stood, cock already stiffening once more, and sat down on the baneful couch. My dick bobbed, listing to the side, and continued to stiffen as she watched.

She got shakily to her feet and walked over, taking my offered hand in hers. Our juices slid down the insides of her thighs like rivers of gold in the firelight. I'd need to plow her properly and often to make sure her womb filled with my seed. And stayed filled with it until she grew ripe with our child. The thought alone had my knot filling swiftly with cum.

"Ride me, Ruth," I growled as I pulled her on top of me. Her knees sank into the couch on either side of my hips. The sight of her on her knees over my lap, the light from the fire limning her lush curves, had me hissing in need. I knocked my head back over the back of the couch and watched with hooded eyes as she settled over me, grasped my throbbing cock in her little hand, and guided me to her core. The moment the tip of my dick pressed against the hot, slippery folds of her pussy, I nearly came. "That's right." My voice shook and cracked as I slid my hands up her dripping thighs to her hips.

Like *hell*, this wasn't the cridhe frenzy. Like *hell*, she wasn't my cridhe mate.

As she sunk onto my cock, inch by delicious inch, she looked me in the eye and moaned my name. I adjusted my grip on her hips and snarled. With one hard thrust, I was fully seated inside of her and she wailed her pleasure. Fuck, she took my cock, all of it, and I'd never imagined she'd be able to with her size, so much smaller than me. But she did, and I loved her all the more for it. Because every thrust was like a glimpse of heaven. Every taste of her breasts in my mouth, a taste of ambrosia.

I'd demanded she ride me, and by the gods, she did. She rocked and gasped and slammed her ass down on my lap, impaling herself on my shaft repeatedly. Wild and wanton, like she couldn't get enough of me. I felt like I was going to burst.

Gods, how I loved this couch now.

Because it was perfect for fucking the shit out of my mate. I loved being able to grasp her ass in my hands, arms curving around her sweet thighs and hips. To help rock her against me how I wanted. I adored how her breasts swayed in front of my face, begging to be sucked and licked and bitten. And how I could brace and thrust up into her hard and fast. Feel how her flesh jiggled and rippled under my hands. How fucking amazing her soft weight felt pressed on top of me.

Unable to take it anymore, I grabbed a fistful of her lovely hair and tilted her head to the side. I set my teeth to her shoulder, snarling into her flesh as I slid my arm up from her ass to clutch her firmly to my body. With her pinned to me, I sank my teeth into her neck, braced as she cried out, and pounded the fuck out of her sweet cunt.

The feel of how her flesh moved under my hands. How achingly perfect her weight was pressed down against me. The delicious taste of her blood as it flooded my watering mouth. It was all enough to push me to the brink of insanity. My knot swelled painfully. I felt her inner walls clenching down hard on my cock, attempting to milk me dry already. Her moans hit a fevered pitch, and I knew she was close, and so was I. So I pulled my teeth free, brought her ear to my mouth, and growled.

"Come for me, my little dove," I demanded. Her hips bucked, her back bowed, and she tumbled over the edge of climax. Her body clenching hard on my swollen cock, her nails scoring lines of pleasure as they raked my back.

"THORN!" She screamed my name like a battle cry and I roared into her hair, knot releasing my pent-up seed as I jerked against her, inside of her. I shattered then. Into slivers of ecstasy and light that pulsed to the beat of my knot pumping my seed inside of my mate. It was a moment of glory incarnate.

Time slipped from our fingers as we slowly wound down from the great height of our orgasm. Something tickled at my chest. Ruth shakily slid off of me, and I easily slipped free of her now that I was spent. I helped her to lie back on the sofa, kissing her knees as she bent them and curled up. As she took my hand, I stole a glance down at my chest. No cridhe marks. It must have been her hair that had caused the sensation.

"I love you, Thorn," Ruth murmured. I looked at my mate then and saw her sleepy smile. My heart melted. If I hadn't sworn myself to her already, hadn't been absolutely in love with her, I was now.

"And I love you, Ruth." I rasped, throat suddenly tight. Her smile was brilliant as the sun.

I got up and snagged the quilt. With some maneuvering, I laid down on the couch and rolled Ruth on top of me. She squeaked delightfully, and I chuckled. I shook out the quilt and laid it over the both of us. She ran her fingers over my chest and sighed, settling her head over my beating heart. I watched as she fell asleep within moments, my entire world loose-limbed and at peace spread over me like a blanket. I smiled, tilting my head back onto the armrest.

Yeah. I *definitely* changed my mind about this damned couch.

CHAPTER 17*

RUTH

His stamina was remarkable. We spent days having sex on every surface in the house. And outside of it. When the days were warm, he'd insist we go on 'picnics' just so he could rut me in the sunshine. He'd spend all afternoon alternating between making sweet love to me, burying his head between my thighs until I was a trembling sobbing mess, and pounding into me mercilessly like a wild animal.

I didn't know love could be quite like this. Thorn doted on me constantly when we were alone and when we were visiting friends. With the chleoc ring finally in his possession, Thorn looked just like a regular guy. An enormous, really *handsome* guy. Julia had taken one look at him, rolled her eyes at me, and had just treated him like she treated everyone else. Bless her.

The amount of attention he'd gotten the first time we'd gone into town together, though, had been staggering. Men and women flirted with him regardless of age, marital status, or occupation as if he were a Casanova. Hell, the sixty-year-old woman who ran the bakery gave Thorn her number right in front of her husband. The orc was an absolute menace. And he got a huge kick out of it, laughing until he cried when we were alone. Sanchez complained Thorn got all the phone numbers of the pretty girls in town and wasn't leaving any for him.

It had irritated me at first because they'd do it right in front of me like I didn't exist. But then Thorn would, without fail, politely decline and either wrap his arm around my waist or bend down to kiss me, making it blatantly obvious he was spoken for and happy about it. The upside to dating, er, being *mated* to an orc? They didn't have any interest in anyone outside of their mate.

Which was a gods damned relief.

So when Brighton and Sanchez started inviting Thorn over for poker nights, I didn't feel an iota of worry or stress. Because I could trust him. Trust him not to break my heart. It was the strangest feeling, and I was happy to get used to it. It didn't hurt that each time he came home, he'd ravish me. As if he'd been away for months instead of hours.

I'd stopped wearing underwear or pants and took to only wearing dresses and skirts. Thorn loved this, and when we were out in public in town, he'd often devise clever ways to get his hands under my skirts to pleasure me. When we were at dinner, when I drove, hell, even when we went to a Christmas tree lighting ceremony in town.

When he wasn't using his hands, we'd end up in a dark corner somewhere fucking like bunnies. He even took me against an alley wall, his hand clamped firmly over my mouth so I couldn't scream. His favorite had been the movie theater to see his first movie. Where we'd sat at the back and I'd given him a blowjob before he yanked me into his lap with my back pressed to his chest. He had spread my legs wide with his thighs and fucked me noisily during the action and sex scenes. No one had noticed, even when he'd pulled the straps of my dress down so he could easily fondle my breasts in his large hands as he rocked up into me again and again.

I loved all of it. I wanted all of it. All of him. And damn me if I didn't want him to make me pregnant. I wasn't sure humans and orckin could make babies, but he made me want to have a family. With him.

When we weren't having sex or running errands or visiting our friends, we were working on the hobbit holes for the bed-and-breakfast. The weatherproofing had been the most troublesome part. Luckily, Brighton knew how to weld and taught Thorn so he could weld the stainless steel corrugated metal together for the outer shell that would support the weight of the earth and keep out the rain.

After that, it was a matter of adding a layer of gravel and rocks for drainage before we added the topsoil. As the guys did that part, Julia helped me with creating the interiors, including the floors and re-purposing thrift store and garage sale finds. Once the soil for all seven hobbit holes was in place, the guys began on the plaster and sub-flooring. We'd never gotten so far without them, and I was constantly thankful for the help of our friends.

The holidays loomed, and we had to break because of the rain that had moved in. We needed the rest anyway, so it was a great time to spend lazing about with Thorn or doing minor projects around the farmhouse. I got to teach him about our human traditions for the holidays, show him how to drive my truck, and have sex in the truck too with the rain sheeting down on the windshield. It was the best time of my life, full of love and peace, and fun.

Something told me it wouldn't be all rainbows and butterflies, though. As if I were holding my breath.

THORN

It was the winter solstice. Ruth called it Yule. She explained what Christmas was to her people and how she celebrated the solstice instead as part of her heritage. We spent the day decorating a small potted pine tree in the farmhouse and making sweets.

We were listening to some cheery holiday music on the radio. She'd put some sort of nut in a heavy metal pan onto the fire. Her hearth and home filled with the oddly sweet-smelling scent. While we waited for the nuts to finish cooking, I lay beside her on the sheepskin rug before the fire, kissing the graceful column of her throat and tracing circles on her bare belly with my human-looking fingers.

Since the first time we'd coupled weeks ago, we'd been unable to keep our hands off of one another. It didn't matter where we were or who we were with. We always found a way to slake our lust. But it wasn't just lust that had taken over. We'd been at a restaurant when I'd gone to the restroom. When I'd come back, I saw a man trying to hit on Ruth. My instincts took over. With one punch, I broke the man's jaw and Ruth had to get between us before I broke more than that.

We'd limited our outings after that. Deciding that until the frenzy calmed down, we'd spend it together at home. It was the happiest point of my life. As if Ruth could banish the darkness from my mind with one laugh. And that delightful woman laughed often. I thanked the Source often for guiding me here. To her.

"So what are these nuts called, then?" I asked, following her lead as she peeled one and blew on it before popping it between her lips. She made cheerful noises as she chewed, and I laughed.

"They're called chestnuts!" she exclaimed around a mouthful of roasted nutmeat. "I love them. They're my favorite snack in the autumn and winter."

As we laughed and fed each other chestnuts, a loud noise outside caught my attention. I looked up to see flickering orange light outside the kitchen windows. I frowned.

"Ruth?" I asked, all merriment gone. "What is that?"

"What's what?" She turned and looked. Her joyful expression

dropped away and her face paled considerably. She cried out and sprung to her feet. Ruth scrambled back into her jeans and sweater that I'd been careful not to rip off of her earlier. "Oh no. Oh no, oh no, oh no!"

"What's wrong?" I asked, getting to my feet and reaching for my kilt. I buckled it on as she ran to the mudroom door and started yanking on her boots.

"Call Brighton and Sanchez! Now!" she cried and was out of the door in the blink of an eye.

I rushed to the phone in the kitchen and dialed the number for the Sheriff's department from the card tacked to the fridge. Then I looked outside the kitchen window to see where Ruth had gone. Brighton answered just as it registered what I was looking at. I wish I could say that I felt something, anything - anger, fear, anxiety, dread. Only numbness and confusion reigned as I watched months of our hard work go up in flames.

"Hello?" Brighton asked. There were merry noises in the background, like a gathering.

"Brighton," I said thickly as I spotted a lone man standing next to a very distinctive car. He had cans of gasoline at his feet and was laughing, his head tilted to the sky. "We've got a problem at Ruth's farm. Hobbiton is on fire. There's a man who set it on fire."

"What?" Brighton almost shouted. "Who would do such a thing?"

That's when the numbness died, and horror took its place.

Because there was Ruth, running full bore at the laughing man. A length of wood gripped in her fists. She swung, and it connected with his shoulder. He staggered and caught himself. Then they started yelling at one another. Ruth made to swing her stick. But he turned and whacked her over the head with a rock. Ruth crumpled to the ground in a heap at his feet. Right next to the gas cans he'd tripped over.

"NO!" I bellowed. Ice-cold pain lanced my heart, and I stumbled. I heard Brighton's voice in my ear, but I couldn't understand his words.

I dropped the phone and sprinted out the back door. The ground flew under my bare feet as I leaped over rocks and fences and brush on my way to my cridhe. I ran, heedless of anything in my way, the burning hillside showing me the quivering, slackening red thread of fate that tied me to Ruth. The world around me fell away as dread gripped my insides tightly until I wanted to throw up. I'd seen the rock in his fist. I'd seen how hard he'd hit her head.

No. No. No. Don't you dare, Ruth! You stay alive!

Lungs burning, arms pumping, I raced towards the burning conflagration of Ruth's dream. And the crumpled form of mine.

RUTH

That fucking *son of a bitch*!

As I hurled myself out of the back door and down Thorn's steps, I spied a wooden hoe handle that no longer held the blade. I snatched it, taking to the trail that led to the hobbit holes. Blood pounded in my ears and brambles left lines of fire on my skin as I heedlessly sprinted through them. My hot breath puffed from my mouth in the cold air to stream behind me. My footfalls barely hit the ground as I took to the uneven path like a mountain goat. Everything was bathed in red, the fire, the glow on the trees. Like torches blazing bright.

Manic laughter rose higher than the sound of splintering wood and hissing steel. The line of hobbit holes with fire spewing from their doors and windows on the hillside looked like some kind of hellscape desolated by a dragon.

That's when I found him. Agent Simms. The bastard stood next to his Impala, cans of gasoline at his feet, grin broad enough to split his face in half as he watched months of work go up in smoke and ash with wild eyes.

Agent Simms couldn't hear my footfalls over the roaring of the blaze. Lifting my hoe handle, I grasped it in both hands. Between one step and the next, I swung that hoe handle with everything I had at his batshit crazy face. The wood connected with his shoulder and head in a satisfying crack that split the winter air like a thunderclap.

"What the hell is *wrong* with you?!" I screeched at him as he fell back from the force of my swing. He kicked over some of the gas cans at his feet, and I could hear gasoline slosh onto the grass.

One of the hobbit holes buckled under the flames and the weight of the earth above it, collapsing in on itself. Crashing timber and the rushing sound of smothering dirt sent a torrent of embers and hot air out into the night, a small imploding star. The shock on his bland face quickly shifted to something ugly and twisted.

"I *know* you've got an interdimensional portal on your property, Ruth!" he screamed, voice cracking with the force of it. "I know it opens tonight, on the solstice! Whatever it takes, I *will* find it. Your land *will* be mine. You can't do a damned thing about it!"

"Don't call me *Ruth* like we're friends, you absolute nutcase! The gate doesn't work like that!" I raised my makeshift baseball bat, ready to swing again.

"Ha! You expect me to believe that?" he shouted. Then his body language changed so fast it was like a switch had been thrown. That odd gleam in his eyes from months prior came back as he held out his hand to me. "Join me, Ruth, let's work together and we can send that monstrous *freak* you've got living with you to Area 51 where he belongs! I'll look out for you, Ruth."

And that's when I finally realized. Somehow, in some way, his distaste and hate for me and the farm had grown into some sort of twisted obsession. It registered that *he'd* been the one calling me, breathing heavy into the phone as he diddled himself before Thorn put a stop to it. I'd denied him every step of the way and he wanted what he couldn't have. The Geata. *Me.*

The subtle signs had been there the entire time. Little red flags I'd pushed aside as unimportant. Just like I'd done with my boyfriend at the commune. Ignored the danger until it was too late.

I went cold.

"I wouldn't touch you if you were the last man on earth," I hissed.

"You *monster fucker!*" he roared. "I saw you fucking that big grey behemoth in the field with a picnic like a damned *hussy!*" Moving swifter than I thought possible, he lunged at me and swung. There was a sickening crunch as something connected with my skull. With a sudden flare of pain, the world went black.

CHAPTER 18 *

THORN

When I reached the car and gasoline cans, there was no sign of Agent Simms or Ruth. I'd lost sight of them for a few moments as I'd run straight for the hobbit holes, foregoing sections of the path as it dipped amongst the hillocks and meeting hurdles along the way. The rock he'd hit her over the head with sat in a puddle of gas, reeking of Ruth's blood. He wouldn't have bothered taking her with him unless she was alive.

She had to be alive.

Snarling, I sprinted after her trail of blood. Her scent cut through the smells of surf, fire, and scorched earth, leading me to her. I thanked the Source for the times I'd bitten her. I knew the taste and aroma of her blood better than the beat of my own heart and it led me to her. Rocks sliced open my bare, human-looking feet, devoid of their claws and tough soles of my orckin origins. But I barely registered the pain as I chased my fate, chest heaving like a bellows in the cold sea air. As I followed the trail of Ruth's blood, I realized where he was taking her.

To the sea cave.

Somehow, he knew. He knew where the cave was. Possibly about the Geata. He'd try to force her to activate the gate, something even I couldn't do. What would happen then when his insane plan fell apart with my unconscious mate at his feet? When the Geata wouldn't open for him?

Skidding to a halt at the trailhead towards the beach, I peered over the edge of the cliff. Cowardly Agent Simms was walking away from the base of the trail towards the sea cave. The sand slowed his steps, as did the weight of my cridhe slung over his shoulder. I bared my blunted human teeth and growled low.

I flung myself from the cliff's trailhead. The cold light from Earth's lone, full moon was enough for me to see by. My strength and endurance were less as a human, yet still greater than one. As I landed fifteen feet down on the switchback trail, my legs gave way, and I scraped my knees on the ground. Hissing, I staggered to my feet and slid down the side of the cliff to the next switchback.

Agent Simms heard my descent and looked over his shoulder. The scent of his fear sparked a feral joy and satisfaction inside of me.

Yes, little man. Be afraid of me. Be very *afraid.*

I reached the bottom of the cliff and sprinted through the sand as fast as my human feet would allow. Agent Simms jerked and dropped Ruth, fumbling with something in his pocket. He held it up and clicked. A small flame sprouted from it.

"Stop!" he shouted over the crashing waves. "I'll burn her alive if you don't!"

I came to a stumbling halt in the sand. And that's when I could smell it. The gasoline soaking her clothes from when she'd fallen into the puddles of it. If he dropped that lighter on her, she was done for. Even if I dragged her to the ocean to douse the flames, she wouldn't survive the burns.

Indecision gripped me, and we faced one another in a standoff.

"You're not human, I *know you aren't!*" he cried. "I don't know how you're human now, but I saw you as a monster! You came from that portal in the sea cave, didn't you?"

"How do you know about that?" I asked.

"Years of fucking *research* and listening to crazy old people in nursing homes!" Agent Simms looked like a madman, holding the lighter high. His hair fell into eyes that were too wide to be sane.

"Why?" I asked.

"Why what, freak?"

"Why do you want the Geata?" It truly baffled me. It was broken. But even if it wasn't, and he went through, he'd end up at the mercies of the clans and likely tortured to death for his troubles.

"Do you know the power I could wield? America is the *greatest nation* on this godforsaken planet. Our country could use the resources on the other side. No one could stand against us!" Voice gone shrill with fervor, his mouth split into a grin made for nightmares as he pulled a revolver from the holster beneath his coat and pointed it at me. "And it's not just the gate I want. But *her.*"

Ruth. He meant he wanted Ruth. Somehow, someway, his warped mind thought he had a claim on *my cridhe*. If anyone had a choice, it was her. I'd rather die than see her fall into his unstable hands. Agent Simms would burn her alive if he couldn't have her. He'd kill me to have her. He'd sure as hell have to because I couldn't live without her.

Her safety and happiness were, and always would be, my priority. Even if it meant my death. I found I was okay with that. So I slipped into that calm center within myself. The place in my mind I went to whenever I faced an enemy. Whether it be rival clan orckin, dorcha'aon, or human bastard.

Ruth. My thoughts whispered her name over and over. A mantra that beat in time with my very heart. It echoed in that calm space in my mind, calling to her as surely as when I'd seen my red thread of fate that led me into the Geata. Like a tremulous sigh, I felt her. As if she'd just taken my heart in her hands. I showed her all the love I had for her in that infinite whisper. That if I died, it would be worth it.

And as if the Source, the universe, was laughing in Agent Simm's face, a sudden wind snuffed out the flame in his hand. As if to say '*not today, asshole*'. Simms panicked as he tried repeatedly to get the lighter to produce a flame. But each time he was successful, the wind rose and snuffed it out.

He became frantic and a dark, half-mad laugh bubbled up from inside of me. Grinning like a wolf, I roared at the man. He froze, eyes wide with terror as he watched me. My chest heaved as I continued to laugh and pulled the chleoc ring from my finger. I felt a shiver rush over me, my form realigning to its true nature. And I watched in glee as Agent Simms paled.

He pulled up his revolver and pointed it at me. Simms blinked, I shifted, and he fired.

One of the best things about poker nights with Brighton and Sanchez was getting to meet the officers from the surrounding towns. They'd taken me to the range. Taught me how to shoot. So I knew, as Simms jerked the trigger, that his shot would go wide. As would every one of his following shots.

I made no sound as I lunged, zigzagging across the beach, sand barely kicking up behind me as I sped towards him on my clawed feet. Feet made for stealth, for varying terrain, for a predator. The reek of his fear as his inevitable demise finally registered in his addled mind was sweet. My mouth watered with the need for vengeance. I reached him in a matter of heartbeats. Flinging an arm out, I snatched his neck in my clawed fist as I came to a halt inches from him.

"Give me one reason I shouldn't kill you, human," I growled, lips pulling back from my sharp teeth. I let my long, black tongue slip from my mouth, let it fall past my chin like some devil. And laughed as he shrieked while I lifted him off the ground. He screamed and screamed, tears streaming from his wide, bloodshot eyes as if I were from his worst nightmares. And maybe I was.

I knew he'd been the one to call Ruth to scare her as he touched himself. Knew he saw what was rightfully mine as his. Knew his warped mind would refuse the truth, and seek to destroy what he couldn't have. He'd scared, harmed, and harassed my mate, my cridhe.

So I'd become his nightmare, drag him to hell with my orckin form as the last thing he saw. I dug my fingers into the soft flesh of his neck, choking off his scream into a wet gurgle. Raising my fist, I clenched my fingers tight, ready to punch a hole completely through his weak skull. Just like he'd tried to sink that rock into Ruth's.

"Don't kill him!" I heard Ruth shout, and I froze.

She was awake. *She was awake.*

I looked over my shoulder, fist still raised, claws dug into Simms's neck, leaving trickling trails of blood to pour down his conniving throat. It took every ounce of determination to keep my hand from spasming and ripping out his windpipe. To play a jaunty tune on it as the light faded from his eyes.

But my relief that Ruth was not only alive but awake, rushed over me like the waves nearby. Cool, soothing, calming the anger and rage and fear. I lowered my fist and dropped him into the sand.

Agent Simms made some warbling kind of sound, and I looked down to see him faint. The scent of urine hit my nose, which wrinkled in disgust as the man lost control of his bladder. A familiar noise reached my pointed ears, and I looked up at the cliff edge. Sirens. Brighton had gotten us help, after all.

I rushed over to Ruth and helped her sit up. She held her head and groaned. Pulling her to me, I ran my hands over her body to check her for wounds. She hissed when my probing fingers found scrapes and bruises, but nothing more serious than that. I heaved a sigh of relief and cradled her to my chest.

I broke then.

Tears slipped from my eyes as I shook from the emotional whiplash. She was alive. Ruth was alive. Sobbing, I clutched her to me and buried my face into the soft waves of her hair. She was my entire world, and I'd nearly lost her. I knew she'd been precious to me before. But now I understood her priceless light.

"Thorn." She patted my back as I choked. "Thorn, I'll be okay, I promise, baby. I'm Irish, and we're notoriously hard-headed."

I barked a laugh and finally allowed her to pull back from my grasp. She frowned up at me in concern and gently wiped away my tears with her sandy fingertips. She cursed, wiped her hands on her pants, then got both my tears and the sand off my face. I smiled a little at her. With a small sound, she braced her hands on my shoulders and leaned up to place a gentle kiss on my lips.

"Is he dead?" Ruth asked me as she pulled away, gaze unfocused as she attempted to stay present.

"No, he just pissed himself and fainted," I told her, cupping her beloved face in my hands. Ruth snorted and allowed me to check her head injury. The side of her head was tender. She likely had a concussion, but at least the bleeding had stopped for now. "We should see about getting you to a healer."

"You mean a doctor?" she asked with a smirk.

"Whatever you humans call them." I shook my head at her. Releasing her face, I slipped the chleoc ring back on, feeling the shiver of change waft over me once more.

"Ho there!" Came a familiar call. Sanchez waved down at us.

A group of ten officers and emergency persons made their way down to the beach. Along with Julia, of all people. In minutes, my poker friends from various local police and fire departments surrounded us and a healer began looking us both over. Ruth refused to release my hand, making my chest feel like it was overflowing with love for her.

"What the hell happened to Hobbiton?" Sanchez asked, hands on his hips, looking pissed. Our project had earned the excitement of the entire town.

"That one set fire to it with gasoline," I explained, my energy draining from me now that we were safe.

"Isn't that Agent Simms?" he asked, as Brighton, with enviable nonchalance, flipped the agent over with his booted foot so he was face first in the sand. He caught the scent of urine and grimaced before bending over to cuff the unconscious pain in the ass.

"What made him pass out and piss himself?" Brighton called over as some officers were laughing. Agent Simms had made no friends at all.

"I threatened to bash in his skull." I shrugged and the officers all erupted into guffaws.

"Can you tell us what happened?" Another officer pulled a little booklet from his pocket and clicked a pen to jot down case notes.

So I told them. About Ruth running out to face Agent Simms after he'd set months of hard work on fire. About how he'd felled her with a blow to the head. And how he'd dragged Ruth down here, screaming about some insane conspiracy and his desire to kidnap her and use her.

No one laughed after that.

RUTH

Thorn had rescued me. He'd come for me when I thought I'd died. I'd felt him call to me in the dark, begging me to wake up. To not leave him alone.

When I'd opened my eyes, blurry from the blow to my head, the echoing crack of gunfire lancing my skull, all I could focus on was Thorn. He'd gripped Agent Simms by the throat and was about to haymaker his head right off of his neck. Thorn had stopped when I'd screamed for him to not kill the agent. If Agent Simms died, there'd be too many questions. If Agent Simms died, the farm truly would be forfeit. So would the Geata and Thorn's very life.

My head was a blistering storm of agony. My eyes couldn't focus for long. Even my equilibrium was off. I couldn't seem to do more than wobble where I knelt. I found myself enfolded in Thorn's arms. They were solid and warm and gray. He released me and slipped his chleoc ring back on. I couldn't remember him removing it.

Everything after that was a stilted blur. I could remember wiping Thorn's tears away with sandy fingers. Sanchez asked us questions while an EMT checked my head wound. It didn't take a genius to figure out I had a pretty severe concussion. Eventually, we'd made it up the cliff back towards the smoking ruins of Hobbiton. My big strong orc mate, back in human form, carried my chubby ass up the cliff bridal-style, to the shock of everyone.

There were rounds of apologies and condolences as the officers saw the destruction for themselves. Months of work were reduced to rubble. Simms woke at some point and hollered to be released until Sanchez, sweet Deputy Sanchez, decked him square in the mouth.

That had impressed Julia off to no end, and she'd given him her number. Thorn left me with the EMTs, so Julia came over to keep me company.

"What was that crackpot after?" Julia asked, settling down on the bumper of the ambulance.

"He believes there's a gate to another world here," I mumbled. My mouth felt like cotton and the meds they had given me for the pain were kicking in.

There was a long pause. Then Julia's dark gaze swung to meet mine. She looked conflicted.

"What is it?" I asked, slurring my words a bit.

"Is it true?" She asked, frowning. Her expression was intense in a way I couldn't understand.

"Gates and portals that can take you to other places exist everywhere. Just gotta know where to look." I laughed then and winked.

"What about different times?" She asked, looking at me sideways.

I paused and looked at her. She'd always been a little odd. Saying things that were a little off. Like using slang I'd never heard of before. Just little things that had set her apart from the rest of the town's residents. She'd never shared her story. But I found it was okay with me. I loved her as my friend for how she was now. Though I hoped she found whatever it was she was looking for.

"I don't know. Probably." I gave her a one-shouldered shrug, and she helped me bring the blanket up around my shoulders. "Love ya, girl."

"Love you too, loopy." Julia chuckled. And just like that, the strange conversation returned to normal. "What are you going to do now?"

"I don't honestly know," I whispered into the night. The flashing lights of the cop cars and emergency vehicles lit up the clouds of smoke from the fire they were still trying to put out.

All my dreams had turned to ash.

CHAPTER 19*

RUTH

Dawn crested the curve of the horizon. Most of the officers had left, as had Julia, the ambulance, and fire crews. After realizing I wasn't in imminent danger of dying, everyone relaxed. Thorn was talking to the officers that remained, so I could have a minute. I sat down on a boulder that Thorn had placed near the seven little hobbit holes. The hobbit holes were now only char and rubble.

A deep well of sadness settled inside of me. I wanted to cry, but I couldn't. I could only stare with empty eyes at the scorched earth and twisted steel of what remained.

Someone cleared their throat nearby, and I gingerly turned to look. Sudden movements made me want to vomit, and I'd already done that twice since I woke up on the beach. A man stood before me in a very pristine suit. He wore horn-rimmed glasses and carried a briefcase with him. There were other similarly dressed men milling about the farm. Much to the ire of the remaining police officers.

"Can I help you?" I asked with a croak. I was fuck all tired.

"Yes, Miss O'Daniels, I'm Agent Forrest with the FBI." He was blandly handsome, but where Agent Simms had a blurry feel to his features, Agent Forrest's were sharp. Sharp cheekbones, sharp jaw, sharp nose.

"Of course you are." I groaned, and he came forward.

"I'm here to debrief you and help cover up this... fiasco. And to apologize, unofficially of course, on behalf of the United States Government for your treatment by one of our agents. His actions were *not* condoned, and he'll be punished for his insubordination."

"Well, that sounds dire."

"With a target as significant as an *interstellar portal*, consequences must, by nature, be dire."

Before I could process *that* bombshell, a commotion nearby drew our attention. Agent Simms was stumbling away from officers trying to hold him back, his hands still cuffed.

"Agent Forrest!" He shouted. "Agent Forrest! *Please*, let me explain!"

"No need. Miss O'Daniels and the local authorities have explained the situation satisfactorily." His voice was sharp and bit like steel. Causing a frazzled-looking Agent Simms to halt. "I put you on leave to address your issues and instead you acted falsely on behalf of the United States Government on an *unsanctioned* investigation. As you have dragged the name of the *FBI* through the mud, trespassed, harassed and caused bodily injury to a civilian, *and* destroyed private property, I'm going to need you to hand over your badge and your weapon."

Oh *shit*.

I looked between Agent Simms and Agent Forrest with wide eyes. Sheriff Brighton and the officers all circled around, including some G-Men that had arrived with Agent Forrest.

"Irons, please relieve Agent Simms of his firearm and badge as his hands are… preoccupied." Agent Forrest's voice brokered no mercy and the agent in question, Irons, a huge African American man who could have been a linebacker for the NFL, stepped forward. He patted Simms down roughly and removed his badge and holstered firearm. "Take him away."

Agent Irons nodded stiffly and grasped Simms by the scruff of the neck. A neck with trails of blood seeping from what looked suspiciously like claw marks. Simms fought, trying to get away from Irons and screaming his head off.

"GO SEE THE CAVE!" Former Agent Simms screeched over his shoulder. Agent Irons paused as Agent Forrest looked to Sheriff Brighton for enlightenment.

"I've seen the cave. There's nothing there. When your agent arrived and started stirring up trouble, talking nonsense about a cave with a magical portal, flapping old drawings in my face, I requested to see it. Miss O'Daniels and her friend Thorn were gracious enough to show it to me. The sea cave contains rocks and seaweed, that's about it." Sheriff Brighton shook his head, then raised his eyebrows at Agent Forrest, spreading his hands in a helpless gesture. "I think your agent's been under too much pressure and cracked."

Thorn stalked forwards then to stand at my side in a much-appreciated show of support. Simms caught sight of him and paled about three shades. To cement the perception of his mental break, Simms thrashed. He nearly brained one of the police officers from the next town over who'd come forward to support Agent Irons in dragging Simms away with his elbow. Breaking free from the arms of the two men, he ran over to us once more.

"Agent Forrest! Have that *monster* take off his ring! He'll transform into the most horrifying thing you've ever seen! Grey skinned, sharp teeth and pitch-black eyes! He chased me down and nearly *killed me!*" Spittle flew from Simms's mouth and splattered against Agent Forrest's glasses. I cringed.

"I'm not taking off my *wedding band* to satisfy your curiosity. That would go against my vows." Thorn scowled down at the cuffed Agent Simms, who was practically frothing at the mouth at this point. To add salt to the wound, Thorn crossed his muscular arms over his broad chest and shook his head, expression sad and pitying. "And I may have chased you down, but I didn't nearly kill you, just scared you unconscious for everyone's safety."

Simms flicked his wild gaze from my cridhe to me. As if he couldn't believe that I'd not only fucked but married Thorn. I mean, I hadn't technically, but I wasn't about to contradict Thorn now, let alone ever. We were mates by his tradition, and that was good enough for me.

"Oh! You two tied the knot, eh? Good on you!" Called Deputy Sanchez with a cheery wave. I blushed full scarlet. We weren't married. Yet.

"Congratulations, Miss O'Daniels." Sheriff Brighton gave me a fatherly conspiratorial wink. I thought my head was about to explode from how hot my cheeks were burning and the pounding that began behind my eyes.

"I won't forget you, Ruth," Simms whispered, gaze fever bright as he drank me in. "I'll be back."

"You LSD popping creep, do me a favor and have the end you deserve." I hissed. "As soon as gods damned possible."

Simms's smile cracked in much the same way his sanity had. He laughed then, high and shrill and absolutely fucking insane. Dread roiled my stomach, and it took everything I had not to vomit all over Irons's shiny black leather shoes.

"Irons, get this criminal out of my face." Agent Forrest said.

His quiet tone made shivers run down my spine. And *not* the fun kind. The kind that told you he was capable of absolutely *unspeakable* acts of violence. Irons complied, and he roughly dragged Simms away. Thorn followed them and clapped the one officer on the shoulder as he rubbed his jaw from Simm's earlier elbow strike.

Once Agent Forrest and I were alone again, I turned and looked at him. Really looked at him. The man was hard to read, but I knew I'd heard him right. I was desperately hoping all of this wasn't the concussion talking.

"So. You know about the Geata." I muttered.

"Of course we know, Miss O'Daniels." Agent Forrest said softly into the frosty morning air.

"Then why are you not following up? Confiscating my land? Running experiments?" I asked, wondering idly if I was hallucinating this entire conversation.

"Because. These Geata have existed for as long as human history. We could do just that, but then our involvement brings speculation, which brings revelations. *None* of which the population at large could handle." His mouth quirked in dark humor and I found I could appreciate Agent Forrest's approach.

"You know what lies on the other side of the Geata?" I asked as innocently as possible. His gaze was cutting.

"I do. The knowledge is a closely guarded secret. One of the many secrets held by the Freemasons who helped found this country." Agent Forrest adjusted a ring on his finger and I groaned, wishing I could just *not* know. Because he was wearing a Freemasons ring.

Of course, he was.

"Thorn will continue to wear his ring, correct?" He cocked an eyebrow at me.

"No shit."

"Good. It would be unfortunate for him to be relocated." The light tone of his words belied their absolute levity.

"Relocated?" I asked, stressing the word.

"Who do you think we keep in Area 51?" With a self-satisfied smile at my completely gobsmacked expression, he straightened his suit and brushed away a nonexistent piece of lint. "I don't think I need to explain how vital it is to keep this a secret. We'll be in touch. If circumstances change here, I am going to have to insist you call this phone number and provide information. Especially if the gate were to... open again."

He handed me a strange business card that was oddly heavy. Engraved on it was a phone number and a code. Damn G-Men were worse than the media made them out to be. I sighed heavily and tucked it away into my jacket.

"Yeah, yeah, I'll make sure I don't give you guys a reason to come calling." I rubbed at the bridge of my nose. "What happens if the gate *does* open again?"

"Then we come calling. To welcome our visitors." He shrugged. "Protocols may change in the future, so I can promise you nothing. Only inform you that not everyone Earth-side wished to end the relationship with the Orckin."

"Well, there's that I guess." I looked at Agent Forrest and he looked at me. We watched the sun rise over the smoking ruin of my dreams.

"You were right, by the way."

"About what?"

"I had put agent Simms on a leave of absence before he came here for his... active use of LSD." I laughed then, despite the pounding it caused in my skull. "Good luck, Miss O'Daniels. And congratulations on your marriage."

With a polite nod, he pivoted on his heel and disappeared. Left alone, I turned my gaze back to Hobbiton. I tried to take stock of what I was facing now that Pissy Pants Agent Simms was permanently out of the picture. At least I hoped he was permanently gone.

I knew that if he ever escaped wherever Agent Forrest shoved him, Thorn would end him and his body would disappear. That knowledge of Thorn should have terrified me. I'd always known he was a warrior since he'd washed up on my beach, but today I saw him in action. Instead, it made me feel safer.

There was only a month left before my six-month grace period ended. Before I had to have the bed-and-breakfast operational or lose the farm from the inability to pay my mortgage. Months of hard work we'd invested into the bed-and-breakfast had gone up in flames. Because of one man's mad obsession.

I was going to lose everything I'd worked for. I was going to lose my dream and my home when it was just within reach. A black cloud obscured my mind. I couldn't see through the darkness, only perch on the boulder and stare blankly at the charred remains of Hobbiton. Just burned out husks. A few of them caved in. All that time, money, and effort gone.

Once the police left, Thorn dropped to sit next to me. I couldn't stop staring at one of the beautiful circular doors that he had made. Now a burned wreck, it swung on its half-melted hinges in the breeze. Little puff clouds of ash drifted by. In my peripheral vision, Thorn braced his elbows on his knees. He released a heavy sigh as he surveyed the damage. We sat quietly together, each lost in our thoughts.

A trembling began in my limbs and before I knew it I was barking sobs out into the early morning fog. I'd barely brought my hands up to my face when I felt Thorn's arms wrap around me, holding me together. He tucked my face into the crook of his neck and began murmuring to me in a low, lilting voice. I didn't know the meaning of the words, but I didn't need to. They were soothing regardless, and I cried harder for his sweetness.

I wept. Big ugly sobbing tears that soaked the T-shirt he'd donned at some point. He didn't seem to mind and only ran his hand over my hair in soothing strokes, avoiding my wound, occasionally kissing my forehead. I was so caught up in my emotions that I barely registered that I had crawled into his lap, feeling small and dainty as I wrapped my arms around his neck. Thorn's arms wrapped around my torso, and he held onto me while I cried.

I mourned for losing all the hard work on Hobbiton. I grieved the dreams of having my home and land that was now shattered. Sobbed for myself and all I'd lost and endured. And I cried for Thorn, who'd left everything he'd ever loved behind to go on a foolish quest to locate his failure of a mate. *Me.*

Broken, messy, constantly pushing him away or keeping him at arm's length. Despite how badly I wanted him, clung to him. Even now, even after all we'd been through.

"It'll be okay, little dove," he murmured into my hair. "I've got you. It'll be okay. We'll figure it out."

"No, it won't!" I cried. "There's no fixing this in a month! I'm going to lose everything! The farm, the bed-and-breakfast, all of my money, and you, too!"

"Me?" Thorn tried to pull back, but I held on.

"You gave up everything to be here. Your life will *always* be at risk! And I'm not your mate! I'm not! I'm just some broken woman who keeps pushing you away!" Dragging in a ragged breath, I pushed on before he could say anything. "You worked so hard helping me, and I can't do anything to repay you! I'm a nobody and you're a damned prince, for crying out loud! You deserve better than me..."

The shaking began again after my tears dried up. A bitter knot of dread formed in my belly as I waited for his response. Certain that he'd finally see that I wasn't worthy. I hadn't realized that the festering wound was there this entire time, despite how I'd accepted his love and loved him in return. But it was. And now I'd shoved it right under his nose.

Thorn sighed heavily and pulled back. I kept my head down, not wanting him to see the mess I was. He took a square of cloth from a pocket on his kilt and lifted my chin so he could look at me. Holding up the cloth to my nose, he indicated I should blow. Embarrassed, I did.

"Are you finished?" he asked me quietly. Face spasming in pain, I nodded. "Good. Now. There is no one better for me than you."

"But your *life* back on Talam," I protested, but he just held a finger to my quivering lips.

"Ruth?" His voice was low and intense as he gazed into my eyes. "There is not a force in this entire fucking universe that could *stop* me from loving you."

I sat staring at him, my heart thundering in my chest, hardly able to breathe. My nose clogged from the snot of my crying, eyes swollen from all the tears they'd shed. Definitely not my best moment. His gaze was full of love and adoration all the same.

"They can try, but it just isn't going to work," He grinned at me, thumb brushing away tears I hadn't realized had been slipping free again. "The Source itself led me to you. We've tested the gate, and it doesn't work. And I'd never go back unless you came with me. My life is here with you now. Not back there."

All I could do was stare helplessly at him. Bewildered, baffled, utterly bamboozled by this orc. He was the real deal. What we had was *the real deal.* He truly loved me.

"Ruth, my dove?" he crooned, hands cupping my face. I made some unholy sound that was almost a grunt. "Would you be not just my mate, but my wife?"

"Don't you guys only marry when you've had children?" I asked, befuddled.

"Yes." His grin was slow and seductive. My heart beat a wild tattoo in my chest.

"But I'm not pregnant yet," I whispered.

"'*Yet*' being the keyword there, dove." A wicked spark danced between us and I could feel my core begin to pulse. Gods, how I wanted him.

"So?" he asked, voice gone quiet and mirth slipping away from his expression. "What do you say about becoming my wife?"

"Yes," I whispered. As if there could be any other option. I loved him with everything that I had. What little there was of it.

CHAPTER 20*

THORN

She'd said yes!

I almost couldn't believe it. My cridhe agreed to be more than just my mate, but my wife. I was so filled with bliss, despite everything else facing us; it felt like my heart would surely burst with it.

Once she stopped crying, I scooped her up into my arms and carried her into our house. Whatever the day brought us, it could wait a while. My little dove needed to sleep and recover first. And maybe... maybe I did, too.

Thinking I'd lost her had changed something fundamental. I couldn't get that moment on the beach out of my mind when I'd felt her soul as I faced down Agent Simms. There was more tying me to Ruth than just the cridhe bond. That much was clear to me. I was unsure if I would find out what it was. As long as I could hold Ruth and cherish her for the rest of our lives, I couldn't find it in myself to care if I did.

Once inside, I set her on her feet and Ruth shuffled ahead of me towards the couch. I placed my hands on her hips and steered her towards the bathroom instead. She mumbled some kind of protest, clearly exhausted, but I refused to let her sit on the couch. She needed to be taken care of. And damn it if I wasn't going to.

"No," I murmured, my love for her suffusing my voice. "We're going to take a shower, wash away the night, and then we're going to bed."

"Thorn, I'm tired." She sighed.

"I know, little dove." I opened the door to the bathroom and ushered her inside. "Let me take care of you. You're my cridhe, my mate. Let me show you what that means."

She looked up at me then as we stood close together in the little bathroom. Eyes brimming with defeat and sadness that were so unlike her. Ruth leaned forward and rested her head against my chest, right over my heart. I wrapped my arms around her and bent to kiss the top of her head. Letting out a breath, she melted against me and nodded her assent.

My heart cracked under the strain of this bittersweet moment. Under better conditions, this would be joyous. But with how badly she'd been hurt, caring for her this way after she'd agreed to become my wife became an honor I'd never known. The knowledge that I'd nearly lost her to the mad Simms, left me staggering. Taking care of her wasn't just a way to honor her, and honor my traditions, it was a way to assuage my fears. Remind me that she was here. She was safe in my arms where she belonged. That I hadn't truly failed her.

I tilted Ruth's face up to me and removed my chleoc ring, so she could see me as I truly was. The ghost of a smile fluttered across her features as mine changed. Bending down, I captured her soft lips with mine, a gentle caress filled with all the love and longing I held for her. She melted against me further and hummed her pleasure against my mouth.

Lust lit my veins and roared in my ears. My instincts, still running rampant because of the initial mating frenzy and from nearly losing her, demanded I take her and fill her until she was overflowing with my seed. Luckily, I'd had a lot of practice resisting my urges these past months. Now was the time for gentleness, not passion.

Stepping back, I cupped her face in my hands, mindful of her wound, retracting my claws as I did so. Her eyes fluttered closed, and she turned, placing a gentle kiss against my palm. Source be praised, she was the most loving female I'd ever encountered. Soft where I was hard, sweet where I was sharp, flexible where I was rigid. My perfect counterpart, balanced in every way.

I took my time, helping her remove her clothing that stank of charr and sorrow. Kneeling before her, a penitent at her feet, I ran my fingers up under her sweater, fingertips skimming her ribs. My face was at her chest height when I knelt like this. And as I guided her sweater up, the luscious undersides of her breasts came into view. My mouth watered at the sight.

Gently, I helped her pull her sweater off over her head. She tossed it to the side and looked down at me as I gazed up at her. She looked exhausted, worn, and defeated. The opposite of how a female should be. How *my* female should be.

Each clan was different, but the Oc'Dellor prized the happiness of their females. A happier female meant more orclings. So it was a matter of honor, of malehood, to turn a female's sorrow into joy. I'd had practice, and I was damned glad of it, as I'd be able to put all of my experience to good use for my cridhe.

I cupped her cheeks in my hands once more, my thumb grazing her bottom lip. She pressed a soft kiss to it, making me smile. My hands slid from her cheeks down to cup her throat ever so gently. A light gasp escaped her, and I made a note of it for another time. My mate thrilled at such attentions and that lit a wicked fire in my blood that was hard to curb.

But now was not the time for such things.

Instead, I laid the palm of my hand over her heart, feeling its beating pick up in pace as my other hand skimmed the top of her breast. I glanced up at her, our eyes locked, and I flicked her nipple with a claw. She let out a soft cry, body jerking. I hummed low in my throat, pleased, as I leaned forward and buried my face in the valley between her large breasts.

Inhaling deeply, lost in my senses, I used my hands and claws to caress and knead her. She mewled softly as she brought her arms up around my shoulders to press my head to her chest. I trailed kisses and murmured words of Teanga Dhubh into her skin, praising her in my mother tongue as my mouth worshiped her in other ways.

The growing shift in her scent was tortuously slow. A spike of impatience had me taking her nipple into my mouth, my sharp teeth scraping against the tender pebble of flesh. She gasped, hips jerking gently against my chest, as her scent plummeted into pure arousal. I sighed against her breast, lavishing it with my black tongue. Ruth's breathing hitched and a soft moan escaped her as she sunk her fingers into my hair, fisting it until my cock jumped.

I moved my mouth to her other breast and my hands moved from cupping the lush landscape of her chest down to her waist. As badly as I wanted to release my claws and shred her jeans from her, I knew she'd be upset. They were her favorite.

Instead, I showed restraint, slowly unbuttoning the fly before skimming my hands up her hips and around towards her ass. I sunk my fingers under the waistband of her jeans and dragged them down. Her ass popped out from the fabric as I pulled them down to her thighs. I loved how, even with hands as large as mine, her curves overflowed them.

She hadn't been wearing underwear when she'd gotten dressed

to go pummel the shit out of Simms. So her scent hit me like a slap to the face. Her juices had already soaked the crotch of her jeans and I hissed against her as I tugged her pants down her long legs onto the floor.

Kissing my way down the soft, generous expanse of her stomach, I turned us both, mouth never leaving her skin as I licked and sucked and growled against her. Skimming my hands up her thighs and hips to her waist, I lifted her and placed her on the bathroom counter. She jumped a little in surprise, then relaxed, leaning back. Her mound was just below my chin as I leaned forward, breathing upon her sensitive flesh. She shivered, a gasp escaping her.

"Thorn." She murmured my name under her breath. A soft plea.

I looked up at her from under my lashes and watched as her chest heaved and her eyes glazed over with desire, soft mouth open in an enticing O shape that I knew from experience was a perfect place to sink my cock. A lopsided smirk threatened to tug my mouth into a full-blown grin. The beauty of my human cridhe as she quivered before me spoiled me. A goddess upon her altar.

Leaning back, I let my hands trail from her waist, over her hips, around, and down her thighs. She whimpered in protest as I moved away from her glistening pussy. I lifted one of her legs, turned my face, and began kissing and licking my way down from her inner thigh to her ankle. Giving extra attention to any sensitive place.

Once I'd finished with her ankle, I hoisted her leg over my shoulder and picked up her other leg, starting with her ankle, and slowly, tortuously, made my way back up to the apex of her thighs. Lavishing her as I went, sliding my hands up the length of her legs as I guided them over my shoulders.

Ruth's quiet cries and shuddering limbs, her long fingers as she reached for me and sunk her nails into my hair as I drew close enough.

How she was now dripping onto the floor from where she perched. It took everything I had to keep from rising to my feet and sinking my aching cock into her in one hard thrust. I was desperate to claim her, frantic to prove to us both that we'd survived.

Instead, I drew close to her once more, my face inches from her delicious cunt. A wicked thought coiled in my mind as I looked up at her again, licking her inner thigh in circles that moved ever closer to where I knew she wanted me most.

"Thorn!" she protested, attempting to drag my head to her core. Resisting her was easy, and I chuckled darkly against her thigh.

"What is it you want, little dove?" I growled as my gaze locked with hers.

"You! I want you!" She cried, thighs quivering around my head.

"Ah. But *how*?" I breathed. "Shall I gently lick your juices from your cunt? Shall I fuck you with my tongue until you lose count of how many times you come for me?"

She moaned. Loudly. I chuckled again, lips against her short curls.

"Or... do you want me to sink my cock so deep inside of you we can't tell where one of us ends and the other begins?" I snarled, panting with the force of my desire from the images that flooded my mind. Becoming drunk on her delectable scent.

"All of it!" She gasped, fingers clutching for purchase in my hair.

I paused, breathing ragged as my gaze bored into hers.

"Beg me," I whispered against her core.

"What?" she mumbled, lust drunk as surely as I was.

"I want to hear you beg me to do these things to you. Be a good little lass. Beg me. And I'll give you exactly what you want." I froze, fingers gripping her thighs, sinking into her plush, silky skin. We stared at one another for a long moment, long enough that I wondered if she'd say no.

"Please." The broken wail shuddered past her trembling lips.

"Och, please what?" I hissed.

"Please, Thorn. Please..." She swallowed. My cock was leaking like a busted pipe beneath my kilt and it jumped each time she said *please*. "Lick my pussy, drink me down. Fuck me with that amazing tongue of yours until I can't see straight. Please. Thorn."

"Is that all...?" I asked in a deep, wicked tone. She licked her lips, and I yearned to nibble them until they became swollen with my kisses. She hesitated a moment, and then all of her words rushed out at once.

"I need you inside of me. I need your cock so deep inside of me that I lose my mind. Fill me, please." She moaned. "Breed me, Thorn."

Breed me.

Something snapped inside of me at those two words. Not 'fuck me'. Not 'make love to me'. But, '*breed me*'.

With a roar, I jerked her closer and sunk my mouth into her slick folds. Ruth cried out, scrabbling for purchase as I suckled her clit. I had her screaming her orgasm to the ceiling with a few well-timed flicks of my tongue. Adjusting my grip, I set to licking every bit of her I could reach. She bucked in my hold, still sensitive from her last orgasm. But I was relentless.

Good to my word, I elongated my tongue and plunged the ribbed length of it into her. Her ragged cry as I drove it in and out of her, her sweet juices coursing down my throat. It had me wanting more of her screams. More of her.

Reaching a hand up, I pressed gently on her stomach above her pelvic bone as I curled my tongue and began flickering it against that spot inside that had her coming undone. I snarled, tongue vibrating with the force of it. Between one panting gasp and another, she was screaming my name to the rafters.

But it wasn't enough. It would never be enough.

CHAPTER 21 *

RUTH

Gods, my mate was more ravenous than usual. As if the fear of losing me was enough to drive him to prove it to the both of us, we were alive. That we'd made it through, together.

I spiraled back into my body after the latest of a series of orgasms. Every inch of my skin was hypersensitive as I sat perched on the bathroom counter with Thorn's face buried between my thighs. My legs were thrown over his shoulders as he knelt on the tile. His arms curled around my hips, locking me in place.

No matter how I jerked and writhed in his grip, he kept me right where he wanted me. His gaze never left my face as he chased climax after climax from me. And gods, it was so good for a while. But after a time, it became too much to bear without a break.

"Stop." I whimpered, body at its limit. "Thorn, *stop*."

He just growled and kept at it, his gaze unfocused as he stared at me in single-minded determination. It registered then that his instincts had taken over. He'd explained the mating frenzy to me and how it could steal the good sense from the best of the orckin. He was normally so in control of himself, always stopping the moment I asked; I hadn't thought he'd succumb. I was damned wrong.

"Thorn!" I bit out, gritting my teeth against the sensitivity. When I tried to pull away again, he snarled and clutched me tighter. Alarmed, I pulled back, trying to think past my singing nerves. Panic and dark memories were knocking on the door at the back of my mind. I knew it would be only seconds before things could go horribly wrong.

So I did the only thing I could think of. I reached forward with both hands and cupped his face.

"Thorn. Please, baby, stop. You're hurting me." My voice shook as I truly started dancing that line between pleasure and pain. The tenderness I showed him seemed to worm past his addled senses, and I saw the haze of lust lift from him as he paused.

"Thorn, stop, *please*," I begged now, tears threatening as I fought the urge to fight him and my memories at once. A traitorous tear fell down my cheek and his gaze sharpened, focused. In a rush, he let me go and pulled away from me. He blinked rapidly as he took in the scene, what I'd said, how I now had my thighs clenched tightly together.

"Source, Ruth, I'm so damned sorry." He rasped, staggering to his feet and slumping against the wall, the back of his hand over his mouth. Thorn looked stricken. Horrified. Worried, I reached out a hand towards him and he flinched as if I'd slapped him. He turned his head then and made to move towards the door. "I should go... I don't trust myself right now."

I didn't know what was worse. Him losing himself to his own emotion and instincts or him being so desperate to flee me and the situation. Ire flared bright hot in my breast. I knew if I didn't do something immediately, things might become irreparable between us. I couldn't let him leave, not now, not after the night we'd survived.

"Thorn," I said sharply, and he froze, gaze sliding to me in anguish. With shaking legs, I got off the counter and stood. He watched me and grimaced at how my legs continued to shake. Recognizing that he'd done too much.

He'd become desperate to please me after nearly losing me. And, in the process, lost himself. Suddenly, the buffeting clouds of memory thundering so close dissipated and a new clarity hit me. A clarity that was only possible because of the healing he'd helped me through. I blinked at him and saw him anew.

This wasn't one of those terrible commune men only concerned with their pleasure. This was the male who'd waited months for me to come around. Who'd shown me infinite patience, love, and protection. He was terrified of losing me, terrified he'd hurt me. He'd gone too far but had stopped. By the gods, he deserved some grace, just like I did.

The tension I'd felt evaporated like morning mist in the sun.

"Come here," I demanded softly and held out my arms.

"Ruth, I hurt you. I lost myself in the frenzy and didn't pay attention. I'm an honorless wretch who should be strung up." Thorn's voice broke and tears threatened. Definitely not the reaction of someone who didn't love me, didn't cherish me.

"Thorn, you are just as scared by what happened as I am," I told him, waggling my fingers until he placed his hands in mine. "You didn't lose me. You protected me and saved me. I'm here."

"Yes, but I-"

"Thorn," I said, and he shut up, eyes imploring me. "You stopped. It took longer than it should have, but you stopped. That's what's important." Silence descended, and it seemed as if he wasn't breathing. "You are my safe place, Thorn. Don't run from me now."

Thorn swallowed hard and jerked a nod. I pulled his hands up to my cheeks and stepped closer. Looking up at him, I let him see everything I felt for him in my eyes. All the love, frustration, forgiveness, trust, and passion.

"Ruth, I'm so sorry, my dove." His voice rumbled, thick with emotion.

"I forgive you," I whispered back, and offered him a small smile. "Now, aren't we supposed to take a shower before we go to bed?"

"I..." Words failed him as I led him to the shower and turned on the hot water. As it heated, I turned and grasped his face, pulling him down for a kiss. It started stiff, but with the same loving patience he'd shown me, I melted him into a scorching kiss.

He groaned shakily into my mouth, hands rising to fist in my hair with the utmost tenderness. A throbbing pulse started in my core, my body raring to go once more. I still needed a bit for the sensitivity to subside, so I'd indulge in something we didn't do often. Something just for him. Steam wafted from behind the shower curtain and I pulled away from him enough to remove his shirt and kilt and lead him under the hot spray. Once in the shower, I sank to my knees before him.

"Ruth." He growled as he watched me at his feet. "This is about you, not me."

I looked up at him from where I knelt, his dick curving sharply up towards his navel mere inches from my face. His knot already straining with cum as it trickled from his tip and down his shaft. I nearly drooled just from the memory of how good he tasted.

He needed to unwind and remember the goodness we shared, too. He needed to know that I truly forgave him and wanted him. It was only fair.

"This is about *us*, Thorn," I whispered. The truth of those words set him to trembling.

I leaned forward and tilted my head to the side, zeroing in on the rivulet of cum as it dribbled down along one of the deep vertical grooves in his shaft. With one long, luxurious lick, I captured the line of liquid against my tongue. The sweet saltiness of him exploded in my mouth and I groaned.

He tasted like salted caramel to me and I'd gladly take him in my mouth more if he'd let me. As I reached the alien tip of him, I pulled back so that he could see his juices on my pink human tongue he loved so much. Thorn's breathing grew ragged as I swallowed the dollop of it and then showed him my clean tongue.

"Good lass." He breathed into the steaming air between us as I took him in my hands, angling his cock where I wanted it. "Gods, I don't deserve you."

"Shut up, you idiot. I love you and it's going to take a lot more than what just happened to change that. We're mates after all." I murmured against the sensitive flesh of his crown. "Learn from it."

He choked on his next words as I slid my tongue between his foreskin and his tip, circling his entire head before slipping my tongue out. With a small sound, I took him into my mouth, careful of my teeth with his girth. I loved how thick he was, how he filled my mouth and stretched my jaw. At the silky feel of him against my tongue. I stopped just above his knot.

I had very little gag reflex, but his size made it so I couldn't get much of him down my throat at this angle. That and his knot was so swollen I couldn't get it past my lips without scraping it with my teeth. So instead, I reached my hands up to cup his sac and the base of his cock as I ran my tongue around his shaft.

"Och, dove. You look so lovely with your mouth full." He growled, his hands moving to cup my face as he stared down at me, a fierce expression of approval etched in his features. Water sprayed onto his shoulders and ran in rivulets down his muscled torso. A sight that had me moaning with him in my mouth. He flung his head back and hissed, fingertips pressing into my scalp.

I opened my mouth wider and pressed him as deeply as he could go. My lips grazed his knot and Thorn moaned long and low above me. Spurred on by the sound of his pleasure, I ran my hands and mouth up and down the length of him. Each time my hands ran over his knot, the pressure sent spurts of his hot, delicious seed into my mouth.

Pulling back, I sat on my heels and suckled at the tip of his cock as I worked him with my hands. I didn't want to waste a single drop of him. Thorn's breathing shifted, quickened, as his hips twitched forward. He was close.

So I did the one thing I'd always wanted to try. I took him into my mouth deeply once more and hummed a tune. It was our song, *Hooked on a Feeling*. The one we'd first danced to.

Thorn cried out, swaying from the shock of it, then laughing as he recognized the song while I continued to hum the tune. He let out a shaky moan, fighting his release, but then I hit the chorus and he roared his pleasure. His cum flooded my throat and my mouth and I groaned, losing the tune as my core throbbed.

I wanted him to suffer in the best way possible. So I palpated his knot, still engorged even as he shot his load down my throat. He shuddered, fisting all of my hair at the back of my head in one hand. I continued to hum the tune relentlessly until he gasped and made to jerk back. I let him go, and he slid from my lips.

Taking a deep breath, I swallowed a few times, the taste of him still coating my mouth. I looked up at him and he had an arm braced on the wall, his other hand still tangled in my wet hair. So many emotions danced across his face as he looked down at me, breathing heavily like a bellows. We stayed like that for a minute, as Thorn got his breathing under control.

"That wasn't fair, my little dove." Thorn chuckled breathily as he released my hair and helped me stand.

"All's fair in love and war, baby." I grinned at Thorn. He pulled me to him roughly and kissed me soundly as we chuckled against one another's lips. When he pulled back from the kiss, he was happy once more.

"All's fair, och?" His smile turned up at the corners in a devastating way, looking all the world like a cat who caught a canary. A shiver ran over my skin. "Time to wash, little dove."

Thorn bent to the side and picked up the bar of cedar soap and my loofah. With practiced ease, he lathered it up and began by washing my hair. With heartbreaking gentleness, he ran his fingers through my wet locks, gently massaging my scalp, mindful of where I'd been hit. It felt wonderful. Sighing, I closed my eyes as he turned me so the hot water could rinse away the suds.

"Thank you," I murmured, feeling relaxed.

"Anything for you, dove."

"Oh, och? Anything for me?" I asked, peeking at him with one eye and a mischievous grin, mimicking his thick brogue.

"Sassy little nocrys, aren't you?" He chuckled. Thorn had told me what nocrys were, and I was envious. I wanted to ride a giant cat too!

"Well, *someone* needs to keep you on your toes," I said matter-of-factly. He smirked at me and began to lather his hands again.

"Och, that I do. I'll be keeping *you* on your toes soon enough." Thorn chuckled and I looked at him questioningly. "You'll see." His eyes burned like twin suns as he slid his lathered hands over my body.

"I'm still a little sensitive." I breathed, already trembling in anticipation. My orc grunted softly in acknowledgment. I trusted that this time; he had himself under control.

Thorn's massive hands slid effortlessly over my skin. A delicious sensation coupled with the callouses on his palms. Especially when he ran them over my aching breasts. My breathing hitched as he ran his thumbs around the taut peaks of my nipples, drawing a panting gasp from me.

"Too much?" He murmured, slowing. I shook my head, sending droplets flying. More than soap and water cascaded down my inner thighs and I clenched them together, in need.

"More," I whispered, and he obliged. His shaft was already at attention once more, pressed against my stomach. I wanted to feel that hard length pressed against my ass, so I turned in his arms and pressed back into him.

"Mmmhh." He groaned as my ass and low back pressed into his groin.

His arms encircled me, one gliding up to cup my throat, his claws slipping through the bubbles. A shuddering breath escaped my lips as I tilted my head back against his chest. He clutched me roughly to him, pressing tight against me until there was nothing between us but his massive cock.

"You want me to *breed* you?" Thorn panted into my ear, his hand slowly curving over my belly, inching ever lower. "Fill you with my seed until you swell with our child?"

A shudder wracked my body at his words, at the desperate edge to them. How his fingers splayed possessively over my stomach. So *that* had been what sent him over the edge. Me begging him to breed me. Fuck *me*, that was scorching hot. I wasn't sure if it would be possible for us to have a child. But it didn't stop the primal need to try.

"Yes." I breathed, voice wobbling as my legs nearly gave way beneath me.

Thorn's arms kept me upright as he turned me to face the shower wall. I placed my hands against the tile, bracing for him. With devastating gentleness, he pulled my wet waves from my shoulder and laid a soft kiss there. Bar of soap in his hands, he worked up a good lather between them and ran them over my body once more.

With loving hands, he caressed the mountains and valleys of my torso, claws leaving tantalizing trails in the bubbles. Then he pressed forward with a low growl, his soapy hands gliding back over my hips to cup my ass as my chest pressed against the tile.

"Have to make sure you're squeaky clean." Thorn breathed, hardly above a whisper. He ran his hands out, around the sides of my hips, up to my low back, then down before he slid one hand between my thighs.

I cried out as his now clawless fingers parted my folds, dipping briefly into my core before withdrawing. They continued their decadent explorations as he slowly reached my clit. He made circles with his two middle fingers. My clit caught between them as he slid them amongst my curls. I bucked, thighs trembling. I was still sensitive.

Thorn removed his hand, then pressed the tip of his cock between my thighs. I made room for him to slip it between them, the soapy suds and my juices allowing him to glide easily. He hissed above me as he took a step forward, pinning me to the tiled wall, his mouth against my shoulder.

"I love your softness, my little dove." He whispered into my ear. "I want to be rough. Will you let me possess you as surely as you've possessed me?"

Thorn slid his hand up to cup my throat again as I panted into the steamy air. My heartbeat scattered and the throbbing of my core became an incessant pounding. This slow, deliberate control he was wielding was devastating me, ruining me. Gods, I wanted him to destroy me. Break me.

"Yes..." I whispered, voice thick from desire and his hand encircling my throat. A throat he could easily rip out but was holding so reverently. His claws the barest caress against my fluttering pulse.

"Yes... *What*?" He demanded, a snarl making his words bite. Knowing I once again held all the cards, I tilted my head back against his shoulder and looked up into his smoldering gaze.

"Yes... *Possess* me. *Breed* me. My cridhe." I breathed against his cheek. I saw the moment that oh-so-special word registered because his pupils blew out, turning his copper irises into fine wire bands. Twin rings like the one on his finger.

"*Good lass*." He growled. I barely had time to gasp my surprise as he snaked an arm between me and the wall, lifted me by my throat and waist, and rammed his cock into my pussy from behind.

He filled me so completely that I cried out in ecstasy. I could feel the tip of him crushed against the opening to my womb and I shuddered at the pleasure of it, hands trying to seek purchase on the tile. Thorn braced his knees against the wall between my spread thighs, my spine bowed and my ass pressed tight against his groin.

I clutched at his hand around my throat like the loveliest of necklaces and my other reached back to pull him tighter against me, deeper inside of me as he ground his hips. His dark chuckle, like thunderclouds rumbling on the horizon, danced along my skin and I felt myself devolving into mewling, needy moans.

The heat of him at my back, the cold tile pressed against my front, and the spray of hot water from the shower sharpened every feeling, every inch of desperate skin. Every time we shifted, my nipples grazed the tile before me and left me quaking.

I needed him to move inside me *now*. As if he knew my mind as his own, Thorn rolled his hips. I cried out, cheek pressing against the cold tile.

"Sing for me, little dove." His words rumbled against my cheek as he began a merciless rhythm. His hips snapping against my ass like thunderclaps. Thorn's knot created wet popping sounds as it moved in and out of me.

Each thrust had his thick cock hitting deep inside of me in brief explosions of pleasure. I cried out with each thrust, panting and moaning, urging him to go faster, harder. All while he pinned me against the tile, my feet only touching the floor with my tiptoes. Like he'd promised.

Thorn's hand spasmed around my throat, without cutting off my air. I moaned low and long at that. I'd never been choked before, and by the gods, I loved it. Thorn's panting breaths became snarls and vicious growls as he picked up the tempo.

"Such a lovely song you sing for me, dove." He growled. "But I think you can do *better*."

He shifted then, mid-thrust, and slid his hand down between my thighs. I reached backward, holding onto his shoulders for dear life as his thick fingers found my clit. The change in angle, the addition of his fingers flickering over my sensitive nub, his hand wrapped around my throat, and how he *ruthlessly* railed me sent me screaming bloody murder headlong into an orgasm that was entirely on another level. I screamed and wailed and nearly blew out my eardrums as he kept fucking me like a wild animal until one orgasm rolled into another and crashed headlong into yet another.

If *anyone* had been outside, they would have thought he was in here brutally murdering me.

With a strangled roar, Thorn quickly lost his rhythm and

slammed home as deeply inside of me as he could get. Hips jerking and twitching as he filled me full of his seed. I could feel the hot wash of it inside of me, feel it dripping down my thighs as I clamped down on him, body unwilling to release him. His knot still throbbing inside of me, not soft enough to slide free.

Each shuddering gasp, every breath, slowly drew us back from the glorious heights we'd shared. The water was now just lukewarm as it sprayed onto us both. We'd outlasted our water heater. Eventually, his knot softened and I stopped clenching enough so he could slide out from me. A flood of cum gushed out of me, down my thighs, to splatter thickly on the floor of the shower before being swept away by the rapidly cooling water.

"Are you alright, dove?" Thorn asked, voice raspy.

Alright? *Alright*? The orc had decimated me and left me loose-limbed and languid. Fit only to crawl under the covers and sleep for the next week. At least it felt that way. All I could do was mumble and nod weakly as he helped me back onto my feet, legs trembling like a newborn colt. Thorn wasn't much better off. He was trembling too, even as he helped me out of the shower and turned the water off.

"I didn't hurt you did I?" He queried, dipping his head so he could look into my eyes. The worry there and the self-censure was alarming.

"You didn't hurt me," I mumbled, cupping his cheek in my hand. "Made me come very good. Can't think. Love you."

"I love you too, and I'm glad." He chuckled then, all that stress melting from him as he helped me to dry off.

When we were both dry, if not exhausted, he guided me to our bedroom, our clothes in his hands. My chest tingled as I tottered to our bedroom, and I rubbed at it absentmindedly. I looked down but couldn't see anything. Must have been from having my boobs pressed into the tile for too long.

CHAPTER 22

THORN

Healing. That's what this was. Healing from the past, from this horrific night, from what threatened to split us asunder. And healing from our fears.

I still hated myself for losing control with Ruth. It should have *never* happened. I was supremely blessed with such an understanding and loving cridhe. One who, instead of showing me hatred and vitriol, refused to let me run away, gently pointed out the problem and reminded me it was about *us*.

Not what I could do for her. Not what she could do for me. But what we could do for each other.

She'd accepted my apology, my desires, and my seed with more grace and love than I thought possible. And I swore I'd keep my head, check in with how she was faring throughout our coupling. Make sure I never made an error like that again. I loved her with everything I was, and I was determined never to hurt her. And if I ever did? I'd make it right, no matter what it took.

I would be her safe place. Just as she was mine.

Our desires had turned darker then, sharper, than usual. Like licking honey off of one of my knives. Decadent, exquisite, luscious, brutal, seductive, and tender all at once. The release we shared had been beyond anything I'd experienced. I loved it was something we could explore together in the future, this kind of mating. But for now? For now, we'd rest and recover. Before we faced rebuilding Ruth's dream. *Our* dream.

After I dried my sleepy cridhe off reverently with a fluffy towel and brusquely dried myself off, I ushered Ruth into our bedroom and kicked the door closed. I helped her get into a clean pair of pajamas. She slid under the covers and I curled up behind her, still naked, tucking her close to me where she belonged.

As the mourning doves cooed outside our window, the late morning sun warmed our space with beams of gold. Ruth fell asleep the moment her head hit the pillow. I watched her for a moment as she slept, her soft snores were lovely to hear. She was the most beautiful female I'd ever seen, and I was blessed beyond the stars to call her mine. I placed a gentle kiss on her forehead and curled around her. Sleep found me swiftly.

We woke hours later to what sounded like a stampede of nocrys thundering down our driveway. I sat up quickly. Grabbing my ring, I slid it on before I snagged my kilt, standing and buckling it on.

"What the hell is that?" Ruth mumbled, still half-asleep and looking lovely with her sleep-mussed hair.

"Stay here, I'll check." I placed a quick peck on her forehead before I stalked from our bedroom. I could see truck after truck coming down the driveway through the front windows. It was a convoy of contractors.

Confused, I opened the front door and watched as someone got out of a car and came up to the porch holding a clipboard. I heard soft footsteps behind me and Ruth came to stand beside me wearing a quilt like a cape. I wrapped my arm protectively around her shoulder, tucking her in close to me. She wrapped her arm around my waist, still hardly awake.

"What the hell is all this?" she asked in sleep-addled shock, the quilt wrapped tight around her.

"The government has paid for the renovation and rebuilding of... hobbit holes?" asked the man who stood at the base of the porch steps, flipping through his clipboard in confusion.

"Looks like the FBI wants to apologize," I laughed and looked down at my mate's stunned expression.

"What?" was all Ruth could get out, shaking her head as if afraid she was hallucinating. "Um, thank you," she called as the lead contractor corralled all the others.

Suddenly, a chorus of honking horns rent the afternoon air. We watched as another caravan of vehicles came rumbling down the driveway. Ruth's eyes were enormous as she looked up at me in absolute confusion. Brighton's truck rolled up to a stop in front of the porch steps. I recognized Sanchez's truck and a few of the guys from poker night. But there were dozens of cars, trucks, and larger vehicles I didn't know.

"Looks like the town's turned out to help us, too." I laughed, delighted at the show of support.

Brighton and Sanchez got out of their trucks and made their way to us. Julia had shown up in a box truck filled with gods only knew what. Each of the guys from poker night had brought tools and supplies. Even their families. Brighton, Sanchez, and the lead contractor sent by the FBI conversed with one another quickly, shaking hands. The rest of the contractors and townsfolk converged, ready to get to work.

"Good afternoon!" Brighton called as he left the knot of contractors, striding up the front steps to us.

"What?" was all Ruth could get out, mouth hanging open as she surveyed the scene in her front drive.

"Well, none of us liked what Former Agent Simms had done here in our town and to you. So, as an apology of sorts, we all got together to help rebuild your Tolkien bed-and-breakfast." Brighton's warm, fatherly smile crinkled his eyes.

"Who would have known the FBI would help too?" Sanchez was grinning like an idiot as he joined us.

"It'll save us a lot of time and materials, to be sure." Brighton nodded thoughtfully, running his fingers over his salt-and-pepper mustache.

"Why...?" Ruth asked, her voice wobbling. She sounded on the verge of tears and we all looked at her.

"Think of it as a *wedding present*, okay?" Brighton smiled kindly and patted Ruth's arm.

"Um, thank you." Ruth offered, blushing furiously. I wrapped my arm around her, a grin set to match Sanchez's on my face. Then she turned towards the gathered crowd and hollered, "Thank you all!"

A cheer went around the small gathered crowd. Julia waved before directing a bunch of ladies who were unloading a variety of furnishings and plants. Sanchez left us to organize a bunch of folk that looked just like him as they unloaded building supplies from a box truck. Brighton shouted to the crowd and pointed the way towards the ruins of Hobbiton before turning back to us.

"You two go rest. Sanchez and I will make sure they're handled.

We'll get everything cleaned up today and make sure we get the build done in time for you, Ruth." He patted Ruth on the shoulder and she sobbed before she flung her arms around his shoulders in a tight hug. Brighton chuckled and hugged her back, patting her shoulders before letting her go and pushing her towards me. "Look after her, would you? Knowing her, she'll insist on joining us, shovel in hand, and end up cracking her head on another rock."

"Those stubborn Irish genes." I chuckled.

"Hey! I heard that!" She glowered at me, and I grinned, turning and herding her inside our home.

And the locals of our small coastal town did well. The next day, I was out there helping remove the heavier debris. Surprising the men who didn't know me and making a few of the ladies swoon.

A few days later, Ruth was back to normal and joined us. With the help of the townsfolk and the contractors hired by the FBI, we were back to where we'd started before Agent Simms had destroyed it in just a matter of weeks. All seven hobbit holes were restored, if not improved upon. It was an immense undertaking but was one that was met with love and appreciation.

And my lovely cridhe was at the center of it all. Offering thanks, encouragement, refreshments, and direction. Including ideas and concepts that people suggested to her, making it a place that was no longer just ours, but a piece of everyone who helped build it.

One contractor even tore down the old barn and replaced it with a new one, since the FBI was footing the bill, after hearing from Julia that Ruth wanted one to host large events. His daughter was to get married in a few months but didn't have a venue. Ruth offered to host it as a thank you and, once word got around, a flood of other folks quickly had us booked for the next eight months.

The ladies from the local nursery had donated a bunch of

plants. A lawn care expert had laid local ground cover over the knolls the hobbit holes were in. They installed dwarf fruit trees and decorative plants throughout the place, transforming it into a quaint, idyllic utopia. It reminded me of Baile Coille strangely, and I found myself less homesick.

A fireplace contractor joined forces with a kitchen crew and they created the outdoor kitchen of Ruth's dreams for her Green Dragon outdoor bar. Even the fire crews showed up to cook and work as hard labor. And in the evenings, everyone would gather and eat after a long day's work. I would watch Ruth in these moments and see the awe and joy that shone from her like a beacon.

Watching my cridhe, the human woman who would be my wife, as we rebuilt our dream, I smiled. Pledging to the Source that I would face all of life's challenges that came our way. As long as I had my little dove by my side.

EPILOGUE

RUTH

Months after the Hobbiton rebuild, I woke up sore and aching in our bed. The build might have been complete and the farm was now officially mine. But we were still fixing up the farm itself. It was long, hard work. My body was protesting the months of labor without a break. The contractors hired by the FBI had added on extra projects like replacing the barn since the government was footing the bill on the rebuild. Yet, there was always more to do.

I'd placed ads with local travel agencies about our bed-and-breakfast and we already had plenty of interest from literary types. Not to mention all the bookings we already had with the townsfolk who had made our dream a reality. We'd already hosted two weddings and a couple of writing retreats, which had been amazing.

Julia had left her job at the supermarket after making friends with the ladies who ran the local nursery and began her own floral business, which became a colossal hit. We'd signed a contract that we would use her floral business for our events, a step that helped us both business-wise.

She'd insisted on doing the flowers for free for *our* wedding.

That's right, Thorn and I had tied the knot. The whole town had shown up. Thorn and I said our vows on the beach where I'd found him washed ashore. We'd both been a laughing, crying wreck as we shared our first kiss as husband and wife.

The reception had been the biggest party the town had seen in years with a local band and Thorn's first batch of his orckin whiskey, uisge-beatha. Everyone had gotten piss drunk, and we'd left them all to party as Thorn swept me off of my feet and carried me into our home. Where we'd spent the entire night worshiping each other. I'd never been so happy in all my life.

Thorn's arm wrapped around my waist, bringing me back to the present, cock pressed hard against my ass as he snored into my hair. I couldn't help but chuckle as I patted his forearm. My wedding band, a simple thing he'd made from the guard of one of his knives, glinted in the morning light.

My laughter caused him to snort in his sleep. He groaned, shaking off sleep in the bright sunlight that filled our room in the farmhouse. Suddenly, Thorn went absolutely, positively still.

"Ruth." Thorn choked, hands frozen on my body.

"What is it?" I asked, suddenly worried. "What's wrong?" I tried to turn, but he held me fast.

"Ruth..." His voice broke and I could swear he sobbed behind me. Terrified, I turned in his arms. Grasped his beloved face in both of my hands and made him look at me.

"What's wrong, baby?" I asked. Dread pooled in my belly. Because Thorn Oc'Dellor, prince of his clan, warrior, and hobbit hole builder... was openly weeping.

"You're..." He breathed a shaky breath, his eyes so full of tears and love as he cradled me to him with such immense tenderness it broke my heart.

"I'm what, Thorn?"

"You're *pregnant*." Thorn broke on the words and pressed his face to my chest. Baffled, I wrapped my arms around him as he wept, trying to process.

"… Well, I guess that makes sense. It's not like we've been using protection. How do you know?" I wasn't as alarmed as I thought I'd be at such news. Slightly surprised we were compatible enough to have children, but not scared. It was then I realized it was because I felt safe. Thorn was my safe space.

And for the first time, building a loving family felt possible. The dream I'd always coveted was now a reality I could share with someone. And not just anyone. But Thorn.

"I can smell the change. The shift in your scent." He muttered against my bare breasts as I gently rubbed soothing circles on his shoulders and gently brushed back his hair. He was shuddering and shaking with the force of his emotions.

"You really want to have a family with me, don't you?" I asked in awe. He pulled back and looked into my eyes, into my soul, with his oddly human copper-colored gaze.

"I really do." He whispered through his tears.

"Well then. I guess I'm really glad we got married. Since I'm officially doing right by you, by orckin culture." I told him, love and joy bursting forth in my breast like the rising sun. He laughed as I beamed a loving smile at him.

"Then you're okay with it? Happy?" He laughed, brushing tears off of his face.

"Of course I am, baby." I smiled at him with all the love I possessed. "I told you I always wanted a family, and I'm blessed to have it with you." Thorn pressed his brow to mine and breathed deep. I could feel the contentment and love settle into our bones, warm like a blanket on a wintry day.

"You've just made me the happiest orc in the universe." He sighed, a smile tugging at the lips I loved to kiss so much.

"The cridhe marks you've talked about haven't shown up," I murmured, fingers grazing his chest where he said they showed up for the orckin. It was the only thing that had held me back from fully believing we were a match.

"It doesn't matter if they ever show up, little dove." He rumbled, cupping my cheek in his giant hand. The chleoc ring glinted on his ring finger in the morning light, his wedding band. "Marks or no, you are my cridhe, and you always will be."

Tears pricked my eyes as I raised my hand to cup his cheek, my gaze and fingers roaming over his beloved face. The poor orc was trying to grow a beard. So he could fit in better. Sheriff Brighton had been showing him how to groom himself according to our human ways. It was a scraggly thing that didn't suit him yet, but I loved it anyway.

I decided then that he was right. Cridhe marks or no. He was my cridhe. Because I couldn't imagine spending another day without him.

"Thorn, darling." I chuckled and tugged at the wiry hair that grew on his chin like some silly billy goat. "Let's get us some goats for the farm. Start adding to our family."

Thorn grinned broadly, eyes sparkling. His blunt human-looking teeth were so at odds with the sharp ones I knew lurked beneath the chleoc ring's magic.

"Family. I like the sound of that. It's my life's greatest joy to look after my family." He kissed me slow and sweet, and I knew in my soul that he was my cridhe too.

Turn the page for an excerpt from:

RHUGER'S PEARL

ORC MATCHED 1.0

Coming 2022!

AMELIA

"Okay," I said, holding up my hands. "Let me get this straight. This is a gate to another planet. Like Stargate or something, right?"

"Yes."

"How do you *know this*?"

I was not ready for her answer. She looked me dead in the eye and the brutal honesty I saw there froze me in place. "Because your grandfather is not human. He came through this gate. He is from Talam." Grandma Ruth lifted her chin at me as she said this. Daring me to refute her.

My brain short-circuited.

"What do you mean, Grandpa wasn't human?" I demanded, shaking my head. "He sure as hell *looked* human."

"That was because of his chleoc ring," Grandma explained. "It was a ring that allowed him to look like us while he was here."

"A *what*?" I asked a little breathlessly.

"A chleoc ring." She repeated.

"And what exactly did Grandpa look like *without* this chleoc ring?" I dreaded her answer.

Grandma Ruth shrugged and lifted her eyes and arms, swinging them around at the cave at large.

Slowly, realization dawned on what she meant.

No.

"He was an..." I swallowed hard. "*ORC?*"

Grandma Ruth nodded and shrugged helplessly at me.

"Are you *insane*?" I asked, horrified.

I wasn't sure if I was asking if she was insane to think this whole situation was real. That Grandpa really was an orc or that this weird carving was really a gate to another planet.

Or if I was asking her if she was insane enough to boink an orc alien.

Of course, she was.

"Okay, so why should I believe you?" I asked, feeling a migraine imminent. I rubbed the bridge of my nose.

"Think about it. How often have you been sick?" She tilted her head, already knowing the answer.

"Rarely."

"You heal fast, don't you? Your mother too? Like baffle-the-doctors fast." Grandma Ruth began ticking off fingers.

"Okay."

"And both you and your mother have always been crazy strong and tall. It's your orckin genes."

"Grandpa was over seven feet tall, Grandma. Of *course*, we'd get some of his genes and be tall." Grandma Ruth just cocked an eyebrow at me and crossed her arms. As if waiting for me to connect the dots.

It was true. Grandpa had been *immense*, both in size and personality. And he hadn't been lanky like a lot of tall people. He'd been built like a fucking tank.

He'd always been weird. Not doing what you'd expect a person to do. A human to do. And he'd been ridiculously good at fighting, even though he'd never been in the military. And there was no record of him before he met my grandmother. Grandpa *never* talked about his life before her. Almost like he'd sprung up in the world, fully formed.

And perhaps he had.

At least on this planet.

I looked at the gate, then back at my Grandmother Ruth. Everything about her expression and body language tasted of honesty and almost... defeat.

"You always talk about Grandpa like he's still alive," I stated.

"Yes."

"You think he went back instead of drowning in here?"

"Yes."

"Why did he leave?" My voice broke on my words. The little girl inside of me ached for the grandfather who had abandoned her.

"I don't know." She whispered before swallowing hard.

My heart broke for her. If this was all true... then she'd been waiting for him to come back for over two decades. She'd been waiting all this time for the love of her life. Been waiting to ask him why he'd left and not come back for her. For his family.

I felt my thoughts tumble around my shocked brain like rocks in a dryer.

"Do you have proof?" I suddenly asked.

"Yes." came her simple reply as she pulled a photo out of her sweatshirt pocket. She handed it over and stood patiently as I looked down at it.

The photo I held in my hand was worn around the edges as if she'd lovingly caressed it millions of times. As if she looked at it multiple times a day. Held it to her heart every day since he'd left.

It took a moment for my mind to process what I was looking at. Because it was my grandfather standing proudly in what looked like the makings of one of the hobbit holes. But he looked... different.

His hair was still silky black and tumbled around his shoulders, just lacking the streaks of grey. He had the beginnings of the beard I remembered. And his smile was broad. But... *those teeth.*

They were sharp, with long canines. Almost like a wolf's.

And his skin wasn't the peachy honey color I remembered. It was the color of clouds in an inbound storm. He was shirtless and black tattoos curled up his tree-trunk arms, over his shoulders, and up his neck.

I didn't remember those.

His hands ended in sharp claws that stressed how tiny the pickaxe was in his massive hands. Despite the joy and love lighting his facial expression, despite how much he looked like the Grandpa I knew and loved, he was *not* human.

"What is he...? What am *I*?" I whispered. There was no denying it now. Not with proof staring back at me.

"Your Grandpa called his kind orckin. Orcs." She shrugged.

"Yo, Grandma... you realize you're a monster fucker, right?" I tried to laugh, to find a joke in all this as the foundation of my entire life quaked beneath my feet.

"Proudly." Grandma chuckled. "I didn't like him at first. I found him nearly drowned just outside of the cave. It was a challenge dragging him up the cliff to the farmhouse. When he woke up..." Grandma paused, a flush on her dimpled cheeks. "He looked at me as if I were the most beautiful creature he'd ever seen. Said as much, too."

"He'd always been so smitten with you," I whispered. Memories of how he'd constantly doted on my Grandma Ruth and his family had tears streaming down my cheeks.

"He grew on me, for sure. He had lost his chleoc ring, and it took us a while to find it here in the cave. The Feds were involved, especially one crazy bastard named Simms who burned down Hobbiton. If it wasn't for the ring, he would have ended up at Area 51 or someplace worse." Grandma paused and shifted on her feet. "Before I knew it, I was in love with him. And the rest is history. The night he..."

Grandma's expression drew tight, and I took her hand, waiting for her to continue.

"The night he... left... he'd had a nightmare and rushed to the sea cave. When I'd gone after him, I'd watched as the gate flashed and snatched him away. It's why I never gave up hope he was alive. I've always known for a fact that he hadn't drowned." She explained in a rush.

Time stretched out between us and I absentmindedly rubbed the back of her knuckles with my thumb. An attempt to soothe us both.

Grandpa was alive.

"Can't we open the gate? Get him back?" I asked, a sudden desperate urge to see my grandpa flooding my veins.

"I've tried. I can't find the seventeenth stone." Grandma just shrugged as she nodded towards the empty divot in the carving.

Turning, I handed the photo of my *orckin* grandfather back to her before taking a step towards the carving. Time seemed to slip for a moment. The world went a little sideways, and I shook my head. Weird. Grandma was frowning at me.

Shaking my head again, I walked up the short flight of stairs to the carving. I traced the carvings with my fingers. The feathers and leaves of the tree were so detailed, that they almost looked alive. As if the wings would flutter at any moment. Each of the rings had strange characters carved along them. I'd never seen characters like that. Sunlight caught in one point of light and my gaze flicked to it. Upon closer inspection, the lights were crystals. Crystals that looked like carved acorns the size of apricots that reflected the sunlight.

I ran my fingers over one and a pulse of sensation singed along my skin. It wasn't electric, heat, or cold. It was some other feeling altogether. Almost like breathing and rushing water all at once. Jerking my fingers back from the crystal, I looked across the wall to where the last divot sat empty of its crystal acorn.

As I stood there, I saw a flicker of light up in a niche in the rough cave wall. Brow furrowing, I strode over to where I'd seen the glimmer of reflected light. Taking the stairs two at a time, I reached the wall and reached up. There was a little ledge just above my head and I felt around. My fingers brushed the item.

I felt something hit the top of my head and drop inside the front of my t-shirt. Rattled, I carefully pulled my hand back and hooked my finger inside the neck of my t-shirt, tugging on it I looked down. Perched between my breasts sat two halves of one of the crystal acorns.

"What did you find?" Grandma called, frozen to the spot by my curious actions.

I didn't answer her.

Instead, I fished the pieces of the crystal acorn out of my boobs and held my hand out to her. Her eyes widened in shock and she rushed to my side. Her hand shook as she covered her mouth with her fingertips.

"Is that what I think it is?" She whispered, tears pouring from her eyes.

"I think so," I murmured. Gently, I took the two halves and placed them together. They fit perfectly.

There had been a flaw in the crystal. It'd been a deep crack in it that the ocean had washed until the edges had worn smooth. Knocking it off of the ledge with my fumbling fingers and having it hit my hard head had been enough to crack it the rest of the way. The newly fragmented crystal was sharp as freshly chipped obsidian.

Careful not to cut myself, I lifted it up into the light. Rainbows exploded on the cave walls around us. Twisting the halves of the crystal in my fingers was enough for the two halves to slip apart. One of the sharp edges nicked my finger and my blood rushed along the crack.

The rainbows turned pink.

Hissing, I pulled my hand from the light and inspected my finger. The cut wasn't deep, but it had hit a vein.

"Amelia, are you okay?" Grandma Ruth's voice was tinged with worry.

"I'm okay. It was my fault." I stuck the injured finger into my mouth as I held the two halves of the crystal loosely in my other hand. "What do you think will happen if we put this in the empty spot?"

"I-I'm not sure." Grandma Ruth stuttered. "It's broken. It might not work at all."

The realization aged my grandmother in front of my eyes, the hope that had flared brightly in her face like a beacon, dimming. I couldn't stand it.

With grim determination and powerful strides, I took to the stairs, my grandmother sputtering and calling out to me. I stopped in front of the empty divot. Ignoring my grandmother's protests, and pleas to stop what I was doing, I slid the two halves back together, now sticking to one another with my quickly drying blood.

I glanced over my shoulder. She was at the base of the stairs, arm reaching out towards me. Beseeching me to stop.

"We won't know unless we try." I smiled at her. Then I stuck the acorn into the divot.

"Eley, NO!" Grandma cried.

But I couldn't hear her. Because the acorn sunk into the divot with an audible *click*. The crystals along the arch of the gate flared to life and pulsed. The three stones in a vertical line at the center of the arch glowed brightly. Rainbows scattered across the cave and down my body. The one cracked in half glowed a reddish-pink from my blood. The rings carved into the stone shifted, sand raining to the uppermost stair, as they creaked and ground into motion.

Everything happened all at once.

It felt like time was flying by and crawling at the same time.

The wings carved into the stone shivered as a seam of light split the tree carving within the arch in half. It widened, and it drew my gaze like a magnet. It was easily the most beautiful thing I'd ever seen. Rainbows and chiming and the susurrus of wind through wings and leaves all at once a tangible sight, sound, and feeling. Everything else fell away from my awareness. All that existed was this light calling me forward, the pull in the center of my being.

I stepped into the shaft of light. A swirling, glowing tunnel of rainbows greeted me. Fresh air breathed towards me and it felt like something was pulling me forwards. I looked down and saw a bright red strand pulse and stretch from my heart, down to my pinky finger, and out into the multicolored glow of the tunnel.

I'd heard myths of red strings of fate.

In fairy tales.

My grandmother screamed my name. Turning to look at her, I saw her reaching for me, tears falling down her face... about to lose her granddaughter along with her husband. The tug on my belly turned sharp, inevitable, and I felt myself being pulled in.

The portal closed behind me, but not before I heard a faint "Fuck!" follow me into the light.

I felt like I was falling forward, unable to breathe. My hair was flying out behind me, my shirt plastered to the front of my body. Within a few heartbeats of flying through the tunnel of light and rainbow and chiming fluttering, I saw the walls of a cave rush towards me. An end to the tunnel.

And suddenly I was falling face-first onto a rocky cave floor. The light behind me cut off abruptly, and I coughed, attempting to catch my breath in the semi-dark of the cave.

I got up onto my hands and knees and looked around.

It wasn't the sea cave. This cave was dry and the walls strangely looked like bark. I got to my feet and glanced behind me. There was another gate carved just like the one in the sea cave. Only this one had complete crystals that shined and gleamed in the low light. The one in the center of the three, the same one I'd placed there back home, was whole. Yet it was the same pinkish-red as the one I'd gotten my blood all over.

I did it.

I'd gotten the gate to work.

Because I was most definitely *not* in the sea cave back home. But then fear froze me to the spot. I had no idea where I was, if this was Talam, or if I'd find my grandfather.

Shit.

For the first time in my life, I'd done something truly reckless. Before I could berate myself for my complete lack of sense, I heard something shifting at the front of the cave.

Great! Now I was going to die by galactic bear mauling! I cast about, frantically looking for something, anything, to use as a weapon. Coming up with absa-fucking-lutely *nothing*, I eased into a fighting stance. I'd survived too much to let myself get taken out by some interstellar mountain lion.

If I went down, I'd go down swinging godsdamnit.

A shadow passed along the walls, and light footfalls grew closer. It hit me then. Whatever it was? It was bipedal. I was about to meet a real-life alien. Fuck. I was *not* qualified to be first contact!

Before my brain could bleat in panic, a giant man stalked in. I paused. His shadowed form was obscured by the warm light from outside that lit the mouth of the cave. He stopped in front of me, surprised to find me there. I looked up at him as he stepped into one of the few shafts of sunlight coming in from the ceiling.

My breath caught as his black and silver eyes met mine.

He *definitely* wasn't human.

He was fucking *tall*.

And when I say that, let me put it into perspective, he was *at least* an entire head taller than me. I was craning my head back to look up into the black sclera-ed eyes and their silver irises that were boring holes into me like I was the weirdo here.

Well, maybe I was?

He was tall. And it was flustering the fuck out of me because not only was he taller than me, but he was also built like he just oozed off of some romance cover for alien gladiators or some shit. Muscles for days! Washboard abs I could do the laundry of an entire army on, arms and thighs the size of small tree trunks, cuts in his hips that looked like they were declaring a V for a vendetta against my last nerve, and hands that were big in manly ways that screamed they'd feel fun all over my ass.

He was making me feel fucking dainty, and I was having a hard time processing this new emote gotdamnit.

He wore a short vest made of some sort of reptilian hide, a leather kilt, knee-high boots made of the same hide as his vest, and bracers. What looked to be an honest to gods torc made of gold cuffed his thickly muscled neck and a band of similar design cuffed his upper bicep. His hair was black and shaved on the sides. The long length on top fell down his back in a braid. He had some sort of tattoos, that crawled from his neck down over his shoulders and biceps. Like that photo of my grandfather.

He wore a belt with two wickedly curved swords at his waist. Straps crossed his chest under his vest and a bandolier showed the hilts of three knives. I spied a boot knife sticking up from the inside of his left boot and an axe that swung on the opposite hip from his swords.

The guy was bristling with weapons and raw masculine power that made me sink further into my stance and prepare to defend myself. I wasn't sure if being attacked by an interstellar cave bear or this guy would be a worse end. He blinked at me in surprise, as if he realized I was prepared to fight him, and I swear I saw approval in his strange gaze.

And despite being roughly seven feet tall, having a skin tone that was somewhere between sage and cucumber, black and silver eyes, hands that ended in black claws, and pointed ears... he was rather handsome.

He had high cheekbones, a firm jaw, expressive eyebrows, a straight nose, and a... very kissable mouth. I couldn't keep the blush from rising at this train of thought. He caught it and one side of that devilishly delicious-looking mouth of his quirked up in a crooked grin that did all sorts of things to my belly.

"What's a lovely pearl like you doing in a dump like this?" His voice was rough and deep, rumbling against my skin and I couldn't help the shiver that stole over me.

INDEX &
PRONUNCIATION GUIDE

Online Pronunciation Guide With Audio:

https://www.authorcarlottahughes.com/orc-matched-pronounciation-guide.html

ALL VOICE CLIPS SOURCED WITH PERMISSION FROM
https://learngaelic.scot/

Please note that not all words have a pronunciation guide or a link to the audio. These words are pronounced phonetically and are the creation of the author.

EVERYDAY WORDS

NAMING:

Cridhe (p. Cridheachan): [/krʲi.ə/] Heart; the title of an orckin's soul-bound partner and mate

Daonna: [/duːNə/] Human

Fògradh: [/fɔːgrəɣ/] Exile

Gaiseadh: [/gaʃəɣ/] Blight

Taobh A'Muigh: [/tuːv/ /ə'muj/] Outsider; usually what someone is called if they are not part of a clan

Neamhnaid: [/Nʲãũnɪdʲ/] Pearl; often a nickname for a princess or female of royal blood or someone with a pearly sheen to their skin

FAMILY:

Màthair: [/maːhərʲ/] Mother

Athair: [/ahərʲ/] Father

Piuthar: [/pju.ər/] Sister

Bràthair: [/braːhɪrʲ/] Brother

ROYALTY NAMING:

Rìgh: [/Riː/] King

Banrigh: [/bãũNRɪ/] Queen

Leanabh Rìgh: [/Lʲɛnəv/ /Riː/] Prince

Leanabh Banrigh: [/Lʲɛnəv/ /bãũNRɪ/] Princess

Fear a Chì (p. Feadhainn a Chì): [/fɛr/ /ə'/ /hee/] Spiritual leader of each clan. They are conduits to the Source and are often caretakers of the orphaned orclings; often female

ROYAL ITEMS:

Seud Iteach: [/ʃiad/ /ihdʲəx/] A feathered ornament that Leanabh Rìgh wear in their hair

Seud Neamhnaid: [/ʃiad/ /Nʲãũnɪdʲ/] A pearl ornament Leanabh Banrigh wear in their hair

SPIRITUAL PLACES:

Craobh na Beatha: [/kruːv/ /nə/ /bɛhə/] Tree of Life

Gàrradh: [/gaːRəɣ/] A circle of trees interwoven like a protective cage with a fire pit and resting places for weary travelers; a holdover from when Talam was first created

Geata: [/gʲɛhdə/] gate, the carved gate within the Craobh na Beatha and the sea cave at Orc Rock Farm

Neach-gleidhidh: [/Nʲɛx/ /gleː/] Sentinel, one of the giant beings that look as if they're made of stone. It is an ancient tale regarding the birth of Talam and how if ever a time came when the planet would be ruined by the orckin, the Sentinels would come alive and wipe the planet clean to start again

SPIRITUAL ITEMS:

Chleoc: [/klɔːxgə/] An ancient type of ring that cloaks the appearance of orcs to look more human-like, a common item left over from the ages past when humans and orcs traveled to one another's lands

Clach Grèine: [/kLax/ /ˈɟɾʲeːnʲə/] sunstones; stones that absorb the heat of the sun during the day and expel the heat at night

Frith-rathad: [/frʲi/ /Ra.ad/] Path; often regarding one's life path or destiny

LANGUAGE:

Common: English

Teanga Dhubh: [/tⁱɛŋgə/ /ɣuh/] Black tongue, the primary orckin language

HEALTH & WELLNESS:

An'sgudal: [/əN⁽ʲ⁾/ /sgudəL/] The wasting illness that strikes the orckin, predominately affecting females and orclings; accompanied by the Dorcha'aon, it is unknown how they are connected

ANIMALS:

Cnuimh: [/krũĩv/] Worm

Cuileagan: [/kulagan/] Flies

Dorcha'aon: [/dɔrɔxə/ /ũːn/] An apex predator with six legs, six glowing eyes, and a maw filled with sharp teeth; they come with the an'sgudal and eat the males and their nocrys

Eun'bogha-froise: [/ian/ /bo.əˈfrɔʃə/] A large bird whose plumage is the colors of the rainbow; they like to fly amongst rainbows after a storm

Iolaire'lasair: [/juLɪrʲə/ /Lasɪrʲ/] Fire eagle or phoenix

Moileasgan: [pronounced similarly to mollusk] Enormous mollusk that is carnivorous and will lie under the sand in wait then snap closed around their prey; neamhnaid are found within the Moileasgan

Nocrys: Large felines which act as steeds and guardians to the orckin; they have black or dark grey fur and scales and choose their rider

Fuar Nocrys: [/fuɐr/] Nocrys that are found in the snowy mountain ranges of the Oc'Blyre; they are white and grey to blend in with their surroundings

FOOD:

Luibh Gaoil: [/Lɯiv/ /gɯːL/] Whiskey spiked with an herb that triggers a state similar to the cridhe frenzy

Uisge-beatha: [/ɯʃgʲə'bɛhə/] very strong whiskey distilled by the orckin

Dearc Ruadh: [/dʲɛrxg/ /Ruəγ/] An edible red berry the size of a cherry that grows on a bush with black leaves; has a tart taste similar to cherries

Tiùbar: [/tʲuːbər/] Edible tubers with a mushroom-like stalk that looks like a dildo. All parts are edible but need to be roasted

A'crathadh Cnòthan: [/ə/ /krahəγ/ /krɔ̃ː.ən/] Nuts from the tree with the waving noodle-like spikes on the trunk; the nutmeat tastes like pumpkin seeds and peanuts

Aran: [/aran/] Bread

Fighe Inntinn Bog: [/fi.ə/ /ĩːNʲdʲɪNʲ/ /bog/] Similar to marijuana but a lot stronger

Caraiceag: [/karɪgʲag/] Pancake-like food

ITEMS:

Concrait: [pronounced similarly to concrete] A building material similar to concrete

LOCATIONS & CLANS:

EARTH:

Earth: The planet where Amelia is from

Orc Rock Farm: A dilapidated farm that Ruth buys and transforms, with Thorn's help, into a Tolkien-inspired bed-and-breakfast based on Hobbiton

TALAM:

A planet with three moons that orbits twin stars in a solar system across the universe from Earth. There are many continents, but none have been explored outside of the primary continent in which the orckin reside.

Talam: The planet on which the orcs live, also the continent on which they reside

Muir Sgàil: [/murʲ/ /sgaːl/] The Shadow Sea, is a large body of water that is a host to all kinds of monster-like creatures that make sailing across it impossible

OC'DELLOR:

A clan of orckin who reside in the forested lands of Talam. They tend to have grey coloring to help them blend in with the shadows, teeth similar to a wolf's, and live in tree homes built into the giant trees.

Baile Coille: [/balə/ /kʏLʲə/] The forest city of the Oc'Dellor

Daingneach: [/daiŋʲgʲNʲəx/] The fortress where the Oc'Dellor rulers live

Craobh Bean Glic: [/kruːv/ /bɛn/ /gliçgʲ/] The wise woman tree where the Fear a Chì and the orphaned orclings live

Craobh Brathaidh: [/kruːv/ /brahəɣ/] The traitor tree where traitors are hung for their crimes; is located next to the fortress Daingneach

Fàinne Sleagh: [/faːNʲƏ/ /ʃlɤɣ/] The stone ring of the caldera that juts up through the trees surrounding Baile Coille as a natural fortification

Noc'tal Forest: The wide forest surrounding Fàinne Sleagh that borders Oc'Sentan and Oc'Turin lands

OC'TURIN:

A clan of orckin who reside in the steppes and rolling hills of Talam. Their coloring leans more towards greens and browns to blend in with the grasses and stones of the steppes. Their teeth have large, sharp canines and flat molars. They live primarily in stone homes with living roofs, blending into the environment. They are often considered the harshest of the orckin as their training is brutal and starts early and they are rigid in their views of females.

Cìp Carragh: [/kʲiːhb/ /kaRƏɣ/] The stone keep where the Oc'Turin rulers live; there are many caves dug into the hard rock of the steppes that are connected to it

Feurach Clachach: [/fiarƏx/ /kLaxƏx/] The name of the steppes and stone grasslands of the Oc'Turin that borders the Oc'Dellor and Oc'Blyre lands

Carrachan Neach-gleidhidh: [/kaRƏxan/ /Nʲɛx/ /gleː/] A Sentinel surrounded by a unique ring of standing stones; cairns are erected for the dead here in a spiral pattern

OC'VELTAS:

A reclusive clan of orckin who reside in the isles on the eastern coast of Talam. Their coloring leans more towards blues and sea greens to blend in with the waters that they often swim in. Their teeth are narrow and sharp. They live primarily in The Citadel in homes made of stone and glass. They

have isolated themselves for generations and have technologies far beyond the other clans.

Tòrr Chathair: [/tɔːR/ /kahɪrʲ/] Oc'Veltas city, also often called The Citadel

Geodha Corranach: [/gʲɔ.ə/ /kɔRanəx/] The crooked coves, channels, and islands that are scattered between The Citadel and the mainland

OC'SENTAN:

A clan of migrating orckin who reside in the jungles and desert of northern Talam. Their coloring leans more towards dun and orange colors to blend in with the rock and sand. Their teeth are the most human-like with prominent canines. They are the most difficult of the clans to track down as they migrate with their mobile homes following the rains. They are excellent trackers and hunters.

Fras Raonach: [/fras/ /Rɯːnəx/] The rain wilds are a mix between plains and desert, the monsoon rains come seasonally and replenish the wildlife

Òrdha Beinn-sheilg: [/ɔːrɣa/ /beiNʲ //] The jungle in which the Oc'Sentant do most of their hunting and gathering with lots of wild edible plants

Fàsach Coinnich: [/faːsəx/ /kɤNʲɪç/] The circular plain within the jungle where the caravans meet up each triple moon cycle to trade

OC'BLYRE:

A clan of giant orckin who reside in caves carved into the mountains in the south of Talam. Their coloring ranges from brows to greys to whites to fit in with their cold, rocky climate. Their teeth are sharp with tusks and can reach over eight feet tall. They are well adapted to the cold and mine the mountains for ore and sunstones.

Niomhair Abhainn-deighe: [/Nʲivɛrʲ/ /a.ɪNʲ/ /dʲejɔ/] A giant glacier that snakes like a river through the mountains

Neulach Callaid Bheann: [/NʲiəLɔx/ /kaLadʲ/ /bjauN/] The mountain range along the south of Talam with peaks so high they're obscured in the clouds

Creagan Speur: [/krʲegʲan/ /sbiər/] A cliff city carved into a mountainside where the Oc'Blyre live

CONTENT AWARENESS*

I have sought to be thorough in identifying potential triggers, both explicit and mentioned, including kinks and mental health awareness. This is for the comfortability of readers who are sensitive to triggering content and because I believe in the informed consent of my readers. If you find any mentions of triggering content that I have not included, email me at *authorcarlottahughes@gmail.com* so I can address it within reason.

Please note that chapter titles marked with an * mean there are explicit scenes. I've included mentions of triggering content below, though they are not specially marked in the chapter titles. Some triggers are generalized throughout the book and aren't specifically identified in the chapter breakdowns (i.e. misogyny). I do not write rape scenes. However, characters have that as part of their backstory and there are questionable consent moments (immediately stopped, addressed, and resolved).

List of General Triggers: Misogyny, Extinction, Gaslighting, Societally Expected Pregnancy

List of Explicit Triggers: Drowning, Stalking, General Violence & Assault, Gun Violence, Fire, Pregnancy, Harassment, Questionable Consent (immediately stopped, addressed, and resolved)

List of Mentioned Triggers: Mentioned Sexual Assault, Mentioned Abortion, Mentioned Family Loss, Mention of FBI Violence, Mentioned Drug Use

List of Kinks: Praise, Knotting, Choking, Pleasure Dom, Breeding, Exhibition, Primal, Bloodplay, Marking, Tandem Masturbation

List of Mental Health Awareness: PTSD, Anxiety, Depression, Panic Attacks

Chapter 01: Mention of drug use, mention of SA, mention of abortion, mention of vehicular death

Chapter 02: Mention of death by plague, mention of general violence

Chapter 03*: Phone harassment, drowning

Chapter 04:

Chapter 05:

Chapter 06*: PTSD, mention of FBI violence, harassment, mention of SA,

Chapter 07*: PTSD, panic attack

Chapter 08:

Chapter 09:

Chapter 10*: Phone harassment/stalking, tandem masturbation

Chapter 11:

Chapter 12*: Police harassment

Chapter 13: Mention of abortion, mention of SA, mention of drug use, mention of societal expectation of pregnancy, mention of family loss

Chapter 14:

Chapter 15*: Primal, knotting, marking/blood play

Chapter 16*: Primal, knotting, marking/blood play

Chapter 17^: Mentioned exhibitionism, fire, general violence, stalking

Chapter 18*: General violence, gun violence, fire

Chapter 19*: General violence, mention of drug use

Chapter 20*: Breeding, primal

Chapter 21*: Breeding, primal, pleasure dom, questionable consent (immediately stopped, addressed, and resolved), choking, knotting

Chapter 22:

Epilogue: Pregnancy

ACKNOWLEDGMENTS

A huge thank you to YOU for reading my book! Thank you so much!

I'd like to thank my parents for helping me escape my marriage, allowing me to move back home, and giving me the time and space to process and write my stories. I'm forever grateful for your kindness and love. Also, special thanks to my mom for being so sweet and excited to read my writing. And demanding more constantly.

I'd also like to thank the members of the writing group I'm a part of, The Degenerate Syndicate: Sara Ivy Hill, Maddie Syn, Ami Wright, L.A. Holloway, Matilda Vega, Ursa Dax, Stella Frost, Krista Luna, Alanna Morgenstern, Brianna Everly, Anne Riland, Chloe Parker, Kimberly Lemming, Clarissa Bright, and Victoria Aveline…. You guys inspired me and provided support as I wrote again, moved across the country, and began my healing journey. You've helped me fight back my impostor syndrome and encouraged me to make this happen. I love you guys and I'm so thankful to have you in my life.

A big ole squishy thank you to my beta readers Luna Wolff, Anne Riland, Elsie Smith, and Jordan Harris.

An immense outpouring of gratitude to Connor. Your moral

support, even from so far away, has built me back up. I've sprinkled our moments throughout Thorn's Dove. I hope you find them all. I love you with every piece of my healing heart. Thank you.

About the Author

Carlotta Hughes is a giant orc-like lady living with her four cats and an enormous book collection. She wrote a creation story with a polar bear at age five and has been writing ever since. When not reading or writing, she's often exploring, hyper-fixating on a new creative outlet, and generally being a bubbly goblin hermit. She loves snacks, being warm, weapons, and snuggles.

Carlotta writes thorny, corny, horny stories with sassy one-liners, alt-human love interests, sexually frustrated characters, lots of simping, and guaranteed HEA. Her stories explore the spectrum of humanity, including disabilities, gender, sexuality, kinks, and survivorship. You know, for science.

- Website: https://www.authorcarlottahughes.com/
- Amazon: https://www.amazon.com/Carlotta-Hughes/e/B09P9S6JVH
- TikTok: @authorcarlottahughes
- Instagram: @authorcarlottahughes

ALSO BY...

ORC MATCHED SERIES

0.5 THORN'S DOVE (2022)

1.0 RHUGER'S PEARL (2023)

1.5 RHUGER'S CRIDHE (2023)

2.0 SHARN'S HONEYBEE (Coming 2023)

2.5 RHUGER'S TINSEL (Coming 2023)

3.0 SIGG'S KITTEN (Coming 2023)

Made in the USA
Monee, IL
29 July 2023

40081145R00154